ALSO BY ISHMAEL BEAH

A Long Way Gone

RADIANCE of TOMORROW

ISHMAEL BEAH

SARAH CRICHTON BOOKS

FARRAR, STRAUS AND GIROUX · NEW YORK

SARAH CRICHTON BOOKS
Farrar, Straus and Giroux
18 West 18th Street, New York 10011

Library of Congress Cataloging-in-Publication Data
Beah, Ishmael, 1980–
   Radiance of tomorrow : a novel / Ishmael Beah.
      pages   cm
   ISBN 978-0-374-24602-0 (hardback) — ISBN 978-0-374-70943-3 (ebook)
   1. Villages—Sierra Leone—Fiction.   2. Sierra Leone—History—Civil War,
1991–2002—Fiction.   I. Title.

PS3602.E2417 R33 2014
813'.6—dc23

                                                        2013036856

Designed by Abby Kagan

Farrar, Straus and Giroux books may be purchased for educational, business, or
promotional use. For information on bulk purchases, please contact the Macmillan
Corporate and Premium Sales Department at 1-800-221-7945, extension 5442, or
write to specialmarkets@macmillan.com.

www.fsgbooks.com
www.twitter.com/fsgbooks • www.facebook.com/fsgbooks

1   3   5   7   9   10   8   6   4   2

For Priscillia, my wife, best friend, and soul mate.

Thank you for infusing my life with love and joy that I never knew existed.

AUTHOR'S NOTE

I grew up in Sierra Leone, in a small village where as a boy my imagination was sparked by the oral tradition of storytelling. At a very young age I learned the importance of telling stories—I saw that stories are the most potent way of seeing anything we encounter in our lives, and how we can deal with living. Stories are the foundations of our lives. We pass them on so that the next generation can learn from our mistakes, joys, and celebrations. Growing up, I would sit around the fire every evening and my grandmother or other older people—the elders, as we call them—would tell stories. Some were about the moral and ethical standards of my community, about how to behave. Some were just funny. Others were scary, to the point that you didn't want to go to the bathroom at night. But all of them always had meaning, a reason for being told.

I bring a lot of that oral tradition to my writing, and I try to let it seep into the words. The places I come from have such rich languages, such a variety of expression. In Sierra Leone we have about fifteen languages and three dialects. I grew up speaking about seven of them. My mother tongue, Mende, is very expressive, very figurative, and when I write, I always struggle to find the English equivalent of things that I really want to say in Mende. For example, in Mende, you wouldn't say "night came suddenly"; you would say "the sky rolled over and changed its sides." Even single words are this way—the word for "ball" in Mende translates to a "nest of air" or a "vessel that carries air."

If I express such things in written English, the language takes on a kind of new mode. "They kicked around a nest of air"—all of a sudden that has a different meaning. When I started writing this novel, I wanted to introduce all these things to my work. They are part of what makes language come alive for me.

After I wrote my memoir, *A Long Way Gone*, I was a bit exhausted. I didn't want to write another memoir; I felt that it might not be sane for one to speak about himself for many, many, many years in a row. At the same time, I felt the story of *Radiance of Tomorrow* pulling at me because of the first book. I wanted to have people understand how it feels to return to places that have been devastated by war, to try to start living there again, to raise a family there again, to rekindle some of the traditions that have been destroyed. How do you do that? How do you try to shape a future if you have a past that's still pulling at you? People go back home with different nostalgias. The younger generation return because their parents and grandparents have told them stories about how this place used to be. The older people are holding on to tradition. You have all of this push and pull; people are trying to live together.

For me, coming from this war-torn place, a place most people had not heard about, writing has become a way to bring to life some of the things I could not give people or provide physically. I want readers to get a tangible, tactile feeling when they see these words, so I try to use words in a way to fit the landscape. This is why the writing in *Radiance of Tomorrow* borrows from Mende and other languages.

There's a saying in the oral tradition of storytelling that when you tell a story, when you give out a story, it is no longer yours; it belongs to everyone who encounters it and everyone who takes it in. You are only the shepherd of that story—it's coming from you— and you can guide it in any way, but sometimes it will go ways you actually don't intend it to go. That's how I feel about *Radiance of Tomorrow*. I'm the shepherd of the story, but I hope you take it in your own direction.

Ishmael Beah

RADIANCE of TOMORROW

1

It is the end, or maybe the beginning, of another story.
Every story begins and ends with a woman, a mother,
a grandmother, a girl, a child.
Every story is a birth . . .

SHE WAS THE FIRST TO ARRIVE where it seemed the wind no longer exhaled. Several miles from town, the trees had entangled one another. Their branches grew toward the ground, burying the leaves in the soil to blind their eyes so the sun would not promise them tomorrow with its rays. It was only the path that was reluctant to cloak its surface completely with grasses, as though it anticipated it would soon end its starvation for the warmth of bare feet that gave it life.

The long and winding paths were spoken of as "snakes" that one walked upon to encounter life or to arrive at the places where life lived. Like snakes, the paths were now ready to shed their old skins for new ones, and such occurrences take time with the necessary interruptions. Today, her feet began one of those interruptions. It may be that those whose years have many seasons are always the

first to rekindle their broken friendship with the land, or it may just
have happened this way.

The breeze nudged her bony body, covered with a tattered cloth
thin and faded from many washings, toward what had been her
town. She had removed her flip-flops, set them on her head, and
carefully placed her bare feet on the path, waking the caked dirt
with her gentle steps. With closed eyes she conjured the sweet smell
of the flowers that would turn to coffee beans, which the sporadic
breath of the wind fanned into the air. It was a freshness that used
to overcome the forest and find its way into the noses of visitors
many miles away. Such a scent was a promise to a traveler of life
ahead, of a place to rest and quench one's thirst and perhaps ask for
directions if one was lost. But today the scent made her weep, starting slowly at first, with sobs that then became a cry of the past. A
cry, almost a song, to mourn what has been lost while its memory
refuses to depart, and a cry to celebrate what has been left, however little, to infuse it with residues of old knowledge. She swayed to
her own melody and the echo of her voice first filled her, making her
body tremble, and then filled the forest. She lamented for miles,
pulling shrubs that her strength allowed and tossing them aside on
the path.

Finally, she arrived at the quiet town without being greeted by
the crows of cocks, the voices of children playing games, the sound
of a blacksmith hitting a red-hot iron to make a tool, or the rise of
smoke from fireplaces. Even without these signals of a time that
seemed far gone, she was so happy to be home that she found herself
running to her house, her legs suddenly gaining more strength for
her age. Alas, as she reached her home, she began to weep. The song
from the past had abruptly left her tongue. Her house had been
burnt a while back and the remaining pillars were still dark from
the smoke. Tears consumed her deep brown eyes and slowly rolled
down her long face until her sharp cheekbones were soaked. She
wept to accept what she knew had happened but also to allow her

tears to drop on the ground and call on those gone to return in spirit form. She wept now because she hadn't been able to do so for seven years, as staying alive required parting with all familiar ways of living during the years when the guns took words out of the mouths of the elders. On her way to her home, she had passed many towns and villages that resembled what her watery eyes now looked at. There was one town in particular that was eerier than the others—there were rows of human skulls on either side of the path leading into town. When the breeze came about, as it did frequently, it shook the skulls, causing them to rotate slowly, so it seemed they were all turning their hollow eye sockets at her as she hastened past them. Despite such sights, she had refused to commit her mind to the possibility that her town would be charred. Perhaps it was her way of keeping hope vibrant within so that it would keep on fueling her determination to continue the walk home. She didn't want to call the name of that home, not even in her mind. But something now took charge of her tongue and made her ask, "Will this ever be Imperi?"

The name of her land had been released into the ears of the wind even with her bewildered question. She found her feet again and began walking around the town. There were bones, human bones, everywhere, and all she could tell was which had been a child or an adult.

She managed to conjure the memory of what the town had looked like the day before she began running away for her life. It was at the end of the rainy season when everyone repaired and refreshed the façades of their homes. There were new roofs, thatch or zinc, and the walls of some houses were painted with vivid colors, increasing the liveliness of the dry season. It was the first time her family had had the means to cement the walls of their house and therefore could paint it black at the foundation, green to the windowsill, and yellow all the way up to the roof. Her children, grandchildren, husband, and she stood outside admiring their home. They didn't know that the following day they would abandon everything and be separated from one another forever.

When the gunshots rang through town and chaos ensued the day that war came into her life, she had turned around to look at her home before running away. If she died, she wanted to at least do so with a good memory of home.

She had returned home because she could not find complete happiness anywhere else. She had scoured refugee camps and the homes of kind strangers for some sort of joy that didn't need entertainment, something she knew existed only on the land she now stood upon. She remembered an afternoon not so long ago that had followed days of hunger and finally an offer of a sumptuous bowl of rice with stewed fish. She ate, at first vigorously, and then her muscles slowed down, straining the movements of her hand to her mouth. The pepper tasted different from the one her memory still held on to, and the water she drank was not from a small calabash that smelled of the clay pot that had cooled the water for her household since she was a little girl. She finished her food and drank to stay alive, but she knew there was more to living than these temporary acknowledgments of life. The only satisfaction that remained after finishing the food was the memory of the sound of pepper pounded in a mortar and, with it, the biting fragrance that took hold of the air around the compound and the laughter that ensued as men and boys would flee.

"It is so easy to drive them away," her mother would say as the other women continued laughing, their eyes and noses not showing any sign of discomfort as the men's and boys' did.

She looked at the bones again, her eyes moving beyond the piles to find strength to leap forward. "This is still my home," she whispered to herself and sighed, pressing her bare feet deeper into the earth.

Evening was approaching and the sky was preparing to roll over and change its side. She sat on the ground, allowing the night's breeze to soothe her face and her pain, to dry her tears. When she was a child, her grandmother told her that at the quietest hours of night, God and gods would wave their hands through the breeze to wipe just a few things off the face of the earth so that it would be able to accommodate the following day. Though her pain didn't completely disappear with the arrival of morning, she felt some new strength within her heart that gave her the idea to pluck herself from the earth and begin cleaning the bones. She started at her house with a pile in her hands that shivered maybe because of the cool morning air or the emotions that came from gathering what remained of others. Her feet took her toward the coffee farm behind her house. She held the bones with a delicate but firm grip, pondering how so many could be reduced to such fragments. "Perhaps it is only when the flesh masks the bones of one's body that you gain some worth. Or is it what you do when life breathes through you that makes your memory worthwhile?" She stopped her questions for a bit to allow her scattered thoughts to coalesce. She felt this was the way to harden within her the memories of those she was now carrying so lightly. Her mind became an anthill filled with smoke. She didn't pay much attention to where she was headed. Her feet were familiar with the ground; her eyes, ears, and heart were on another journey.

She rounded a corner and dropped the pile, her heart sinking to her waist-bone at the resounding thud of the bones hitting the dusty earth. Her feet gave way under her body as she saw the back of a man sitting on his knees tying bones together as one would a bundle of kindling. She could tell that this was an old man, as his hair was the color of stagnant clouds. The man's movements expressed his age. This brought her heart back to its proper place, allowing the rest of her body to resume its many functions.

The old man, sensing a shadow behind him, spoke. "If you are a spirit, please pass by peacefully. I am doing this work to make sure that when people return to this town, they may not see this. I know their eyes have recorded worse, but still I will spare them one last image of despair."

"I will help you, then." She lowered herself and began picking up the bones she had dropped and some more, making her way toward him.

"I know that voice. Is that you, Kadie?" He trembled, his hands unable to do what they had been doing since he'd arrived as the sky was wiping the last residue of sleep from its surface. Kadie answered quietly, as though afraid to disturb the deep silence that had come about just at that moment. His heart hesitated to give permission to his face to turn around and greet his friend. He sat for some time watching his shadow move. And all the while, he could hear Kadie rattling the bones and sighing as she continued her work. Turning to see her would give his heart the burden of coming to terms with whatever condition she was in. She might be amputated, deformed in some way or another. He sat some more in his torment, and Kadie decided to end his hesitation, as she knew why he had hidden his eyes from his words. She came before him and sat on the ground. His eyes had dug themselves deep into the earth.

"Please remove your eyes from the body of the earth and see your friend. I am sure your heart will perform a joyful dance when you see that I am as well as I can be." She placed her right hand on his shoulder. He held on to her hand and slowly, like a child caught making mischief, he lifted his head. His eyes surveyed the body of his friend while his mind confirmed: her hands are both there, her legs, too, nose, ears, lips . . .

"I am here, Moiwa, all of how I came into this world is here." Her voice stopped his mind's roll call on her body parts.

"Kadie! You are here, you are here." He touched her face. They embraced and then sat apart looking at each other. He offered her water in a small old pot. She smiled as she took the water in a fractured calabash that sailed on top of the water. He had one of those round and dignified faces that always had a pensive demeanor and could hold a smile only for a short time. His frame, hands, and fingers were thinner and longer.

"It was all I could find in the ruins that could hold water."

What he didn't say was that a week ago he had come nearer to Imperi, near enough that his eyes could see the big mango tree in the center of town, but he hadn't had the courage to enter it. His mind had immediately stopped longing for home and replayed the horrors of the war. It started with wails of people who had passed, people he knew. He had made a temporary home in one of the many burnt vehicles by the river. Those vehicles had once belonged to the mining company that had been preparing to start operations six months before the war. The company had refused to build a small bridge across the river, which it regretted when the war came, as it couldn't get its new cars and equipment across. The foreigners who were supposed to start working for the mining company had at first dismissed the possibility that they would ever have to abandon their cars, loaded with food, clothes, and other provisions, but the first gunshot had sent them running with only a bag each, packed in canoes that almost sank, shaking with their nervousness. They pleaded with eyes wide open for the canoe owner to paddle faster.

Moiwa asked his friend Kadie only how she had brought her spirit into town and which route she had taken.

"My feet touched this land on the day that gave birth to this one. And I walked the path, as that is the way in my heart." She wrapped her fingers around one another and rubbed them to summon warmth.

"I should have known that, my dear Kadie!" She hadn't changed her ways at all. Kadie almost never walked on the roads. She did so only when there was no path. She believed in the knowledge of her great-grandparents, who had made the paths and knew the land better than those foreigners who just get into their machines and carve roads into the earth without thinking about where the land breathes, where it sleeps, where it wakes, where it entertains spirits, where it wants the sun or the shade of a tree. They laughed, both knowing that part of the old ways remained, though they were fragile. At the end of their laughter, words were exchanged, briefly, leaving many things unsaid for another day that continued to be another and yet another. Some things were better left unspoken as long as handshakes and embraces could manage their emotions—until the voice could find the strength to leave the mouth and bring out what was in the guarded mantle of memory.

Mama Kadie and Pa Moiwa, as all those younger would respectfully call them, spent weeks removing things that did not belong to the surface of the earth. They couldn't tell which bones belonged to those they had known. At some houses there were more bones than the people who had lived there. Bones were littered around the town and the nearby bushes. It was the same for the many towns and villages they had passed through; some were burnt and some had become forests, with trees growing inside houses. So they made a decision to take the bones to the cemetery and pile them there until it could be agreed upon by the whole town, when enough people had returned, what to do with the remains. During the entire process, they never cried; they spoke very little to each other except when they rested. And even then, it was in the most general terms, about the past before the land had changed.

"I do hope the other towns will come alive soon. I am fond of wandering down the path to another village or town at midafternoon to sit with its elders." Pa Moiwa surveyed the four paths that came in and out of the town.

"Just as in the old days. You think all such simple things can become our lives again?" Mama Kadie asked. She didn't want an answer and her friend gave none. They became quiet, each thinking of the day their lives had been shifted in another direction that they were still trying to return from.

———

Imperi was attacked on a Friday afternoon when everyone had returned from the market, from farms, and from schools, to rest at home and pray. It was that time of day when the sun came to a standstill and flexed the brightness of its muscles so intensely that even for those used to the dry season it became absolutely and unbearably hot. People sat on their verandas or under the shade of the mango trees in their backyards and drank hot tea or something cold, whispering to one another, as even their voices needed rest. The excited voices of children, however, didn't need any respite. They came intermittently into town from the river, where they swam and played games, chasing after one another, their school uniforms strewn on the grasses at the riverbank.

There were three primary schools in town and two secondary schools nearby. While they didn't have sufficient school materials, there were a good number of benches and desks. And the buildings were solid, though they had no doors, windows, or roofs. They did have the openings where these "ornaments," as the headmaster called them, were supposed to be and where sometimes patches of zinc hung on the rafters. The teachers used to joke, "Who needs things covering the roofs, doors, or windows when you need the breeze to blow through your classroom all day or the heat will teach you more of a lesson than what you had planned for your students!"

The teachers were lively and the students were even livelier, in their colorful uniforms, so eager to learn that they would sit on the bare earth under mango trees or under the hot sun, excitedly reciting what was taught to them.

The inhabitants of Imperi had heard of the war that was hundreds of miles away, but they didn't think it would enter, let alone severely wound, their lives. But that afternoon it did.

Several rocket-propelled grenades introduced the people of Imperi to war when they exploded in the chief's compound, bringing down all the walls and killing many people, whose flesh sizzled from the explosions. These were followed by gunshots, and screaming and wailing, as people were gunned down in front of their children, mothers, fathers, grandparents. It was one of those operations that the fighters called "No Living Thing"—they would kill everything with life. Anyone who escaped such operations was extremely lucky, as the fighters would ambush towns and attack, shooting at will.

Chaos had engulfed Imperi, and some people, especially the very old and children, were trampled on. The passing soldiers, mostly children and a good number of men, shot those who hadn't died when they came upon them. They laughed at the fact that by creating a stampede, the civilians had helped to make their operation easier.

Mama Kadie had watched the bullets tear into her two eldest sons and three daughters. They each hit the earth with eyes wide open, filled with surprise at what had just happened to them. Blood poured out of different parts of their bodies and then at last their teeth were covered with red saliva as life departed them. It had all happened so quickly, and she ran toward them not knowing exactly why, but her heart as a mother had been shattered and this was all she could do. She had no fear for her life. But someone seized her arms from behind and dragged her away from the bullets, away from the opening and near the bushes, where she was left to wake up from the shock and where her instincts to live emerged. In such circumstances, one has to abandon not only the feeling of pain but also sometimes even maternal instincts, and it must be done with immediacy.

She thought about her grandchildren. What if they survived, since they were at the river? Even though the voices of the children had ceased coming through the wind since the gunshots started, she wanted to go to the river, but sounds of heavy firing were coming from that direction. She deliberately turned to see her home one last time before she took up all the speed her age could bear, with bullets flying and catching people around her as she ran out of Imperi.

———————

Pa Moiwa woke her from her thoughts with a deliberate coughing fit. Her face, the slouching of her cheekbones in particular, had given away that difficult memories consumed her just now.

"I was here on that day, at the mosque," he said, "and I ran away from the prayer mat. I think God understood because he let me live through that day." With a stick, he drew some lines on the ground, a way to distract himself somehow so that the thoughts of that day didn't get a complete hold of him. They knew they had to put off for a while speaking about this part of the past. But their thoughts diverged. Pa Moiwa's mind dwelled on the fire that had burnt his house that afternoon. His wife had been at home in bed recovering from a small illness and his twenty-year-old granddaughter had been tending to her. When he saw them run out of the house, slapping the fire off their bodies with all of the remaining might they had left, he thought they would live. But two children, a boy and a girl, had gunned them down and carried on shooting at other people and laughing. He knew he had to go before the children saw him.

"Well." Mama Kadie's voice waited for strength.

"The spider sometimes runs out of webs to spin, so it waits in the one it has spun." Pa Moiwa used the old saying to assure his friend that more words would come to her and she might be able to dwell on things other than the horrors of the past. They were still holding on to old times, to old things, to an old world that didn't exist anymore. Fragments of it worked every now and then, though. She regained her voice.

"Well, I eventually ended up on a small island near Bonthe. A fishing village that had nothing but fishermen, their families, and huts that the wind tossed into the air and set back down every other evening as though searching for something." Mama Kadie leaned against the guava tree under which they sat.

"I just wandered everywhere for years, sleeping wherever night found me," Pa Moiwa said. "My old age became a blessing many times on those days when everyone wished that their youthful qualities were behind them." He said nothing more for a while and Mama Kadie didn't ask. He was thinking again about the war, specifically about the numerous times he had escaped death. About the time the soldiers decided instead to chase after the young people, saying, "He is old, so don't waste the ammunition on him. He can't go far, so we will catch him and use the knives when we get back." A group of boys who could have been his grandchildren had run after more agile folks, shooting at them.

But when Pa Moiwa spoke next, he described something different from what had possessed his mind just then. "The bones and muscles in my feet never felt tired of wandering; in fact, they felt restless. It was only when I set foot here—" He placed his palms on the ground and rubbed the dirt with his eyes closed for a few seconds before continuing. "It was only here that my feet and spirit suddenly felt tired." He let his tongue rest for the passing wind to speak.

The only time they allowed whatever was inside of them to take hold of their faces, driving away their shiny wrinkles even in the presence of the sun, was when they came across bones of children, especially when there were too many of them in one area. They both had several grandchildren; Mama Kadie had five and Pa Moiwa counted six. Mama Kadie would sometimes look at certain piles of bones so intensely that her eyes watered. She hoped that she would recognize something on the bones that might reveal to her that it was one of her grandchildren. After a long period of separation, not knowing whether they were alive or dead, it was sometimes easier to want to bury them; the pain of unknowing was severe and never ending.

"This is truthfully of a girl," she whispered to herself while examining a pelvic bone. "And these are of boys." Three of her grandchildren were always together, so she wanted these bones to be them. "If only the clothes on them didn't rot."

Pa Moiwa would often press the palms of his hands on the small bones and wait to hear the voice of one of his grandchildren, to feel something that reminded him of one of them, but nothing occurred. Only the faces of the children and the sound of the school bell that morning before the attack filled his memory. He was convinced that the bones communicated with him, even if generally. He used to walk his grandchildren to school every morning and greeted people at every household. He would sigh as this memory ached his entire being.

The two elders had been in town for almost a month and had managed to clean up quite well. Every morning, Pa Moiwa would rise earlier than Mama Kadie and go to the bush to check the traps he had set the previous evening. Whenever he went into different parts of the forest, he saw more remains. These he would hide under shrubs or bury so the animals would not find them. He returned with whatever animal had been caught in the traps—a porcupine, a guinea fowl—which he would cut into pieces and have Mama Kadie cook for them. He didn't tell her about the skulls and chopped hands he had seen and how he had examined the ones that had bits of flesh for the birthmarks of his children or grandchildren.

She would go wandering around the old farms looking for potatoes, cassavas, anything edible that grew in the neglected plots to cook with the meat that he brought back. Mama Kadie also saw skeletons, hung in farmhouses with fracture marks from bullets or machetes on the bones. She did her best to set them down and find resting places for them. She said nothing of this to Pa Moiwa. They took care of each other during the day, but at night they went to the ruins of their own houses. Each had found a corner to sleep in shielded on one side by a wall and the other by sticks and thatch. They struggled to find sleep on the mats that separated their bodies from the earth. The tattered blankets couldn't warm their old bones. But they were home, where they knew exactly which tree the first sunrays would pierce through, a signal for God to connect with humans, every day. They had to be in their homeland for that—one could, if possible, hear God only through the words of one's own land.

One morning after the first month and while they were both gone to look for food, another elder, a man, arrived in town. He also had come by the path and saw the footprints around town. He didn't know whether they were friendly ones, so he hid in the nearby bushes and waited. The war had ended, but the reflex of disbelieving in the kindness of a quiet town remained with him.

He had come from the capital city, where he had eventually ended up after searching every refugee camp for his family. At each of these camps he'd had to register as a refugee, so his pockets were filled with ID cards. He didn't like the squalor and congestion in the camps and so had started making traditional baskets, which he sold for enough money to rent a one-bedroom in the western part of the city. His new neighbors felt sorry for him and gave him food every day, and their children took a liking to him, but the relationship hurt his heart. They made him remember his own grandchildren. Still, he would sometimes walk the children to school. The children thought he did it because he liked it, but in truth he had been going from school to school in search of his son, Bockarie, who was a teacher. Wherever he stayed, he would visit all the schools and observe all the teachers. There was no sign of his son. He knew that if he was to find some family members, if luck was to smile his way, he would have to get back home. Therefore, as soon as it was announced that the war had ended, he began making plans to return to Imperi.

When he got nearer to his town today, he began remembering the day he had run away, the day of "Operation No Living Thing." He was at the mosque and the gunmen came inside and started shooting everyone. He fell and bodies piled on top of him. The soldiers fired some more at the bodies to make sure everyone was properly dead. He held his breath. He didn't know how he lived through it. After they left, he waited, hearing the sounds of men, boys, girls, and women crying in pain as they were tortured and then killed outside. He knew most of the voices, and at some point his ears cut him off of their own accord. He stayed under the bodies until late at night when the operation had finished and there was no sound of any living thing, not even the cry of a chick. He pulled himself out and saw the bullet-ridden bodies, some hacked. He ran out of town covered in the blood and excrement of those killed on top of him. He could not feel or smell anything for days. He just ran and ran until his nose reminded him what he was covered in. It was then that he searched for a river and washed himself clean. But water wouldn't clean the smell, sound, and feeling of that day.

As the sun was stretching the cold bones of morning with its warmth, Mama Kadie and Pa Moiwa returned to town. They both noticed footprints that weren't theirs and became worried. As they whispered about what to do next, a voice spoke from a concealed position under the bushes: "The marks you see on the earth are traces of your friend Kainesi, whose words of greeting come from the coffee trees behind you."

Meeting old friends had become strange. "I am now going to place myself in front of your eyes." He pulled his thin body from under the bushes whose leaves had left pimples of water on his face. He was wearing a blue hat with the letters *NY* that young men wore in the city. He had found it on the ground somewhere and wore it to cover his head from the wrath of the sun and because the initials on the hat were the letters of his family name, Nyama Yagoi. He removed the hat to reveal his much-wrinkled face, the scars across it and his skull. A young boy had slashed lines on his face with a bayonet and tried to open his head with a dull machete, proclaiming that he was practicing to become a "brain surgeon."

At first, Mama Kadie and Pa Moiwa didn't want to look at their friend, but in each other's faces they found courage to do so. They embraced him, squeezing him between them until he laughed, making the scars on his cheeks magnify, resembling a second grin.

"Well, you came out of that madness with an extra smile!" Pa Moiwa commented, and they shook hands, their old, warm fingers holding on to each other for a while, each man's eyes fixed deeply on the other's.

Mama Kadie wanted to ask, *How are you, your children and grandchildren, your wife, their health?* as greetings were in the old days, but she held her tongue. These days one must be careful to avoid awakening the pain of another. She placed her hands on each of their shoulders, gently releasing her friends from the stupor of all that had come to pass. She thought, *We are here, alive, and we must go on living.*

"Now I have two men to take care of me. Two old friends whose strength may equal a young man's." They all laughed.

"We still have laughter among us, my friends, and hopefully some of those we have shared it with so deeply will return and we will be waiting," Pa Kainesi said.

And the three old friends walked into the ruins of their town, the air sailing a bit livelier, waking the trees from their slumber and making a small tornado of dust as though cleansing the air for the possibility of life again.

2

PEOPLE HAD BEEN AWAY from Imperi for seven long years. During that time, the days became drawn out as they waited, restlessly, to start living again. They had seen the fire of war lick their town so viciously that even when the war was said to be over, it took them over a year, and more for some, before they started thinking about returning home. It wasn't that they didn't want to go back. Rather, war had taught them not to trust what they heard on radios, through rumors, and, for those who lived in the capital city, read in newspapers. They knew firsthand that the madness didn't cease immediately just because someone signed a peace accord or some useless ceremony honored those who were not close to the realities they had just proclaimed to have stopped with a signature. It would take months for fighters in the deep countryside to get the message, and even longer to believe in it. Those who returned were coming from refugee camps in the outskirts of cities and in neighboring countries where they had waited all these years in tarpaulin houses to go home or start life somewhere else. The waiting had had no fixed end date. Every life seemed on hold. Nothing was sure in either direction;

everything was temporary, and yet it went on for years, no one wanting to accept that it could become permanent.

"We are permanently waiting for the temporary war that is nearing ten years to end," a musician had said in a popular song. Some people couldn't wait in one place, so they wandered about, making themselves vulnerable to other exploitations—police brutality, or mistreatment by the employers, relatives, and friends for whom they worked in exchange for accommodation and meager earnings. Nothing had been easy for anyone. Children born toward the end of the war had no understanding of it; by the time they could form memories, the guns had silenced. And no one wanted to explain what had happened—because they didn't want to remember and they couldn't find the right words. There were other children, though, who had known only war, since they were born in it. No matter how, they were all returning to Imperi.

They began to arrive in groups when night gave birth to a day brighter than the previous ones. Mama Kadie, Pa Moiwa, and Pa Kainesi had woken earlier than usual, before the crow of the only cock that had begun to announce the life of another day. They were resting from their daily tasks, sitting on the logs at the edge of the older part of town, watching the road, summoning those who hesitated to return. Today, this morning, the road spat out people from refugee camps, towns, villages, hiding places deep in the forest that had become homes, from wandering and from many other places where the world now found their presence sour and where they could no longer see the growth of their shadows.

It began with about ten people carrying small bundles wrapped with tarp or cloth. Their children, about six of them, all no more than ten years old, walked beside them. They had been traveling for two days now, starting in a passenger vehicle for five hours and walking the rest of the way. Vehicles hadn't resumed their routes to Imperi. As they entered town, their pace slowed while their eyes ran ahead, surveying the bullet holes in walls, the dark spots where fire had licked with its red tongue, the grasses that had grown in the remains of what used to be homes. Then their eyes would return to their children as an assurance to continue into the belly of their hometown. Their hesitations were in every part of their bodies, the way their arms were tightly tucked to their frames, their lips pulled in, their eyelids quickly closing and opening. But as they ventured into the town, they gradually relaxed, and one of the children, a young girl whose face was clearly filled with another story that she had heard of this place, asked her mother, "Where is the place you used to sit and hear stories and is that happening tonight?"

The mother's smiling face looked down upon her child, her palm cupping the little girl's face. She did not respond, but her arms began swinging freely to their natural rhythm, her body and stride now showing an ease that comforted the girl, who buried her sharp cheek in her mother's palm. Others came with plastic bags that the wind almost knocked out of their hands, revealing the bags' near emptiness. They had walked the entire way—three days' journey for those who could walk fast—as they had no money to pay for transportation. They came two or more at a time. No one said much, even though they knew one another from before. There were only acknowledgments in their eyes, filled with fear, that held the tongue from saying more.

The majority of people walked into town with nothing. Some came with families and with children they had given birth to elsewhere. Other mothers arrived alone and stared anxiously at the faces of every child, every young person, to see if they could find their own. Sometimes they ran after a child and when he or she turned around, the mother would fall sluggishly to the ground, defeated. Most had searched for seven years, and this was their last chance to free the burden on their hearts.

Children and young people came by themselves with no parents. In the beginning they came one at a time, then in pairs, followed by four, six, or more in a group. They had been at various orphanages and households that had tried to adopt them. Some had even been at centers to learn how to be "normal children" again, a phrase they detested, so they had left and become inhabitants of rough streets in cities and towns. They were more intelligent than their years and had experienced so much hardship that each day of their lives was equal to three or more years; this showed in their fierce eyes. You had to look closely to see residues of their childhood. They knew where their parents were from and so they had returned to this place that they hoped would ease their suffering or grant them the possibility of reuniting with family. They had walked longer than everyone else who had arrived in Imperi. Among these children was a young girl no more than sixteen, who came with a child on her back, a boy, about two. She was taller than most her age, with a long face and narrow eyes. She walked with her lips tucked in as though to muster strength for every step she took. Her breasts told that the child was hers. Her eyes, especially when placed upon the child, held love and deep hatred. Mama Kadie rose to meet her, this daughter of her neighbor who no longer walked the earth in physical form.

"Mahawa, welcome home, my child. I am glad you remembered the way back. May I hold my grandchild?" Mahawa reluctantly removed the child from her back and gave him to the old woman while she continued to search her memory for something familiar.

She must have known me before, which is why she calls my name that I haven't gone by in so long. Her voice spoke inside her as she looked into the eyes of the woman whose delight for the young boy was instant. She was rubbing her nose on the child's belly, making him laugh. She never asked who the father was. Mahawa was already dreading having to explain how this child had come to this world, a story she didn't want to remember, not yet, perhaps not ever. She wanted people to make their own assumptions and leave her out of it.

"You can stay with me and we could help each other. I need a daughter, and the gods have returned you just in time. Take him to

the house over there." Mama Kadie pointed. "Feed him and yourself with whatever is in the pots. You will introduce yourself properly later on." The elders were silent with an inkling of the ordeal
that the child carrying the child had endured. Their silence was,
however, short-lived as more young people arrived, in particular a
group of four—three boys and a girl. Three of them carried pillow-
cases filled with things and tied with ropes to prevent their contents
from spilling out. The oldest, who was eighteen, walked ahead of the
group, his muscular body erect in a manner that showed discipline
and purpose. His eyes were as strong as his cheekbones, and they
were attentive to everything. His face was so hardened, dark, and
harsh that you knew that no smile or even smirk had passed on it for
years. His eyes surveyed the town not in the way the other arrivals
had, with hesitation, but more with a confidence that showed he
feared nothing. He walked, almost running, toward the elders.

"Good day Pa, Pa, and Mama. My name is Colonel." He shook
the hands of the elders strongly and looked deep into their eyes,
forcing them to turn their gaze away, something that usually happened the other way around. He pointed at and spoke the names of
the others: Salimatu, the girl, sixteen; and the boys, Amadu, the
same age, and Victor, seventeen. Their faces looked like children but
their mannerisms were those of adults, and they seemed to have
been with one another for a while. The elders didn't ask Colonel
for his real name, which they knew, on that first encounter. Would
they do so? This was to be determined by circumstances.

"They are my brothers and sister. Our parents are from here so we
have come home, like you," Colonel said to the elders. The young
people shook the right hand of each elder and sat on the ground facing them. Colonel remained standing, his hands now in the pockets
of his trousers, removing them only to gesture when he spoke.

"We will take one of the burnt houses and rebuild it. We know
which one used to belong to Amadu's father. We can be security for
the town if there is a need for that," Colonel said, not really asking

or waiting for the elders to respond. He was tall for his age and had an air of forcefulness about him. Even when he asked politely for something, it sounded as though he was demanding it, and you couldn't say no to him.

"You are all welcome back in peace," Pa Moiwa responded. Colonel said no more but nodded to the elders and walked to the house he had spoken of, which was at the edge of town. Amadu, Salimatu, and Victor followed him.

"Well, at least those alive are coming back, even if some are in the clothing of the strangers they have become. That boy in charge of the others. I knew him before all that madness happened," Pa Kainesi said, scratching his head as if to think some more.

"We must let him be Colonel as long as he chooses to be. The others with him are clearly now his responsibility, so we must let him take care of them as he has been doing. We can observe and steer him on the right path gently if necessary," Mama Kadie told the others in a whisper.

The elders refreshed their faces for other arrivals, and indeed there were more who needed to be welcomed without the burden of those who had come before them. Not long after Colonel and his group arrived, there came a man named Sila and his two children. Sila carried a small sack that used to be a rice bag, balancing the luggage effortlessly on his flat head, which seemed bigger than the rest of his body. He had a smile so wide, so brimming with happiness that the sun hid behind the clouds for a while to give permission to the display of unrestrained delight within him. His expressions conjured smiles on the faces of the elders even as he neared and they saw that his right hand was missing, his arm cut off above the elbow. Hawa, his nine-year-old daughter, was missing her left arm; Maada, his son, eight, was missing both, one cut above the elbow and the other below. The children, too, were smiling, walking on either side of their father. They had learned by watching him how to manage the awkwardness that came about when people saw their condition.

Sila and his children had been in the area around Imperi for two years before the war ended. He had been able to escape the attack on the town with only his two children, carrying the younger one and pulling the other along. Sila had kept them together since, hiding in the forest, moving to other towns until they were attacked, and then back to the forest. Then one day he had decided to take his children to the capital city to register them for school. The war wasn't coming to an end as quickly as he had thought. That evening, after walking all day, he and his children stopped to pass the night in the ruins of a town about eight miles from Imperi. Unfortunately, a squad of armed men and boys had also been passing through and decided to spend the night in the same burnt village, which had two houses whose roofs were somewhat intact. The men captured Sila and his children and tied them to a tree until morning. The children were seven and six at that time. Their father's eyes told them not to cry. He couldn't speak, as he had been beaten on his head earlier when he tried to plead for his children not to be tied so tightly. His swollen jawbone and head had pained him all night, but he couldn't cry because he wanted to remain strong for his children.

In the morning, the commander asked a slim little boy with a long, rough, pimpled face—they called him "Sergeant Cutlass"—to chop off the family's hands.

"I am in a very good mood, so you will only have your hands cut off. You can keep your lives for today," the commander had said.

"I am giving you my best man for the job. He is so good that by the time you think about it, it will be finished." He laughed and called on the sergeant. The young boy's sunken face was as cold as the blades he carried. All of them had residues of blood and flesh, and some were dull while others were very sharp. Depending on how much pain the commander wanted his victims to feel, he would ask for either a dull or sharp machete. This young boy had been forced at gunpoint to do his first cutting when he was nine years old. And they were the hands of his mother, father, grandmother, and two uncles. Afterward the commander had killed them because the boy didn't do the job to his liking; "It wasn't as clean as I wanted," he had said before shooting all of them. The commander had then made the boy part of the group to fight as a soldier and with the special task of chopping off hands only.

"Okay, bring them here." The commander asked for Sila and his children to be brought to the log near the bushes. "Sergeant Cutlass, go on and we move out after. One last thing: if any of you make any noise, I will have you all shot."

He laughed as the hands of the children were first placed on the logs and cut, and then it was Sila's turn. Sergeant Cutlass had cut many hands, but this was the second time that it tormented him—the first had been his family. He didn't know what it was, but something about this family got to him. He had also never witnessed such silence from cuts—even when the commander threatened to shoot people, they cried out. Not this family, though, and the silence made him hear the sound that the machete made when it went through the flesh, the bone, and then the flesh again, finally hitting the log.

The sound echoed in his head from that day on. The commander had told his sergeant to cut with a combination of "long sleeve" and "short sleeve," which meant a cut above the elbow (short sleeve) and below the wrist (long sleeve). The squad left right after they had chopped Sila's and his children's hands. The commander had thought that they would die bleeding, but Sila had lost enough people already. He rolled on the ground to gain some strength, got up, looked for some old cloths, and, using his one hand and mouth, tied the fresh wounds of his children and himself. It ceased their bleeding just a bit. He begged his children to forgive him because he was unable to protect them and also encouraged them to be strong, to stand up and walk with him. They did, all of them weak and staggering from the loss of blood. They continued, though, their father calling, "Hawa, Maada, you are still there. Don't leave your father alone."

"Yes, Papa," each would say, and sometimes Hawa would reach

her right hand to wipe the sweat off her younger brother's face. They went on in this manner until they hit a main road, where they all fainted on the earth at the side of the road.

They awoke at a hospital in the capital city on beds next to one another, their wounds bandaged. The nurse explained to Sila that a driver who had said his name was Momodou had kicked all the passengers off his vehicle and loaded Sila and his children inside, forfeiting all the money he could have made, especially at such a difficult time for the country. He had brought them to the hospital and paid for the initial treatment, adding, "This man and his children are brave to have walked all that way," pointing at their tattered bare feet, "so someone must do something to complete their will to live despite all this." Momodou had said nothing more and left. Sila and his children were at the hospital for a week, and from the nurse he learned that he would have to pay the remaining bill. He didn't have the money and wouldn't have for many months, if ever. So one night he quietly woke his children and they escaped the hospital and went to an amputee camp. The camp seemed like a good idea in the beginning. But then people would come by to watch them as though they were animals in the zoo. Sila left with his children after two weeks. He found a job carrying loads, which enabled him to rent a shack on the outskirts of the city. Doing menial jobs that came with cruel comments bruised his dignity. But he was a strong man physically, emotionally, and psychologically. Every morning, he would chant to himself under his breath before going out for the day, "I can always restore my dignity, and may my ears become deaf to negative voices today." He never showed his despair about his situation outwardly, perhaps for his children's sake. And his children learned from their father to carry themselves with dignity even when looked upon with questioning eyes. It did take getting used to, though, how to function without a hand or hands. Sila couldn't wait to return home and saved up so he would be ready.

Other people who wanted the same jobs as him called him

names and suggested that he wasn't as capable. On one occasion, while a group of desperate young men were trying to convince a trader to hire them to carry his loads instead of the "one-arm useless man," he proved them wrong by picking up the two huge bundles one at a time with his only hand and loading them into the vehicle without any help. The young men were going to do it together and had been negotiating payment for four workers. They had walked away angry, and the trader happily paid Sila for the job of four people. He left with his children on the first day he knew he could safely do so.

En route to Imperi, they passed through the town where they had been amputated. There was no other road. It was the only time tears came down all their faces. They walked quickly, saying nothing to one another, but someone heard their heavy footsteps. It was Sergeant Cutlass, who was no longer a soldier but was being hunted by them since his squad had been dismantled at the end of the war; he had come to the town and stayed in its ruins. He had been there for a week, unable to sleep, tormented by everything about the place—but still something held him there. He couldn't believe his eyes when he saw Sila and his children. He thought they had died. He was happy, a bit, that they were alive, but all that had happened that day came back vigorously in his mind. He sat on the ground, sighing, his sun-beaten face twitching with so much pain that it no longer had its youthfulness. He decided to follow Sila and his family, thinking he needed to make amends, but he didn't know how. Sila and his children were unaware that he was behind them. They strode home, finally happy, as their father had told them they would have a simple and perfect life there in their own family house, never worrying about getting kicked out because they couldn't afford rent.

"Greetings to you, all my elders, to the trees, the land, and all that remains. Sila is home to where his spirit brightens." He bent to the side so the bag on his head fell toward his left hand, which caught it swiftly and set it down on the earth.

"Welcome back, Sila. Your house is the only one in slightly better condition than most in town," Pa Moiwa said, feeling a bit awkward about not knowing how to greet Sila properly. Greetings were customarily done with the shaking of right hands. The elders bowed slightly to acknowledge Sila, who was in his forties. "My children, Hawa and Maada. We lost everyone else." He said the last part quickly and went on. "But blessings that our house is somewhat standing. We are home, children, greet your grandparents." The children each walked to the sides of the elders and awkwardly thrust their little frames forward for embraces. The elders held them as best as possible so they didn't feel different, but the extra care to avoid their stumps was enough to show the discomfort. As the embraces were completed and smiles resumed, someone's voice rang in their ears. No one had heard the person arriving because of his dead footsteps.

"Greetings to my elders and to all of you." A stammering sixteen-year-old boy spoke and everyone turned to see who he was. The smile and joy on the faces of Sila, Hawa, and Maada extinguished abruptly as soon as they looked at the boy whose right eye was twitching incessantly. His face was less pimpled but still rough, and they remembered him even though it had been some years. There was a heavy silence, which made everyone's body tighten with fear. The sun came from behind the clouds to replace the lost delight that Sila had brought with him. The sixteen-year-old boy avoided eye contact with everyone.

"Let us go home and find some water to feed our thirst and wash," Sila's shaking voice said to his children, who hurriedly followed, fear in their eyes as they looked back at the boy who had just arrived.

"My name is Ernest. I don't know where I am from but I followed them here." The boy pointed to Sila and his children, swinging his body and placing his hands crossed behind his back. Out of the corners of his eyes, he followed the movement of Sila and his children to see which house they were going to occupy. He didn't need to say more. The twitching of his eye and his stammering got worse when he spoke of following Sila. The elders could see the story in his eyes. They kept their refreshed faces alive to make the boy feel as welcome as possible, knowing full well that more needed to be done to mend what had been broken. Pa Moiwa told Ernest to go to the house of Colonel and to say that the elders had sent him to stay with them.

"We have to make sure that no one feels afraid to be here or unwelcome," Mama Kadie said to her friends.

"The war has changed us, but I hope not so much that we'll never find our way back. I could have never imagined a world where the presence of a child brings something other than joy." Her friends agreed with only hums, looking at the boy as he walked away, his apprehensive shadow seeming to dodge the sun, painting itself in strange forms on the earth.

Ernest didn't go immediately to where he had been told to go. Instead, he walked around town looking for a bucket or jerry can. He found two buckets on a veranda and took them without asking, since no one was present, and went to the river to fetch water. He brought the water and placed it under the stoop of Sila's house. Then he knocked on the doorframe—the home had no door—and ran to hide in the nearby bushes. Sila came out asking, "Who is it?" but there was no one. His eyes caught the two buckets of water and he smiled, surveying the area more, hoping to thank the person for this kind gesture. He patted his own shoulder; this was how he clapped these days, with his only hand, to thank whoever had done him this good. Ernest saw it all in hiding from under the coffee trees. He didn't smile; even though he had made Sila happy, he felt a twist in his heart—this man couldn't clap normally anymore. After Sila went back into his house, Ernest lay in the bushes for a while, his hands folded under his heavy body until they became numb and unusable. He struggled to get himself up without the use of his hands, deliberately letting his body roll in thorns and against trees. He did things like this to himself frequently, sometimes wishing his hands would stop working forever. He made his way to the house where Colonel and the others were, his hands still waking up from their numbness.

He didn't go inside but looked through the window to see who these other youngsters were. He could tell that Colonel was the head of this group, as he sat facing the others, upright, his head higher. When Colonel spoke, they all quieted and listened. Ernest knew that Colonel would test him before allowing him to join this group. When he walked into the house, he had already accepted being under the command of Colonel. He was attacked by Colonel as soon as he came closer, thrown to the ground. With a knee in his back and his face in the dust, he explained that he had been sent to them by the elders. He was let up and told where to sleep. He sat away from Colonel and his group, all of them observing him and whispering things they didn't want him to hear. He sometimes averted his eyes to avoid the strong stares from Colonel. Ernest's mind was too occupied with Sila and his children to worry about becoming an outcast from this group for now. But he didn't mind sitting near other youngsters, who he knew understood things about war that he didn't have to explain to them. This was a small but necessary comfort.

What was common among most of the arrivals was that in whatever conditions they found their homes, they started to live in them. Gradually, they cleaned and fixed things, erecting walls of mud brick instead of cement and patching with any materials that were available in nature. Soon, some of the houses had a mixture of tin roof on one side and thatch on the other.

Among the returnees were those for whom the older people couldn't find faces in their memories. These groups brushed spaces for themselves and built huts. They waited for weeks, and if no one arrived to claim the abandoned houses, they moved in and started renovating. The elders agreed that all were welcome. People had lived temporary lives for so many years that they needed any form of stability. Sometimes this meant building a hut or mending a home. They did it slowly, fearing it would be destroyed again. But when others came to town and weeks passed without any disturbances, their anxiety lessened and they rushed to complete whatever they had been working on. The simple joy of finishing something without running away from it or watching it be destroyed or disintegrate had become rare and was still gaining trust in the minds of these returnees.

Something unexpected happened one afternoon while the elders sat on the logs greeting more arrivals. The heads of two girls, three boys, their mother, and their father emerged in the distance. Pa Kainesi felt the wind about him warmer than it had been. He could not explain why he suddenly felt the presence of his heart more strongly. He stood up, and his friends asked if he was well. His legs took him toward the path, and it was there that he set eyes on his son, Bockarie, and his family.

Bockarie, his children, and his wife had gone missing during the war, and Pa Kainesi hadn't heard anything about their existence. Bockarie had also thought that his father had been killed, since he couldn't find him anywhere. They were one of those few lucky families who had not lost many members. Bockarie had managed to keep his family together throughout the war with a few separations here and there. His wife had gone missing for four months, and he and his children had found her at a refugee camp on the Liberian border, one of the countries next door. Their oldest daughter, too, had been lost and spent months homeless in some town in the north. The oldest son had escaped multiple recruitments. They had all known hunger and suffering intimately; they had all been close to death. Bockarie told his family that as soon as the war was over and things were safe, they would go home, even if it meant walking for weeks.

Upon arriving now with two additional children—twins, a boy and a girl born during the war—Bockarie passed by his former secondary school, where he had taught before the war came. The school was deserted, overgrown with trees and grasses, the floors now harboring roots and littered with leaves. He had hoped he would be able to resume teaching. His family had seen the disappointment on his round face when he surveyed the school compound. Nonetheless, he was glad to be home, and the rest would work itself out.

Pa Kainesi smiled at his son, who couldn't yet recognize this old man with a distorted face. But as he peered into the face, he saw the eyes of his father. He then allowed his father to embrace him, his wife, Kula, and all the children. Pa Kainesi didn't ask many questions but wept as he pressed his palm on each forehead, looking at them and wrapping his arms around them again and again as though to reassure himself that this moment was real and not just another of the dreams he had been having.

"Father, who is this man with this strange face?" Thomas asked, hiding behind his father's leg after the old man had released his arms around him.

"He is your grandfather, my son." Bockarie lowered himself to his child. He had not spoken much about his father for fear that his children would ask whether he was dead or alive. He had no answer to that question at that time.

Oumu, Thomas's twin, then held her grandfather's hand and shook it until he brought his face to the height of her bright, curious eyes. She passed her fingers over his face, touching the scars, and in her innocent voice asked, "Were you born like this, or is this what happens when you become so old?"

Everyone laughed without answering the little girl. She was of the generation that didn't witness the war and had been told only good stories of this land, so she still believed that people get old and then die and that marks such as the ones on her grandfather's face were a result of old age and not of other consequences.

Pa Kainesi's friends had now joined him and welcomed the family, but sadness was in their voices. They still had no news of any of their children or grandchildren. Sensing the mood of his friends, Pa Kainesi announced to the wind, "Kadie and Moiwa, our children have arrived. We now have permission to be old!"

This brought smiles and laughter to the elders, and they all walked to his house and had a feast that evening of cassava and groundnut soup with bush meat that had been caught that morning. The evening brought back one of the old ways and feelings, which was that children were everyone's and that they belonged to all adults, who had the responsibilities to care for them. Mahawa and her child were part of the family gathering. Pa Moiwa, noticing that Mama Kadie was half present, one foot in happiness and the other in sadness, spoke directly into the ears of his friend: "There is no need for too much sadness. There are enough children in town to be fathers, mothers, and grandparents to. You already have two." He pointed to Mahawa, who was playing with her child.

She went to them and gave her voice out to the young woman. "What is his name?"

"I haven't given him one." Mahawa wiped the sweat from the boy's forehead and went on. "But I have thought about it a lot and I have decided that whatever way he came into this world, he is my truth. So I would like to call him Tornya." She looked at Mama Kadie for confirmation. *Tornya*, the word for "truth."

"Yes, I agree. Tornya."

The boy smiled and made a few incomprehensible remarks followed by saliva coming out of his mouth in abundance. He quieted when they smiled and put his hands tenderly on his mother's face.

"He wants to say more than his tongue is ready for," Mama Kadie told Mahawa as they both held a hand of the child. They then moved closer to everyone to become part of the gathering.

"Father, where is the river that you told us you played swimming games in?" Thomas asked his father.

"Yes, and the big mango tree that always had a mango? I would like to try some." Oumu followed her brother's questioning.

"We have time to see all these things. Be patient. For now, let's eat," Bockarie told his children, tickling them under their armpits.

Oumu had been eyeing Mama Kadie ever since the gathering began. Now that there was a small quietness, she walked over to the elder and sat beside her.

"I have been expecting you." Mama Kadie placed her hand on Oumu's forehead and looked into the face and eyes of the little girl.

"I asked Mother who knows the most stories and she said it was you. Can you tell me all of them?" Oumu asked, her voice thick with excitement.

"It isn't about knowing the most stories, child. It is about carrying the ones that are most important and passing them along. I have already decided to tell you all the stories I carry. You have to be patient, though, for the stories can only remain in the mind and veins of a patient person. Come visit me anytime you need a story."

She never stopped to ask if Oumu understood what she was saying, as she usually did with other children. There was a calm seriousness on the child's face that convinced whoever spoke to her that she had heard the words deeply. Oumu said nothing that night and just sat by Mama Kadie until it was time to eat, and she went to assist her mother and older sister in getting the drinking water and plates ready.

All the men and boys ate together and the women and girls did the same, bringing a lively aura to that evening that resembled the way things used to be. There was music coming from the old cassette player, slow traditional music in harmony with the wind. Kula started dancing, her smile and eyes inviting others to join. Bockarie was the first, and then the older people got up one at a time and swayed around for few minutes before sitting down. They continued nodding and shaking their bodies in the chairs and benches they sat on. The children observed and laughed, playing games with their hands in between their laughter. Every so often a passerby would join and dance vigorously, showing off his or her dance skills, and everyone clapped. The visitor would then bid them good night and hum the next tune as he or she went into the night on the way home.

A good part of the sky was red, as though it were on fire or someone were cooking on it with firewood. The hue was not that of a threatening fire but of something playful and inviting, with such richness that the red deepened the more the eyes marveled at it. The clear blue around the surface of the red formed patterns that resembled openings and ladders. The evening grew older and became night.

That night, curiosity engulfed the face of the sky, its stars and moon, and they turned their eyes to Imperi to see the unimpeded spirits that had returned home despite all difficulties. Something within all of them, however small, had propelled them back here. Some did not even know what, how, or why.

Colonel was in the veranda room that he had chosen to be able to guard the others, who were asleep—except Ernest, who for now was on the floor in the parlor, lying on his hands with all his weight. Often in the night, Colonel would come into the rooms where Amadu, Victor, and Salimatu were sleeping and stand over them in the dark. Sometimes he would sit at the doorway looking into the night before going back to his own room.

"I know you are not asleep. Take the empty room in the back. There is a mat and some old blankets there," Colonel said to Ernest as he walked through the parlor on one of his rounds. Ernest went to the room, but before he settled, he left the house through the back door and went to see if Sila and his children were safe. He observed them through the window that had been left open to invite the cool breeze inside. The children were turning in their sleep and their father was awake. Ernest felt he knew what they were reliving. He encountered Colonel as he came back in.

"You cannot undo what has been done. Your heart is in the right place, though, so don't give up trying to mend it." He towered over Ernest and stepped aside for him to get by.

The sky turned its face to different parts of the town that night and ended with Mama Kadie, Pa Moiwa, Pa Kainesi, and the rest. The merriment had ended and they were preparing to return to their various houses, where the habits of despair waited for some. For Mahawa, it was staring at the face of her sleeping son, a reminder of many things that made her lips tremble from the pain that remained inside her body. The visible ones heal quicker.

Nights like this had been rare, and in the past the sky had removed itself farther from the town, but now it came closer, listening to the wind, which was no longer accused of carrying news that stuck needles in the hearts of the living.

After many years of only partially allowing the heart to drum life through their veins, people gradually heard the full drumming of what life used to be. The birds had returned and resumed their vigorous chanting to welcome the day. Children's voices filled the town once again. Every now and then a hesitant air would blow through and quiet things for a few minutes.

3

THERE WAS A TIME when the days in Imperi were longer and marked by elaborate conversations, tales, visiting friends and family, lying in hammocks under the shade and welcoming strangers with a calabash of cold water, going to the river for a swim or to watch children play diving games. The elders still clung to these moments and wanted them back. Aspects of this life were there but without the previous enthusiasm. Perhaps it was because a large part of the population was unsure what to expect out of their lives; they had gotten used to the fragility of things. But they knew they wanted something different from the elders, something new, though they didn't know exactly what or how to set about attaining this new life in their current condition.

The simplicity that had once been life had become a burden, especially when it seemed everyone waited for something to do. In the silence of that waiting, memories of war were awakened, bringing restlessness and irritability. People didn't spend much time on their verandas anymore. Besides the farming that had started on a very small scale just for people to feed their families, everyone just sat around, afraid to find pleasure in most things. Only incidents brought them together and reminded them of the need to mend themselves and their community.

The day after his arrival, Bockarie decided to show the town to Thomas and Oumu. The twins held the long hands of their father as they ventured into the realities of stories he had told them. His quiet demeanor and even his strides were calmer than his children's, whose impatience made him laugh, a slow, drawn-out laughter that made others smile. Oumu and Thomas greeted people, the few who sat on verandas, the way their father had told them about how things used to be.

"Good morning. Was sleep generous to you and your family? Has the world greeted you kindly this morning . . . ?" the children repeated to everyone they encountered. Most of the people ignored them and went inside their homes because these questions reminded them either of the families they no longer had or of the fact that the world was still cruel to them, and they wanted to forget for just a bit before facing the day. Some of the people laughed because they knew these old words didn't belong to the children who spoke them.

"Father, how come they do not respond the way you had told us? Is it because we are small and they don't know us from before?" Oumu asked.

"No, children, it isn't because you are small. They will answer better with time. I am sure they will," Bockarie said slightly ponderously, as he wasn't sure when this would happen. The children didn't give up, and the next person they greeted was Sila, who was standing under the stoop of his veranda, looking at the sky and breathing in the morning air with a vigor that made the children laugh. When they greeted him, he responded in detail about how he and his children were and how they had slept, and he asked the same questions to Bockarie. While Sila was speaking, Hawa and Maada came onto their veranda and sat on an old wooden log, listening to their father and watching the visitors with eyes that hadn't completely been freed from sleep. Oumu's and Thomas's faces filled with joy as they experienced what their father had spoken of so many times. Afterward, they giggled and poked each other as the adults had a long conversation about the way things had been—how in the morning there used to be a man who would play the drum at 5:00 a.m., then again in the evening for dancing, and finally deep at night, singing a quiet melody that summoned sleep for everyone.

"I used to dance to that drum every time I walked by to my farm. The sound cheered me up all the way to work," Sila said, mimicking some of the moves, crossing his feet over each other quickly and making the drum sound with his mouth. He was dancing so well that looking at him the children forgot about his missing hand. Bockarie joined in dancing while telling Sila that he, too, had liked the drum, closing the night in particular. He also said that it was actually how he met Kula, dancing in front of the drummer in the evening.

While the adults reminisced, the children watched one another. Oumu and Thomas clearly wanted to know why Hawa and Maada were missing arms and hands, but they didn't know when it was appropriate to interrupt the adults. So they stepped onto the veranda closer to their age-mates to see if they had just put their hands inside their clothes as children do sometimes, especially in the morning when it was a bit colder. Oumu even touched the stump of Maada's arm—he smiled awkwardly, trying to understand why this little girl didn't seem to understand that his hands were gone. Thomas began to emulate the dancing of the adults as an excuse to get closer to Hawa and Maada to observe them more. The adults were too consumed with one another and their past to notice what was transpiring among the children. Perhaps it was a good thing that they learned to be with one another on their own without the adults, who made the situation more awkward at times.

"You should come to my house this evening. The children can

play together." Bockarie tapped Sila on his shoulder and waved good-bye to the children, who giggled, knowing they would have play-mates later on. Their shyness had subsided a bit, and Hawa, with her only right hand, waved to Oumu and Thomas, who hesitantly waved back. Sila wasn't worried, as his children had been through this so many times that it was no longer a worthy conversation. Bockarie knew that his children would ask him questions about this family. "Your mother will explain better, so wait until we get home," Bockarie said before the children let their inquisitive tongues loose and while their eyes remained on Sila and his family as they walked home. He had to say something but he hadn't the words, nor did he know how to explain why or how Sila and his children were like that.

Just then a man came running as fast as possible and halted next to Bockarie, almost hiding himself behind him and his children. The man pointed to the path and shouted, "Someone is coming again to do away with us all. Run, everyone!"

A few people who had left their verandas returned to see what the commotion was all about. Most of the others already had their bundles ready to run into the bushes. Soon enough, Colonel emerged from the path holding a machete. He was walking hurriedly with deliberate intensity, marching like a soldier, holding the machete not like a farmer but as someone ready to use it for a fight, his strong arms raised and ready to strike. This was out of habit. The man had seen him from afar; now Colonel saw the man pointing at him and the many hesitant eyes directed his way. He stopped, dropped the machete on the ground, and waited. Victor, Salimatu, Amadu, and Ernest came into view with bundles of wood on each of their heads. The man sighed with apologetic eyes as people now turned to look at him, some relaxing and bringing their bundles back inside their houses. Who was to be blamed? A machete in someone's hands these days, especially in a young person's hands, had a different mean-ing. The man went toward the path and shook hands with Colonel before passing, perhaps his way of saying it was not his fault that he feared Colonel.

"We have wood for sale if your household needs some. Please tell everyone we are at the house at the end of town near the oldest mango tree," Colonel said to the dispersing crowd. He didn't introduce himself to Bockarie or anyone else as he walked on. Bockarie later learned about him and the others from Pa Kainesi.

As soon as they arrived home, Thomas and Oumu went to their mother and asked why Hawa and Maada had no hands.

Kula looked toward her husband, whose eyes said, *I didn't know what to say.*

"Well, it was an accident that happened in this country when you were just babies, and it happened to many people," she told the children, and then she preempted their follow-up question. "It is an accident that people do not want to speak about just yet. So don't ask questions, okay. In time you will know if necessary." She hugged them both.

"Mother, we also saw a man running away from a young boy and then he realized he was wrong!" Oumu said.

"So many stories already this morning! Go in and eat with your brothers and sister." She released the children from her arms and placed her head on her husband's back, leaning on him and folding her arms around his waist. He turned to face her. She always had a smile waiting for him that made him feel at peace. He put his hands around her waist and squeezed her until she giggled and playfully pinched him. They laughed and stood together for a while, holding each other to gather the strength that was needed for this day, another day of waiting.

"Mother, Father, I am going to see Mama Kadie. She said I should visit whenever I need a story for the day." Oumu distracted her parents, who looked at each other and nodded to her request. They knew she would go anyway, or harass them to tell her stories.

"What story do you need for today, if I may ask," Bockarie said, kissing his daughter's forehead.

"Mama Kadie will know when she sees my eyes," Oumu said and skipped off.

On that same day, when the sun was in the middle of the sky, a group of children had ventured into the river for a swim. As they splashed in it, making the water swing harder to both shores, they had shaken loose a body that had been hanging from the branch of a tree for who knows how long. The children's frightened shouts filled the air, waking the town from its slumber and bringing adults running with heavy hearts. They found a stick and fished the body out. All they could tell was that he was a young man whose genitals had been cut. Memories of that particular past filled everyone's minds again and they quickly covered the body, as though this would halt the invitation of unpleasant sights into their minds. The children who had been swimming in the river were all too young to know what had happened not so long ago. They had seen burnt villages and houses and holes in walls, and their minds had told them it was fire from a burning farm that had consumed the houses. The adults were happy to agree with such innocent explanations. But as everyone stood with the children at the banks of the river, Oumu, whose innocent mind still thought people died only of old age, asked her father, "Why is this man dead in the river? He does not look older than grandfather." Bockarie and all the other adults searched one another's faces. He cleared his throat and said to his daughter, "The young man was drowned by a bad genie, a water spirit, because he went swimming at night, and by himself."

The children looked at the faces of their parents to confirm this explanation. The adults asked them to head to town, announcing that storytelling would take place that night about humans and water spirits. The children were delighted—their parents had told them of such gatherings, and now they would witness one for the first time. Mama Kadie said she would tell the story at the town square. They raced one another to their various homes, leaving the adults by the river. Pa Moiwa called out to Colonel, who had been sitting on a stone by the river observing things.

"Man in Charge, could you and your caboodle help us with some firewood for tonight's gathering?"

"Yes, Pa Moiwa, and you will have the firewood for no charge. Our contribution to the town." He turned away to look at the river. Pa Moiwa went back to the adults' discussion about the body.

Before they took the body to be buried in the cemetery, they decided to take canoes early the following morning to look for any other bodies that were floating under bushes at the edges of the river and to clean up as best they could. They knew they couldn't clear everything. A massacre had happened on the river, and though the blood no longer cloaked the surface of the water, there may have been all sorts of things underneath. A fisherman among them suggested he would use his nets to dredge whatever he could from the bottom of the river. What he didn't say out loud was that in that process, he would also catch fish, which he could sell to them.

Sila and his children arrived at Bockarie's house all dressed in colorful, embroidered traditional clothing. Their clean Vaseline-covered bodies were shiny in certain spots and dry in others. Sila carried raw rice wrapped in a cloth, which he gave to Kula as soon as they arrived. It was a tradition to bring a particular kind of red rice to signify that one was grateful for the friendship of the person whose house you visited. She hugged him and kissed his cheek, his smile growing wider. She then wrapped her arms around Hawa and Maada, squeezing them at the same time. They giggled—it was the first time they had met someone who didn't make them feel uncomfortable, someone who hugged them with no hesitation. Sila admired the attitude of this wonderful and beautiful woman. He stared at her, hoping to catch her eyes to thank her, which was more genuine than the handshake he lacked these days.

"I see that you have come to take my woman away from me!" Bockarie joked.

"Well, now that I am missing an arm, women don't find me threatening, and I don't complain when they come closer." He laughed and put his left arm around Bockarie's shoulder. Bockarie didn't know whether to hug him or shake his hand.

"But the hugs and kisses are only accepted from women, man!" Sila said. They walked to the front of the house, where most of the family was gathered. Miata, Bockarie's older daughter, Mahawa, and Oumu had gone to the river to bathe and fetch water for the evening. The visitors began their round of greetings to the elders. Mama Kadie was holding Tornya.

"Shake my hand with your left, and we should do so from now on, as this hand now has the responsibility of both," Pa Kainesi said to Sila.

"But this isn't proper. The right hand is customary for greetings."

"Times have changed and so must certain traditions. The respect for the tradition is in your eyes and mannerisms. So from now on I choose to shake your left hand." Pa Moiwa and Mama Kadie shook Sila's hand and rubbed the heads of his children. Maada and Hawa felt comfortable knowing that the elders treated them the same as all the other children.

As the adults settled on benches and hammocks to talk, Manawah and Abu, Bockarie's oldest sons, and Thomas took Hawa and Maada to the other side of the veranda. First they rubbed the Vaseline properly on parts of their faces that were dried and then they played word and riddle games, avoiding activities that required both hands. There were moments when they felt themselves thinking too much about the fact that Maada and Hawa were amputated, forgetting to look at their faces. Maada at one point stood up so the stump of his hand was at Manawah's eye level. He swung himself around and his stump slapped Manawah. He laughed, falling playfully to the floor. Manawah got the point. They would get used to it eventually and would play naturally together.

When the girls returned from the river, they helped to serve the food: country rice with chicken, fish stew with onions, and eggplant cooked in coconut oil with hot pepper and spices. While the food was being spread out on large plates, Bockarie boasted, "My wife's cooking is so good that when you smell it, you start thinking of stealing the pot for yourself, running with it into the bushes, and eating until your stomach is as tight as a drum." They all laughed, the smell of the stew now stronger; they could taste it. The first plate was placed in the circle of the men, and they called on the boys to join them. Mama Kadie left her friends to sit and eat with Kula and the girls, who had their own plate of food. The feasting began. The adult men fed Maada, taking turns shoving rice and pieces of meat in his mouth. The boy was content sitting on the ground against his father's leg. Hawa ate using her right hand, as did everyone else, and was assisted only when she wanted water.

By the time they finished, the sun had successfully hidden itself from the eyes of the sky and put out its fire. They decided to move to the town's square, the adults walking slowly while the children ran ahead, hiding behind houses and jumping out with noises to scare one another on the way.

The light from the fire painted the dark shadows of everyone on the walls of the houses behind them. The young people weren't as plentiful, and some sat reluctantly by the fire. The eager ones were the generation of Oumu and Thomas, who had heard of moments such as this from their parents, and some exceptional ones like Hawa and Maada, who, despite what they had endured, had a joy within them that such a tradition sparked even more. The other few, who had arrived in town without parents and roamed about, helping here and there to get some food, sat by themselves. They listened to the story with one ear focused on the gathering and the other on guard. Colonel and his brothers and sister were among this group. He had gathered every young and parentless individual in town to fetch wood and prepare the fire. During that work he had also told them it was their duty to make sure that things went smoothly, to prevent any outside intrusion, and had assigned each a position and task for the night.

No matter who was present, and why, the entire town had come to hear a story from Mama Kadie and from whoever else would be moved to tell. This was the tradition—the elders, mostly women, would tell a story, and other elders would join in afterward. Some nights it would go on until even children were called upon to retell stories they had heard. Tonight, Mama Kadie stood up inside the circle and walked around the fire as she told the story, adjusting the wood every so often to make the fire brighter or duller depending on the mood of the tale. Some of the boys who had sat away gradually came closer.

"Story, story, what should I do with you?" she had shouted, the call for the teller to start, and the audience responded, "Please tell it to us, so we can pass it to others." She went on a number of times until everyone was asking to be told the story.

"Once upon a time, when the world had a common voice for all things on the surface of the earth and beyond, the chief of the humans, a woman, was a dear friend of the god of the water spirits. She would go to the river very early in the morning to have a conversation with her friend, who emerged from the river in different forms and sat on the banks with her. Sometimes she came as a beautiful woman, as half fish, half human; other times she came as a muscular, handsome man. All these forms were what the human chief had committed to her mind and thought about before their meeting. They talked about their worlds and the need to maintain the purity of the river, which was the source of life for both their peoples.

"In those days, no one drowned in rivers, as the water spirits aided everyone who swam in them. The humans were required to stay away from the river only at midnight for a few hours so that the water spirits could perform their bathing ceremonies uninterrupted. The relationship went on for centuries until one night a callous young man, who had arrived very late on the other side of the river, decided he must cross into town immediately even though he'd been warned to wait just a few hours. As he rowed the canoe across, he frightened the water spirits; some of them hid and others transformed into strong currents because of the shock. He struggled to row against the currents, and one of the water spirits, in the form of a beautiful girl, decided to aid him. She made herself visible and guided his canoe to shore. The young human and water spirit fell in love and started meeting each other to swim when no one else was around.

"One night while they were playing together in the river, the young man, not listening to the girl, went to a deep, turbulent area of the river and drowned. This brought about distrust between the humans and the water spirits. Before the chiefs on either side could speak about what had happened, the man's father, a hunter with too much temper, had already killed one of the water spirits with his arrow."

"Did the hunter have guns or just arrows? He could do more with guns and grenades that he could just shoot or throw in the water and kill all the water spirits," a young man interrupted, with eyes redder than the flames and memories of the recent past in his imagination. He called himself Miller. Colonel had not noticed this young man before and made a mental note to find him the next day. Mama Kadie walked over and sat next to him and told the rest of the story as if only for him.

She told of how in those days there were no guns or grenades, of how a small misunderstanding had changed the relationship between the humans and the water spirits, and how the act of one person whose heart had been quickly consumed by negative fire had caused the water spirits to hide from humans forever. So every now and then when a human laid eyes on any water spirit, it would try to protect itself by drowning that human, especially adults whose minds would conjure only the worst image of the water spirits. It was only children whom they did not attack, except in rare circumstances, for the water spirits still saw them as the only pure humans.

It was an important point that needed to be made about the nature of distrust and how it can spiral into violence. It was also a story to reassure some of the younger ones that their innocence was not to be feared any longer, as it had come to be during the time of the war. Sometimes a story does not make immediate sense—one has to listen and keep it in one's heart, in one's blood, until the day it will become useful.

The sighs of relief from the children filled the night when they heard that they were exempted from harm. The muscles of the night shook with a slight wind, rejoicing as they received these innocent sighs once again.

The last story, told by Pa Kainesi, brought about tremendous laughter in the crowd, something none had done in a while. He began:

"There was a man who always complained about his condition and was unhappy with every aspect of his life, especially about his only pair of trousers, which had holes in them everywhere. Parts of his flesh could be seen through the trousers, so it looked from afar as though he had on checkered pants. When he got closer, you could not help but laugh at the natural beautification of his trousers. Soon all the young people whose pants had holes in them were referring to it as a new style, 'skin to cloth.'

"The tailor in town was of course unhappy about this and blamed the man with the holes in his trousers for ruining his business. No one came to get things mended anymore; natural beautification had taken over. The tailor followed the man everywhere, waiting for the perfect time to steal and destroy his trousers. Late one afternoon, after the man had returned from his farm, he decided to bathe in the river. He took off his trousers and carefully washed them. Then he laid them on the grasses to dry and went into the river. He submerged himself in the water to get a nice soak. The tailor, who had been hiding in the bushes, decided this was his chance, but as he was preparing to move toward the trousers, another man came out of the bushes, took the trousers, and disappeared. When the man came out of the river, he couldn't believe his pants were missing. He called out, 'If this is some kind of a joke from gods or any human, I am not laughing.' He waited awhile, but no response. Then he saw the footprints of the thief and began laughing so hard he fell into the water and struggled to pull himself out, still laughing. He said, 'There must be somebody worse off than I am, and if so, please enjoy whatever is left of my trousers. Thank you God and gods for not making me the poorest of men.' He danced in the grasses while the tailor watched, still not happy because he knew the thief would use the trousers. He wanted them destroyed.

"When the man walked down the path toward town, the tailor rose from hiding. He thought he should clean and cool himself off. He took off his clothes and dove into the river. The naked man heard the sound of the water and ran back, thinking he could see who had stolen from him. He saw no one, only some fresh new clothes: long pants and a shirt. He looked around, but the tailor was deep under the water, enjoying its coolness—even the top of the river had calmed. The man danced as he wore the new clothes, thinking that this was a wonderful day.

"When the tailor came up for air, he noticed that he had nothing to wear. It was a strange thing to see a naked tailor running through town."

The gathering was in a fit of laughter. Colonel, Ernest, and Miller were the only ones to whom laughter didn't succeed in introducing herself. Ernest's eyes searched for Sila and his children. Watching their happy mood brought a stroke of peace in his heart. Colonel looked around to see whether he could determine who the thief had been. Miller had witnessed too many hardships to think about stories, to feel the functions of them. He got up and walked away, as though the laughter was tormenting him.

The children of Oumu's generation laughed purely and repeated the funniest lines to one another. The adults laughed even more because they knew the story was true. The tailor was among them and the checkered-trousers man was there, too. But who was the trouser thief? No one admitted it, as usually things are mended at such gatherings.

After the laughter died down, the adults and elders formed their own circle, leaving the children to themselves to talk about the stories. The adults and elders started a serious conversation about godliness. The imam and the pastor agreed that all human beings embody God within them.

"Then how do you explain what happened during the war?" someone asked. There was no answer for a while, and then Pa Moiwa spoke. "When we are suffering so much, I believe whatever godliness that is within us departs temporarily. During the war and all that it brought about, we as a people of this land chipped away at the embodiment of God within us and all the traces of goodness that were left after God departed. And now there are many who are empty vessels and therefore can easily be filled with anything. I think stories and the old ways will bring them in contact with life, with living, and with godliness again. Of course, these aren't the only things. There are practical measures that must be taken."

There was silence among them, but the children were playing games, laughing and clapping.

If God could be anywhere, this was where he or she was tonight.

No one could have anticipated that this was the last of such gatherings. The elders would have told other stories if they could have seen the strange changes that were in the wind of time. But at such beginnings, it was too early to hope for more; they had hoped only for incremental changes and reintroductions of old ways. They couldn't think too far into the future.

Oumu didn't go home with her family that night. Instead she went with Mama Kadie and the two of them stayed up late into the night sitting around a small fire, their hands stretched out to receive its warmth. Mama Kadie told Oumu many stories until her voice became a whisper as the silence of the night deepened. She went on until Oumu's eyes said she needed no more. It was the beginning of such gatherings for them and it continued for many other nights. Mama Kadie would sometimes ask Oumu to retell stories she had told her. The little girl would do so in a voice that was not of her age. Mama Kadie would smile, knowing that each story had found a newer vessel and would live on.

4

WAITING CAST A SPELL OVER EVERYONE in Imperi, and it ended when they found something to do. It wasn't necessarily something life changing, but anything that brought about a routine that promised possibilities. Those who found nothing either left for other towns in search of employment or sat around, restless and irritable with everyone and everything.

Since the first day that Mama Kadie's feet landed in Imperi, the town had begun shedding its image of war, starting with its physical appearance. Now, a year later, it was difficult to see that most of the houses had been bullet-ridden or burnt. Everyone had done their best to change the condition of their houses so they regained their vibrancy with yellow, white, gray, green, and black paint. Those who didn't have paint plastered their homes with fresh brown and red mud.

The sounds, too, had changed, from hesitant winds and deep silences to the voices of children playing games, chasing one another, or playing in the river. The population had grown, but everyone still knew pretty much everyone else. Nearby towns and villages had also come to life, so the elders sometimes visited friends and vice versa. They would sit together eating cola nuts and discuss the old days when they were children and walking on the path was a pleasurable discovery. You would hear a man working on his farm, whistling tunes so beautifully that he put the birds to shame. Women and girls sang sweet melodies as they fished with nets in the river; farmers would lay out fresh cucumbers on the path for those going by to take a few and eat. Such things had returned during the latter part of the first year of Imperi's revival.

There were only a few unexpected occurrences. Some bulldozers came humming into town, clearing the roads that had been dead for years. Men in suits that made their foreheads sweat too much came with an air of self-importance to discuss the reopening of the only secondary school in the area. They had a meeting by the roadside, standing and squatting around documents they laid on the earth and held down with stones. They couldn't go into the school because it was still overgrown. But they decided that the campus would be cleaned and the school reopened even though it was far from town. A few weeks later, the school was functioning again, although no major repair had been done. The old bodies of the buildings were painted to make them look new. There was no ceremony for the reopening. A short, very dark jovial fellow with a round flattened head like a tadpole and red eyes and glasses stood at the junction on the road, handing out flyers. The incentive was printed in bold, while the words he feared would scare people off were faint and diminished in size. YOU WILL ONLY BE ASKED TO pay YOUR CHILD'S school fees AT THE END OF THE FIRST SEMESTER. That same fellow had come to Bockarie's house two days after the school was declared opened. There were no students yet.

"My name is Mr. Fofanah," he introduced himself to Kula, holding a black briefcase, constantly standing on his toes as though reaching for something or perhaps to look taller. "May I speak with your husband, Bockarie?" He wiped the sweat off his forehead with a handkerchief.

When Bockarie came outside, Mr. Fofanah wasted no time in offering him a teaching position. He had been told that Bockarie had attended the school and had also been a teacher. He wanted him to teach the subjects he had taught before: English, geography, and history.

After Mr. Fofanah left, Kula hugged her husband and he gave that half smile and hum that only she knew meant he was extremely happy. He wasn't one who showed emotion as others did.

"Will you help me prepare for lessons, my dear?"

"I miss when we used to do that. Sit, I will get a pen and some papers." She smiled.

"Yes, my lady. I miss that stronger commanding personality of yours whenever we start intellectual things." He sat and she laughed as she ran into the house.

While he waited, a tall man with a medium beard came onto the veranda and said his name was Benjamin.

"Mr. Fofanah told me to come and introduce myself." He spoke fast and his eyes opened wide whenever he did.

"Welcome to my homeland. Where are you from?" Bockarie spoke slowly.

"I am from Kono, the diamond area, but don't ask me why I am here. I got a job offer, man, so here I am with my family. The rest isn't interesting. Okay, man, I will see you in school or on the way there. I must go prepare for my lessons." Benjamin tapped Bockarie on the shoulder and walked away. He jogged a bit with one hand in his pocket, dribbling an invisible ball, then resumed walking.

"Were you talking to someone?" Kula returned with some wrinkled pages and several pens, as she always had to go through a bunch before one of them worked.

"Yes, the Benjamin fellow that Mr. Fofanah spoke of. He went back home to prepare for his lessons as well." Bockarie made room on the bench for Kula to sit next to him. They began from memory, from their school days, laughing and giggling as they teased one another with questions.

The following morning, Benjamin and Bockarie encountered each other on their three-mile walk to school. They strode quietly at first, the morning dew soaking their faces.

"You know, all of my life I have had to walk in the morning. At first it was to the farm, then to school, to work . . ." Benjamin started, and before Bockarie responded that he, too, had had the same experience, Benjamin spoke again. "The good thing about it is that I have always made a good friend on each of those walks. Okay, teacher Bockarie, let us walk like young men with life in them." Benjamin started pulling Bockarie along as he hastened his steps and they laughed, walking as fast as they could. When they arrived at school, Mr. Fofanah, the principal, gathered all the teachers and gave them the first month's salary followed by a talk about how wonderful it was that they were all there. Things looked promising.

"Don't worry about the lack of school materials. The board of education has promised to send things right away. For now we have the basics, chalk and a blackboard and some desks and benches to start with. And here come the students." The principal was distracted by a large group of young people walking toward campus. He guessed there were more than fifty, and that would suffice. More came as the day unfolded.

That same morning, Kula had gone to the river to wash some clothes and saw a woman she hadn't laid eyes on in town. She was humming a tune while rinsing her laundry away from the other women. She was very tall and thin, with big brown eyes that brightened her narrow face.

"You must be the wife of the new teacher in town. What is his name, by the way?" Kula placed her hand on her forehead as she often did to remember something.

She stopped humming and responded with a smile. "Benjamin. That is his name and yes I am. My name is Fatu."

"I am Kula. Please come by my home anytime if you need any help knowing the area. You have two young ones?" She washed her bucket.

"Thank you. I will, and yes, we have a girl and a boy, Rugiatu and Bundu. We just got here and don't really know anyone, so it will be good for them to have friends and me, too. My husband was looking for something different and wanted to leave his hometown, Koidu, you know, in Kono, the diamond area. You must be the wife of Bockarie. My husband spoke of him." She held the cloth between her knees so that the river wouldn't take it away and extended her hand to Kula. They, too, just as their husbands, went on to become friends.

It had been many months since Mr. Fofanah came to Bockarie's house and hired him and on that same day he had met Benjamin. Their teaching jobs and lives hadn't unfolded as they had hoped. They continued walking to school every morning, now along with Bockarie's three older children, Manawah, Miata, and Abu, and most of their students and colleagues. The three miles of dusty road with patches of tar here and there had become unbearable for them. To start with, though there were few vehicles on the road, when one was heard in the distance, teachers and students ran into the bushes, holding their noses. They hid themselves from the dust that looked for clean bodies, clothes, and hair to settle on. The leaves were already cloaked with enough dust that their colors couldn't be seen. So running into the bushes was only to lessen the amount of dust that could find them. During the rainy season, they still ran, though not into the bushes but away from the many puddles to avoid being splashed on. There were too many puddles, so one had to zigzag strategically to this and that side of the vehicle or find a spot near the deeper holes where it almost came to a halt, the driver worried about getting stuck. If you had an umbrella, you could hold it against your side. But not many could afford umbrellas.

During the year of teaching, the materials that the principal had promised on the first day of school still did not arrive. Therefore, with barely any materials, the teachers continued preparing lessons from memory, from their own school days, and tried to write on the blackboard as much as possible whenever there was chalk. Otherwise, they dictated lessons and students wrote in their books, interrupting with a raised hand to ask for the spellings of certain words. For eleven months now, the department of education in Lion Mountain had sent only lengthy letters that the principal would read out loud to his teachers, his facial expression showing his disbelief in the message. "We have engaged on a remarkable revamping of our educational system," the letters would start, and they'd end the following way: "Educational Ministry of Lion Mountain, working for the people, always." One day while the principal was reading the letter, he couldn't contain himself. "They manage to send me these useless letters every week but not school materials, not even a box of chalk," he said and stopped before more words slipped out. It was clear that things were worse now than in the past. The neglect of this part of the country had increased. Before the war, they at least sent some school materials even if a month or sometimes a semester late. Salaries, too, unprecedentedly lagged behind. In nine months of teaching, the teachers had received only three months of salary that came every three months. As a result, Bockarie had started selling cigarettes, chewing gum, batteries, mosquito coils, and other small items at night on his veranda. He laid the items out in a small wooden box with a lamp that cast a dim light on the goods. This was also where he corrected students' papers and prepared for lessons, sometimes using a flashlight when he had no money to buy kerosene. It was difficult to provide for his family, and he continued teaching only because as a teacher he received a reduction in school fees for his three older children. His pay was 150,000 leones, which could barely buy a bag of rice. Kula helped by selling food items such as salt, pepper, and maggi cubes at the market, but they still struggled to make ends meet. They were, however, better off than Benjamin, who, with the same salary, had to pay rent and feed his wife, Fatu, and two little children, Bundu and Rugiatu. Since he wasn't from Imperi, he had no family house as Bockarie did.

"Sometimes, I think I should have stayed in my home, Koidu. I thought I could do something different with good pay, something less dangerous than mining diamonds . . . I also thought my wife could find work as an apprentice for her nursing career," Benjamin had said once to Bockarie when he came by to keep him company on his veranda.

At school, everyone functioned as best they could. The excitement of the school's reopening had lasted only for a semester, until they realized that this time around they would not receive the necessary support from the government. Nowadays, by the time teachers and students reached the school grounds, whatever happiness had been on their faces had disappeared with the long walk, the dust, the heat, the thirst and hunger. Looking around you couldn't tell who was hungrier, the teachers or the students, but all of their demeanors announced that most of them wanted school to end earlier; in fact, the moment they arrived they couldn't wait to return home. Coming to school for teachers and students had become a routine just to nurture whatever possibility of hope was left. Sitting at home all day, one is likely to fall in the way of the heavy wind of bad luck.

The only constantly lively person in the school was the principal, who had a brand-new motorcycle, and no one could figure out where he got the money to buy such an expensive thing that could pay for more than ten teachers' yearly salaries. Every morning, in his annoyingly exuberant mood, he would gather the teachers and lecture them on the need to "inspire the students, to rekindle their fire for learning and show them the importance of education.

"I believe in you and I'm only here to guide all of you to achieve your best," the principal would go on, walking on his toes, buttoning and opening his jacket and adjusting his tie, while sweating.

"Any questions that I may answer? No. I guess I made things very clear. Okay, let us go and inspire those youngsters." He would end with a big smile, which no one in his audience of teachers returned. Under his breath he would sigh and then raise his head again with that jovialness painted on his face. The teachers could do little with his inspirational messages. They were missing all the ingredients: salaries, school materials, and faith in the educational system itself.

Bockarie had tried talking about the importance of education in his class, and one of the students had asked, "Sir, you are educated, but I do not see any significant changes that education has made in your life. So why should we waste our time and money that we could use to enjoy our lives now as opposed to investing it only to be miserable later?"

"You have made a good point, but think of it as planting a mango tree. It takes years before you can begin to see the fruit. You can also plant something that grows quicker, like cassava or potato, but you want mangoes, too. I hope you get my point, since you are also studying agriculture." Bockarie walked slowly up and down the classroom, making sure that he made eye contact with every student regarding his last point.

"I understand, sir, but you still see my point that what we see of those educated isn't encouraging," the young boy persisted.

"It is indeed not an easy question, but it is worth thinking about." Bockarie wanted to flog the boy for his tone, but he respected the intelligence in his thinking and also knew the importance of his question. It was difficult to convince anyone to invest in education if those educated were worse off and couldn't find better jobs for themselves. So his response was, "Times are difficult for many people these days. There used to be a time when an educated person lived better. But that is not the only purpose of education. Its purpose is far greater than just improving your economic condition. In your case, you all need education so that you can be in a position to take advantage of opportunities that will come along. You cannot wait for the opportunity and then get an education when it arrives. You'll be too late." The students were quiet, even the young man who had asked the questions.

Bockarie was not sure whether he believed what he had told his students, but he felt that it would do for that moment. At home that evening he spoke to his father, Pa Kainesi, and his friends Pa Moiwa and Mama Kadie about what had happened in school. He remembered how exciting school was when he was a boy and the children had a thirst for learning. All the elders could offer him now was a popular maxim that "no condition is permanent" and that what he was doing was noble. He wanted to respond that although he believed in the maxim, in this part of the country, the condition of their lives and the despair were bringing about changes in people that would become permanent even after the conditions that had brought them about had changed. But one must have faith in the words of the elders and sometimes allow hope breathing room. He resorted to that thought instead.

He went for a stroll, keeping his frame within the darkest body of the night to avoid greetings and conversations. He soon forgot his thoughts and started to observe how some closed their day. At the edge of town he stopped, and his eyes caught the bottom of the veranda where Colonel and his group were tying up bundles of wood for sale. He walked closer to the nearest mango tree, carefully minding the sounds of his feet so that his footsteps didn't give him away. He leaned on the tree, watching this energetic group of youngsters. They were calculating the amount of money to be made from selling wood.

"Five bundles and one for free so that she will continue buying from us," Salimatu told Amadu, who jokingly saluted her and started tying the extra bundle. She laughed and continued instructing Victor, Ernest, and Miller how to pack the bundles so that it was clear which was to go to what house.

"That makes it six supplies," Victor called out to Colonel, who wrote something in a small notebook while standing on a bench over everybody. They all moved quickly. Colonel sat on the ground and started counting their income for that day, which he pulled out of a small bag, looking around to make sure no envious eyes from the outside were on him. Bockarie hid himself some more in the darkness. Colonel separated the money into two piles, one for saving and the other for food and whatever else they needed.

"If we continue saving this way, all of you will start school again next year." He spoke looking at Salimatu, Victor, Amadu, and Ernest. Though Colonel had brought Miller under his care, he had yet to make him fully part of the family. Therefore, nothing was said about his prospects for school. He didn't seem to mind.

"Okay, let's eat. Miller, my man, bring out the food," Colonel ordered, and Miller ran inside, smiling a bit that he had been given this task for the first time, a sign of a developing trust by Colonel. Miller returned shortly with a big bowl of rice with cassava leaves. They ate together, scooping from a bucket and passing a plastic cup of water around to whoever was thirsty. Bockarie wondered whether Colonel himself would like to go to school or find some work. It was then that Colonel noticed someone in the belly of the darkness and looked directly at where Bockarie stood. He walked away as quickly as possible before Colonel could get up to ascertain further. On his way he passed by Sila's house. He was teaching his children the alphabet with the letters cut out from old cardboard that he held in his only hand. When the children got a letter right, he would ask them to make a sentence, sometimes acting out a word with a smile always on his face. Sila had started a farm, growing cassavas and potatoes that he sold in exchange for things he needed. He had also, after several visits to Mama Kadie's home, gotten her and Mahawa to agree to cook for him and look after his children. It all started at that first gathering at Bockarie's house when they joked with him about what he fed his children.

"Besides the obvious fact that I am missing a hand, I am a man and do not know how to cook as well as you women. So whatever I know how to cook best, which is plain rice, actually plain every-thing, is what I will make for my children. If you don't like it, help. Please help?" He had laughed and continued, "I am sick of my own cooking." He pulled his tongue out and twisted his face to indicate how bad his meals tasted. His children concurred, making faces as though they had just tasted a bitter medicine and quickly turning away when he looked in their direction.

Bockarie remembered admiring how honest Sila was, without any care about what others thought. He continued, his eyes' final feast turning to Mama Kadie's house. Mahawa and Mama Kadie sat together by a dimly lit fire chatting about something that made both of them laugh and then embrace. The old woman's face was filled with joy as she stared at Mahawa and Tornya. Mahawa, on the other hand, had one of those calm faces that showed satisfaction but with a deep torment in their stillness. Bockarie sighed, not really knowing whether it was for him or for others. What he did know was that he had to return home before Kula started getting worried. When he arrived home, his children and wife were reading or doing homework. He watched them quietly, a sight that changed his mood and summoned the dancing of happy spirits on his face.

"What are you reading, Kula?" he asked, and the children ac-knowledged his presence either with a wave or with their eyes and then went back to what they were doing.

"Someone threw this on the street. It is a novel and in good con-dition. I just started, and if it is any good I will lend it to you for a price." She chuckled and motioned for her husband to come and sit on the bench next to her chair.

The day after he had the conversation with the elders, Bockarie left for school early to avoid the melancholic faces on the road, including those of his children, whose doldrums especially tormented him. However, he encountered Benjamin, who was in a better mood, and

that cheered him up. He just stood by the road smiling, clearly waiting for Bockarie.

"I have an idea that will make us some additional money, young
teacher friend who always looks serious." Benjamin started walking
backward so that he could face Bockarie as he spoke.

"What is this idea and please explain slowly, not too fast." Bockarie tried to catch up with Benjamin, who was now moving faster.

"You don't even know when you are funny sometimes. So I
could speak slowly and walk faster or walk slowly and speak faster."
His actions mimicked his words.

"Okay, save your answer. The plan is we should start after-school
lessons, particularly for students who are going to take the national
exam." He jumped in the air and now walked forward, and at a slow
pace.

"It is indeed a brilliant plan, my friend," Bockarie responded,
laughing a bit.

"I did not see any excitement from your body language, just
your voice went up a bit. Anyhow, let us meet and discuss later,"
Benjamin concluded as they neared the campus. They decided to
meet in the small windowless staff room at lunchtime.

When they arrived at the staff room, the principal was sitting in
a corner hunched over a book and a bag filled with cash, new notes
that hadn't yet been worn out by the hands of everyday survivors.
They froze and thought, *Finally the rest of our salaries have arrived.*
His back to the door, the principal was consumed with the contents
of his bag, licking his fingers to carefully count the stacks of bills.
He would make a note in the book next to him on the ground
whenever he paused in the counting.

Bockarie glanced at Benjamin with eyes that said they would
have to either say something or leave quietly. Benjamin thought that
any movement would reveal them, so they might as well announce
their presence.

"Good afternoon, sir." The principal's body jumped with surprise and his fingers halted. He slowly turned his face to look at them while making sure that his body shielded the bag from their view, and as he stood, he covered the bag with the long book they now recognized as the ledger listing the teachers, their salaries, and attendance records. The principal held their eyes, making sure they didn't drift to the bag on the ground. He inhaled deeply, perhaps searching for words, and his forehead was sweating now. Bockarie and Benjamin looked at each other, trying to understand why their superior was acting so strangely.

"So, gentlemen, this is a surprise for me to see that teachers indeed are making use of this room." His nervousness was now apparent even in his tone.

"Mr. Fofanah, we can go somewhere else, sir. We just needed a place to have a private conversation." Benjamin pointed to the back of the building.

"No, gentlemen. I should leave you here and go to my office. I only came because some workers were fixing a cabinet in there." The principal lowered himself, again placing himself between the bag and the men, and slid the ledger between the handles of the bag. With a series of nervous nods, he made his way toward the door, but as he was walking out, his hands shook and the ledger fell.

All three pairs of eyes landed on a page that listed the names of more than twenty teachers, teachers who were not at the school. And next to their names were the salaries they'd supposedly received for three months of the year. The principal froze; he could not bring himself to pick the book up off the ground. Bockarie leaned over and handed it to him. The principal plucked it from his fingers and hurriedly left them standing there speechless.

Bockarie sat down on one of the benches. "Well, now we know why he is always in a good mood."

"What are we going to do about what we just saw?" Benjamin asked.

"It is a difficult situation, my friend. We are getting our salaries. He has not tampered with that, as you saw. He has just added a lot more teachers than we are here. And we do not know anyone up top to bring this complaint to. They are probably all in on this behavior." He pondered. "Let's think about it for a few days."

"Now to our meeting," Benjamin said, to get their minds off the situation. He outlined the after-school lesson idea and they agreed on first printing flyers, which cost money, to hang around town and on the school grounds about the lessons at Bockarie's house. They needed only a blackboard, which they could take from the school's pile of old and unused junk. They both would save chalk, when it was available during school hours, by writing less and dictating more.

At the conclusion of school that day, they stayed behind and looked through the old blackboards until they found one they could easily rehabilitate. They carried it awkwardly, each holding an end, walking the miles home. They stopped every now and then to rest and joked that at least they didn't have to run into the bushes to hide from the dust, as the blackboard took most of it. At the bottom of the hill during a respite, the principal approached on his motorcycle. He blew the horn more than necessary to get their attention.

"This is the school's property and you have removed it without permission. Therefore, I must report it and you will be sacked for stealing." He stopped and got off the motorcycle.

"It is an almost rotten blackboard and you were going to throw it out anyway." Benjamin's fury was apparent in his deep, resonant voice.

"I will be the judge of whether I was going to throw it out or not," he sternly responded.

"We will take it back, then," Bockarie said, as he didn't want himself or Benjamin losing his only job.

"It won't make a difference. You have already stolen it." He got back on his motorcycle and started the engine as though he wanted the sound of it to cover the things he said next.

"Now, if your memories can erase what your eyes saw earlier, then I saw nothing of this. Why do you need this old thing, anyway?"

Bockarie quickly explained their plan, and the principal agreed that it was a great idea not only for making extra cash but also for providing needed assistance to some students. He said if they kept their mouths shut, he would even help them print the flyers for free using the printer in his office. Of course, this meant he would have to start the generator that required petrol that he said he would gladly provide and also some chalk to start with. He left without waiting for their response, as he knew they had no choice in the matter; he had the power to fire them and they couldn't bring their case to anyone. They knew no one and wouldn't be granted an appointment to see the educational district officer, who was currently being investigated for worse. They also needed the work to take care of their families. So quietly, and feeling defeated, their morals imprisoned by necessity, they conjured whatever meager courage they had left to carry the blackboard, which had suddenly gotten heavier.

They got the flyers printed by the principal, who still continued his inspirational messages. He told Bockarie and Benjamin that he wasn't doing anything wrong so he felt no guilt. He continued with an expression that they hated, as the very idea had already destroyed the country: "Where a cow is tied is where it grazes." He added that it was "my time to graze and the school is my field, my little portion of the bigger grazing field for those whose time it is to eat."

Bockarie stepped in front of Benjamin to make sure he didn't hit Mr. Fofanah. Benjamin's hands were shaking as he uttered his response under his breath. "If it is his time to eat, what about other people who must eat, too? We all must eat, otherwise there is no peace." This was exactly what every struggling man, woman, and child felt, but this sentiment was never heard even when spoken as loudly as possible because those who were eating now had become deaf, even though they had been on the other side of the fence a short while ago.

They went home defeated and worked on making the blackboard usable. They knew a trick from when they were students, which was breaking open old D and A batteries, extracting the black substance in them, then crushing and mixing it with water. They thoroughly rubbed the substance on the surface of the board and left it to dry in the sun. Later they wiped the residue to make the board smoother for writing.

"It looks new, man. We could sell this thing back to some other school if there was another in the area," Benjamin exclaimed.

The lessons started a few days later, and some money was coming in to lighten the burden for them. Still, they had to literally threaten parents in order to get the fees. Parents promised to pay but would hide whenever they saw the two teachers in town. Bockarie and Benjamin had to do one of the things they hated most, which was refusing to teach eager and intelligent students. However, if they made one exception, then the whole business would fail because all the parents would no longer want to pay, knowing that the teachers had a weakness for students who wanted to learn. Such was the game of testing and juggling morals among people waiting for their conditions to change. The only person who paid fees consistently without waiting for the impatient words of the teachers was Colonel. He had decided to enroll Amadu, Salimatu, Victor, and Ernest for introductory English and mathematics classes. Miller said he wasn't interested, but he always went along with the others and sat at ears' distance of the lesson. The teachers never sent him away.

"Teachers B to the power of 2. I would like to do a 'sibling payment' so that they can start preparing for school next year." Colonel had approached Benjamin and Bockarie, pointing to the others. The teachers had laughed at the humor and cleverness in his sentence, but he didn't. He discussed with them a reduction in price

and promised to pay on time, guaranteed. Afterward the teachers
considered inviting Colonel to attend school, but something about
his demeanor made them hold back. When the discussion came up
with the elders, they remarked, "You are speaking about Man in
Charge? If he wants to attend school, he will do so on his own."

"Bockarie, my brother, you are too patient. We have been thinking
too long about what to do with the business of the principal," Benjamin whispered, as some students were around and the elders, too,
weren't too far.

"Speaking of our devil." Bockarie shouldered Benjamin, whose
attention was turned to make sure the students had all brought their
notebooks. He looked up to see the principal arriving on his motorcycle, its engine revving up the tiny slope to a halt. Benjamin tried
to subdue his anger while urging the students, who had been hanging around on the stoop waiting and comparing notes, some pro-
voking their friends who jokingly chased them off in the yard, to
take their seats on the bamboo mat on the floor of the veranda.

"Good evening, students and teachers." The principal parked his
motorcycle and walked onto the veranda in between the two groups
of children separated by an opening for the teachers to be able to
walk on and off the veranda.

"Good evening, Principal Fofanah," the children said in unison
as they did in school and turned their heads to the blackboard. They
had to tilt their heads to properly see the raised board. They stared at
one blackboard that had two different lessons. Benjamin flanked
the board on the left and Bockarie on the right, with a thick white
line in the middle of the board separating the teachers' handwriting.
They had wanted to saw the board in half but the carpenter had
asked for too much money for the task.

"I have never seen this sort of efficient usage of a blackboard
before. Two teachers using the same board to teach two separate

lessons? Carry on, gentlemen," the principal said and walked to where the elders sat.

Bockarie eyed Benjamin to keep calm. Benjamin was teaching grammar and Bockarie was teaching Shakespeare's *King Lear*.

"You, stand up and give me a sentence using a reflexive verb and pronoun." Benjamin pointed his long cane at a girl, who stood up and made a sentence. He pointed at another student, a boy, who stood to point out which word in the sentence just made was the reflexive verb and which the pronoun.

Immediately outside the veranda were young boys hanging around, mostly orphans, former soldiers and currently not in school. They enjoyed the lessons and quietly guessed the answers to one another, sometimes betting money. The older people were seated in the yard. Pa Kainesi, who didn't know about what had transpired between the principal and the two teachers, greeted him.

"Principal, welcome, sir. It is a good thing that you are doing for all the children in this area. Please make sure they don't close our school."

"Thank you, Father, it is great to get my small work acknowledged by such wise elders as yourselves. I will continue to work hard for our children." He pointed toward the veranda and made a show of his support for what Benjamin and Bockarie were doing. When he was done, he went behind the house to urinate. Benjamin told his students to write a sentence so as to turn their attention to their notebooks. He also made sure that no one was looking when he climbed over the stoop and threw a stone at the motorcycle. Bockarie's eyes caught him just when the stone was about to leave his fingers. It landed on the petrol tank and the motorcycle fell on the ground, its side dragging in the dust. The principal came running and knew one of the teachers was responsible but couldn't prove it. He said nothing, just picked up his motorcycle and left. Bockarie eyed Benjamin hard, and he shrugged, indicating the principal deserved it.

The lessons resumed with the voice of a boy reading out loud a line from *King Lear*, " 'When we are born, we cry that we are come to this great stage of fools.' "

"Again." Bockarie pointed his ruler at the boy, whose voice the wind carried until the appointed time when nature began its call for the departure of that day's blue sky.

5

———◆———

IT WAS A SATURDAY that everyone in Imperi would remember. They were woken by a sound that wasn't part of the daily call for the arrival of morning. A siren began to wail around 5:00 a.m., and people came outside onto their verandas and into their yards with inquiring and confused faces. They looked at their neighbors for some explanation, but no one knew anything. The women began packing a few things and preparing the children to run away if it came to that. Meanwhile, the men hurriedly dressed and gathered at the compound of the acting chief of the town.

"I do not know what that is, my people," the old man, who had barely been present as a chief, told the men before they even had a chance to speak. They all stood around listening to the siren that resumed every five minutes. After an hour, they saw dark smoke rising in the distance. Some guessed that it was coming from the place where a mining company had tried to set up before the war. As they whispered among themselves, they heard many vehicles coming toward town. This was unusual, so the men dispersed, running to their homes to get their families and depart. However, they stopped as they soon saw that the vehicles were filled with nervous-looking white men, more nervous than they were. Behind the convoy of about ten vehicles were several trucks filled with machinery, equipment, fridges, and boxes of food. Most of the town's population came to the main road and watched the convoy go by to the hills beyond town, where the mining company later built one of its staff compounds.

They had come to mine rutile, a black or reddish-brown mineral consisting of titanium dioxide, which forms needlelike crystals in rocks in the earth. Rutile is used as a coating on welding rods; as pigment in paints, plastics, paper, and foods; and in sunscreen to protect against ultraviolet rays. And wherever rutile is found, you also find zircon, ilmenite, bauxite, and, in the case of Lion Mountain, diamonds. Not that the mining companies reveal they are mining all of these minerals. They obtain permits to dig up only one—rutile. So it is rutile alone that is mentioned in the reports it sends out, but the workers come to learn the truth.

Soon after the convoy passed, and people had returned to their homes, still on alert and making sure all their family members were within arm's reach, chiefs from the surrounding towns arrived to meet with the chief of Imperi. None of them had been advised of the arrival of the mining company, and they wanted to collectively send a message to the paramount chief demanding an explanation. At the very least, the fearful population should have been spared the anxiety of thinking war had returned. The chiefs decided to pay a visit to the paramount chief the following day.

The next morning, as though whoever had given permission from the government anticipated dissent from the people of Imperi who owned the land that the mining company would start operating on for minerals, a number of private security personnel arrived carrying heavy weapons and ammunition. The sight of such uniformed and armed men aroused fear and anger in the dispirited people. They didn't want to return to anything closer to what had happened here not so long ago. When women and children who were on their way to the river, to farms, and to markets saw the 4×4 vehicles filled with armed men, they dropped whatever they were carrying and ran either toward town to alert their families or into the bushes. The foreigners in the front seat of some of these vehicles laughed at what they considered an uncalled-for and silly reaction. By the time the armed men and foreigners passed through town, people were already packing up whatever little they had acquired and running away. The commotion of women screaming for their children and hurried footsteps filled the air. When some of the men learned that these were personnel for the company, they ran about town calling for calm, but half the population had already made it far into the forest and only returned days later. The town was tense that night and some days that followed.

The ease that some of the young boys and girls who had been in the war had started feeling was immediately replaced by the habits of survival because of the guns and uniformed men that passed through town every so often. Most of these children no longer slept; their eyes became more vigilant and they spent nights in the bushes at the edges of Imperi.

The paramount chief was the head of all the local chiefs in various towns around Imperi and was the direct representative of the people to the minister of the province, who resided in the capital. Thus, all grievances beyond local matters went through the paramount chief. All the local chiefs who had agreed to ascertain why the arrival of the mining company hadn't been discussed with the people, or at least announced to them, made the journey to visit the chief two days earlier than they had planned because of the arrival of the armed security.

She lived in one of the dilapidated villages, her house the only one in good condition and with a generator. When the chiefs arrived, having walked five miles from Imperi, where they gathered for the journey, they were treated to cold water, a rarity in this part of the country and sometimes enough to distract people from pursuing their grievances—and this was exactly what happened. The paramount chief told her guests, while supplying them cold water and soft drinks, that she would take up the matter with whoever was in charge. She added that they should be happy for now, as the mining company's arrival was a good thing.

"They are bringing jobs!" she exclaimed, but no one shared her excitement. She had no intention of looking into the complaint and wouldn't mention anything to anyone. She knew of the company's arrival and had received her bribe and some of the supplies the foreigners had brought. Nonetheless, the chiefs had faith in her and believed that she would represent her people. Perhaps it was because of what had happened during the war in their land that they thought no one would work against their people in the very early wake of that madness, or perhaps it was something else. Whatever it was, they were mistaken.

The week that followed brought about changes that no one anticipated so soon. Starting that Monday, very early in the morning before the cock crowed, until deep at night when the world shivers from the cloak of darkness, the machines rattled as they were assembled and tested. Each time the engines started again after a quick interval, it seemed their sounds chased silence farther out of the land. The ugly din interrupted the chanting of the birds so much that they stopped singing and instead listened, bobbing their heads on the treetops as they looked around inquiringly. The sounds of the machines were followed by thick smoke from the bowels of their engines; the smoke quickly blanketed the clouds and cast a dark glow around town. The smell made even the dogs sneeze, some chewing on plants perhaps to cure themselves.

The people of Imperi were beginning to believe in the new life of their town. They no longer leapt up when children suddenly shouted in joy while playing. They remained relaxed on their verandas when strangers emerged from the paths. But the town's revival was fragile.

If the elders had been asked, they would have advised the company to let Imperi become stable before beginning operations. But this wasn't the case, and the presence of the mining company took the town and its people in a direction of "many crooked roads," as the elders said, softening the truth about the devastation that gradually became accepted as the only condition possible for the inhabitants. The direction to the crooked roads began with the arrival of mostly men, including the foreigners, as employees and those looking for work. They were everywhere in their hard hats—surveying the roads with long poles and equipment, while the children gathered around to marvel, waiting to be picked up by vehicles for work, sitting by the roadside to eat their lunches.

Then, older students, mostly boys over eighteen, stopped going to school and sought employment. The possibility of an immediate salary was enticing in a place where it was difficult to find any way to earn income. Soon, some of the teachers followed their students to labor in hazardous conditions for just a few more leones—not a significant difference from what they had earned, but at least it was steady pay.

Machines were everywhere grading only the roads that the company needed to use for its work and nothing more. Water pipes were laid past the town to the quarters for workers. At the end of the day, the same workers who had laid the pipes all day would send their children to look for water miles out of town for them to wash their dirty bodies. They would buy cold water to drink, if they had money; otherwise, they drank the same water that they washed with, which made their bodies itch.

Electricity poles with live wires passed through the town to power mining operations, headquarters, and living quarters. The electricians were issued flashlights to navigate the darkness back to their homes after work, where their children studied under dim kerosene lamps, their eyes struggling to see their old notebooks.

"Here, son, use my flashlight and move that lamp away. I can see the dark smoke settling inside your nose," a father said, setting his light on the stoop of the veranda. The boy smiled up at his father and resumed his work, writing neatly in his notebook on the lop-sided table that he propped up with his foot to keep straight. The next day his father walked home in the darkness; his battery had died and he was warned that next time he would be sacked if he used his flashlight for any purposes other than walking home after work or going to dark areas where they needed electric cables laid out. Therefore, he didn't sit next to his child on the veranda that night, and nights after, afraid that he might not be able to restrain himself from turning the light on for his son.

More bars opened in town, and at night music blared out and drunken men harassed the young women who walked by. The elders no longer told stories in the town square, as the fracas from the bar prevented the quiet necessary for stories to pierce the hearts and minds of the young. With nothing better to do, the younger people went to the bars and stood around observing the white and black workers. They called it "going to watch television." Most nights ended with heated conversations and bottles thrown at walls or heads; or else swearing accompanied by laughs so hurtful to the ears they could come only from wounded souls. Sometimes one of the senior workers—he could be black, he could be white—would stagger out of the bar and, barely able to stand, urinate in public, shaking his penis at whoever was around. Then he'd climb into his Toyota Hilux and, not caring if anyone was in the way, drive away fast.

One night, one of the white workers around the age of thirty-five (or so he looked; one could never tell with sun-beaten white men) pissed all over the town hall where the elders gathered. He had a bottle of Heineken in one hand, and the other hand controlled his privates as he turned around in circles, soaking benches, chairs, the ceiling, and the floor, shouting, "I am Michelangelo and I am making my masterpiece." The young people watched in amazement and shock. The man threw some money at them and demanded, "Clap,

clap for me," as he went on. The young people scrambled for the money and clapped for him. Pa Moiwa had heard the commotion and come to the scene. With his presence, the young people ceased clapping and the man stopped to see why they had suddenly gone quiet. His eyes met the old man's.

"You clearly do not know what comes out of your mouth. If you want to be funny, you could say you are Jackson Pollock, not Michelangelo. But you are neither of those people." Pa Moiwa shook his head in disgust. "Do you behave in such a manner in the land you are from?"

The man burped. "You speak good English, old man. I was just painting here a little bit!"

"In your land, do you urinate in public spaces? Isn't it a public health violation?"

"Are you getting smart with me?"

"Not yet. I am not sure if I should waste my words on an idiot who thinks he can paint with his piss."

The man zipped his trousers and brushed against Pa Moiwa as he turned back toward the bar. "I am going for more paint, my work isn't done," he said loudly. "When I am finished, you will always remember John." He laughed.

Pa Moiwa turned to the young people standing around, who wiped the smiles off their faces, ashamed they had laughed at the man's actions. "Why do they always give good names to such misguided spirits? And why do you watch such behavior?"

Pa Moiwa mumbled to himself. He had wanted to explain to the man that he was pissing on sacred ground where wise men and women had sat for generations to discuss important matters about this land. But it was not worth telling him these things.

"Go fetch some water and wash this place clean, all of you. This is your punishment for standing by and encouraging the white man."

As the young people set about doing what they had been ordered to do, Pa Moiwa went to see his friends and recounted what had happened. Pa Kainesi and Mama Kadie agreed that they should speak to one of the senior supervisors in charge of all the foreign and local employees, a stocky light-skinned fellow by the name of Wonde. Wonde was easy to find in town—he parked his vehicle outside the house of whichever woman he spent the night with.

Colonel had arrived at the end of John's misbehavior. He stood in the dark, away from the gathering by the town hall, and waited until everyone had dispersed. He knew the arrogance of the fellow would bring him back after more beers at the bar.

Hours passed, and most people were already in their beds when screams rang out. Men came running with flashlights. The elders came, too.

On the ground, in front of the hall, was the splayed-out figure of John. His face was swollen from blows and his hands had been tied behind his back with his own shirt, which had been torn to make a rope. He couldn't speak—a beer bottle had been stuck in his mouth and he was struggling not to swallow the liquid in it as he lay on his back. When someone removed the bottle, he spat out repeatedly.

"I am going to find that savage and kill him," he shouted.

"Who are you speaking of?" Pa Kainesi asked.

"One of you attacked me for no reason! I was just joking around . . ." One of the armed men who had arrived untied him and took him away, the crowd's eyes following them as they climbed into the company vehicle.

"It is urine in the beer bottle that he was drinking," Miller said, sniffing, as he held the bottle at arm's length. The crowd turned their eyes away from the vehicle and regarded Miller.

John had urinated in the bottle with the intention of throwing it at the walls inside the town hall building. But before he completed his task, someone had turned the tables on him.

In his room, Colonel lay on his back, his eyes fixed on the spider-web in the corner of the ceiling. The veins on his forehead came alive and his teeth clenched as he fought to hold at bay the tormented images dancing in his mind. The spiderweb had a calming effect on him. He admired how resourceful the spider was in catching prey and living without any external help.

That morning, the elders sent some boys to look around town and locate Wonde's vehicle. They quickly found it and relayed the message to the elders, who waited for Wonde by his Toyota.

Emerging on the veranda, yawning, he stopped in his tracks when he saw them, then he turned his back to them to properly zip up his trousers and button his shirt. Turning around, his body language and face projected cunning, so the men knew that whatever he said wouldn't be the truth.

"Good morning."

The elders returned his greeting, searching for the honest part of his face. They asked to have an audience with him about the behavior of his workers in general. The elders limited their words when they had something important to say.

"Yes, I would want to hear your concerns more than anything else," he said. "I am rushing to work now, but please come to my home tomorrow for some respectable sit-down and chat."

He climbed into his vehicle and left without offering the elders a lift back to their homes. This was not a respectable thing to do. One always asked to accompany the elders, even on foot, and even if your eyes could see where they lived, and especially after they had walked to seek a discussion with someone younger.

But even though Wonde's behavior made the elders shake their heads with doubt, they knew they had to try, as there was more at stake than tradition. Tradition can live on only if those carrying it respect it—and live in conditions that allow the traditions to survive. Otherwise, traditions have a way of hiding inside people and leaving only dangerous footprints of confusion.

The path to the hill where the mining headquarters was and where Wonde lived no longer existed. It had either been flooded or replaced with dusty roads that offered no suitable place for human feet. The elders managed to walk slowly on the side of the road. They wondered why Wonde hadn't sent a vehicle to collect them, but they went anyway, hoping a conversation would mend whatever had been broken and prevent further problems. It was the weekend, so there weren't many vehicles on the road. The four miles felt longer than usual, and when they arrived at the company's living quarters, there was a gate. There, the security guards told them that they must have an appointment to continue beyond the metal post. They tried to explain that Wonde had invited them to come by.

"Why would we walk all this way if we had no business here?" Pa Kainesi asked the guards.

"We are only allowed to let in people who have appointments, and if you do, your names should be here." One of the guards flipped through the pages of a book.

"Do you have a note in there that says three elders?" Pa Moiwa tried to lighten the situation. No one laughed, though.

"Your individual names will be here if the person you've come to visit wants to see you." The guard looked through the book some more with eyes wide open, as if he wanted the names of these elders to appear on one of the pages even though he knew they wouldn't.

"You must be able with that walkie-talkie in your hand to call Wonde and tell him we are here," Mama Kadie said, pointing to the radio.

Now caught between respecting his elders and afraid of losing his job, the guard called on his radio to inquire. As soon as he said hello, Wonde angrily instructed him to go to the telephone in the security booth. The elders were perplexed. They waited, their ears catching only the guard's voice, and he pressed the phone to his ear as though he didn't want Wonde's insulting commands to escape and reach them.

"Yes sir, yes sir, yes sir . . ." The guard nodded on and on. When he hung up the phone, his face became that of a person who had been told to convey words that tormented his spirit. The only thing he could do was keep most of the message—the parts that made his eyes ashamed of being on his face—to himself. He simply told the elders that Wonde would not see them.

They didn't understand. Wonde was a cunning fellow, but this was out of the ordinary and completely unacceptable.

"Did Wonde tell you what his reasons are?" Pa Moiwa searched for the frank part of the young man's eyes. He didn't give them to the old man.

"He cannot see you." The guard motioned for them to walk back the way they had arrived. The elders could have walked up the hill to find Wonde on their own, but there were private security guards standing in formation along the hillside. They weren't dark skinned, they were white, but the way they acknowledged the presence of the elders showed that they weren't from afar, that they understood some African customs. And their mannerisms—bowing their heads just a bit even in their military uniforms to give way to the elders— showed that they were Africans. They were South African mercenaries from the former Rhodesia. The sight of them made Pa Kainesi think about conversations he used to have with his son and friends about the fact that there are Africans who are white-skinned in North Africa and elsewhere. And some of these white-skinned Africans didn't like dark-skinned Africans at all, for no apparent reason. "It is because they are disappointed Africans! You know they are not black as Africans are supposed to be," his son would respond. Pa Kainesi looked at the armed men again. There was something in their eyes that detested the very fact that they were familiar with the customs of the place in which they now found themselves. The elders avoided gazing too much at this well-armed group and turned to the guard one more time to express their disappointment with looks that wounded deeper than words could have.

A vehicle heading in the direction of Imperi approached the gate, and the guard tried to convince the driver to give the elders a lift.

He refused, as they weren't allowed to give natives a ride in the company cars. He whispered this into the ear of the guard. Pa Moiwa heard him though, and commented, "A native in the car says natives aren't allowed in the company's car." A strained smile came across his face. The gate was lifted and the driver sped off.

The elders began walking back home, their old bones becoming weaker under the hot sun. They said nothing to one another throughout the journey and parted as soon as they arrived in town. Bockarie saw his dust-laden father dragging his feet. His clothes seemed to sag on his old frame, and for the first time, his face had lost its glow.

I have never seen my father's countenance like this, like that of a man who just lost his last ounce of dignity. He has been through so much, why now? Bockarie thought to himself. He took his father's hand in his for a while before going inside to bring him a cup of cold water. Pa Kainesi drank the water and looked up at his son.

"We returned here to repair ourselves, but this isn't the way to begin. We need to maintain how we sit down respectfully with one another." He said no more and just sat in his chair under the mango tree in the yard all afternoon and evening, mumbling to himself, eyes fixed on the distance.

That evening, Amadu came to deliver wood from Colonel's group to Kula. Colonel, with offers of free bundles of wood, had gotten Kula to be one of his many customers. While Amadu was stacking the bundles of wood by the mango tree, he overheard Kula talking to her daughter Miata about how the elders had been mistreated.

"This is why your grandfather is so quiet this evening. He is a man of few or no words when he is angry or bothered deeply by something," she said. Kula had turned to look in the direction of Amadu, but not because he was eavesdropping. She had put aside a dish for Colonel and his group, something that had been agreed upon by the elders and her husband. It was customary in small towns and villages for mothers and women in general to put aside portions of food that they had cooked for their families for children with no family of their own or sometimes even single men. Also, Colonel always sent a bit more firewood than Kula paid for, and she wanted to return the favor of goodness.

"Please take this to your Man in Charge for all of you." She handed him the bowl of rice with beans, dried fish, and palm oil soup on top. Miata laughed at the name Man in Charge, but also at Amadu, whose face lit up when he smelled the food.

Upon Amadu's return, Colonel whistled with two fingers in his mouth, which was a signal for all the boys and the girl to gather immediately. Miller, Ernest, Salimatu, and Victor left their various tasks and rushed to the bucket of water to wash their hands. Victor, who had difficulty eating hot food, usually came with a bowl so that he could take his share as they all dug in and wait for his food to cool.

This evening, though, Victor didn't bring a bowl, which made the rest of them laugh as they congratulated him. They then devoured the food as though they hadn't eaten for days.

"She cooks better than Salimatu. I feel I have actually had food after this meal," Ernest said, and Salimatu slapped the back of his head. Colonel turned the other way to smile just for a second before his face returned to its customary state. At the end of the meal, Amadu told Colonel what he had heard. Colonel listened pensively and said nothing afterward.

Deep in the night, when the stars themselves were drowsy, dulling the brightness of the sky and causing it to nod, Colonel left his room and went into town. He stopped at the carpenter's workshop, where he quietly took some nails and borrowed a hammer and screwdriver. He searched until he found Wonde's vehicle, the only one in great condition, parked carelessly outside a woman's house. Colonel went to work, driving nails into all the tires. Using the screwdriver, he opened the vehicle and removed the battery from the walkie-talkie that was on the passenger seat. He threw the battery in the bushes and quietly closed the door of the car. He returned home passing by the bar to see if any men were misbehaving so that he could ambush them afterward. They were drinking and shouting but nothing beyond that as far as Colonel could see. He returned the carpenter's tools and went home to wait for another night to pass, as he was still learning to sleep.

Wonde, as usual, emerged from the house in the morning and finished tucking in his shirt and fastening his belt on the veranda. He had a bottle of water, and he rinsed his mouth and spat before drinking some and washing his round, bearded face. He strutted to his car whistling with an air of self-importance. His mood was soon spoiled when he saw his flat tires. He looked around, scratching his head for answers, then got down on his knees to see if the tires were at least manageable to drive on. Confirming that none of them had any air whatsoever, after he had repeatedly pressed them, he kicked one in frustration, then reached inside for the radio to call for help, but the thing wouldn't come on. When he noticed the battery was gone, he threw it back in the car, slammed the door, and went to sit on the veranda of the house he had slept in to think, holding his head in his hands. He raised his head with a smile when the idea came to him to pay someone to deliver a note for him at the company's main site. Surely someone would come get him immediately.

What he didn't know was that word had spread about how he had mistreated the elders, and no one wanted to help him. Wonde began dangling money in front of people passing by. "You could get all of this if you do a quick errand for me," he coaxed. "Come on." But everyone ignored him, even those on their way to labor for a week for much less than he was offering them for that day.

"I cannot believe that no one wants money for a simple errand," he grumbled after many more failed trials to entice someone with his wad of cash. After an hour or so, Miller walked by and Wonde took out even more cash, wiping his sweaty face that was used to the air-conditioned car and office but not the sun and humidity that drove away the fresh air of morning.

"Young man, take this money for a small errand. Be smart."
Wonde held out the money, his voice exhausted. Miller walked toward
him, nodding. Wonde explained his demands and gave him a note to
deliver, and Miller nodded again, pocketing the money. Then he
tore up the note and threw the pieces in the air before walking away.
Wonde stared in a stupor of disbelief, so used was he to getting his
way with every inhabitant.

It was then that Wonde began the trek to the mining site. Everyone was at work, so he couldn't catch a ride from one of his workmates. Passenger vehicles passed him, and as if the dust, too, wanted
some revenge, it rose thickly and coated his stocky face. He coughed
and spat on the ground and cursed, and he walked as though his
feet had forgotten their natural tasks. For days, that story of Wonde
was told all around town. It made the people laugh. It made them
believe, too, that the world still had an arsenal of consequences for
those who disrespect the elders and the land.

Miller handed the money over to Colonel and described the
surprise on Wonde's face when he tore up the note.

"I wanted him to follow me for his money so I could take him
into the forest and deal with him there," Miller said as he pulled out
more of the money he had in his pocket. Colonel tried not to smile,
even though he loved the story. The two of them had done things
that bonded them so much more than they could ever say to any of
the other youngsters. Often they reacted to the same sounds and
acknowledged each other afterward. This act today, though, this
handing over the money to Colonel without him asking for it or even
having knowledge of it, was the birth of the two of them becoming
partners in future actions.

"This is yours and you can do whatever you like with it," Colonel told Miller.

"I know, man, and I have decided to hand it to you. You can de-
cide how to use it best for the group. Also, I will only get into more
trouble with that money in this town in particular," Miller said,

looking up the guava tree for that one fruit he had been waiting to ripen. Colonel held back another smile. He knew exactly what Miller was referring to, a habit to manage memories of the past. They agreed to add the money to the small pile they were saving to pay the school fees of the others. They sat quietly, and Colonel patted Miller's shoulder before he disappeared into the night for his regular walk at the edge of the bushes around town, making sure that even the light from the moon, let alone the lamps, didn't deliver his shadow from the night's dark embrace.

Everything was in disarray during the preparations for full-scale mining to commence. Huge trucks, bulldozers, and other monstrous-looking machines came from out of nowhere and in full speed traveled down roads to start digging. They provided no proper passage for the travelers who had no other means but to walk, so with the persistence of bare feet finding a way around the roadblocks, people made paths in the bushes by the roads. But the mining vehicles rolled on in groups, leaving a thick fog of dust. It took minutes to be able to see where you were going, whether you were in the bushes or on the road.

Bockarie had started making his children Manawah, Miata, and Abu leave for school with him earlier than usual to avoid these dangerous commotions that now came with daylight. Benjamin, however, waited until it was bright outside. "What difference does it make, man? At least I can see them coming and run for my life." He laughed.

One morning, as Bockarie and his children walked in the last brushstrokes of night, they heard boys shouting in agony down the road. Bockarie, trailed by his children, ran as fast as he could toward the cries. As they came to a halt, gasping, they saw what had happened. A young boy, sixteen years old, one of Bockarie's students, had stepped on a live electric wire in the dark. The blood in his body had been sucked dry and his remains looked as if he had died a very old man. By the time his friends pulled him from the wire that continued to spark, burning his peeled flesh that had been left behind, it was too late.

This was the first death since life in the town began after the war. The boys just stood there weeping, and whoever came along did the same. A few men screamed at the vehicles passing by; others threw stones at them, breaking their side and rear windows, but the vehicles didn't stop. As the group grew—students, teachers on their way to school, mothers and fathers who had come to see what the commotion was about—the more agitated the crowd became. They began uprooting electric poles and destroying anything with the mining company's logo on it.

Bockarie put his arms around his children. It was the only way he could assure them that they were safe, since it could have been any of them. Benjamin came strolling up a while later. Nodding to Bockarie, he joined those shouting at the vehicles carrying the foreigners and local workers.

Before too long, three vehicles with police officers in riot gear pulled up. They threw tear gas into the crowd until the group dispersed, coughing, with burning noses and eyes. There was no school that day. Under the cloud of tear gas, a group of men took the body of the boy with them back to town, where the police chief and his men patrolled the streets, announcing through a megaphone: "Watch where you walk on the roads and there will be no deaths or problems."

The police did nothing further. Instead of investigating what had happened, they blamed the boy who died for his carelessness. They neglected to mention the fact that there had been no danger signs alerting the presence of live electrical wires, or that the wires should have been covered in the first place.

The mining company's work continued uninterrupted. The town grew tense with the people's quiet fury. The atmosphere was so stiff that the wind didn't move, and for the rest of that day it felt as though something was about to break. The police, sensing that something might happen, issued a direct warning that anyone caught sabotaging the mining company's equipment would be arrested.

In near silence, the town formed a procession to take the boy's body to the cemetery. But to make matters even worse, it was impeded by another procession, that of mining company machines. The local men operating the machines stopped to let the mourners continue. But soon one of the foreigners pulled up in his vehicle. He was exasperated and ordered the men back into their machines to proceed. Otherwise, he said, they would be sacked. The men argued that the procession would take only a few minutes to pass and that he should have respect for the dead. But he was already on the phone calling the police, who arrived immediately in two trucks, with batons and rifles with live ammunition this time. They began pushing the crowd out of the way so the machines could pass.

"Why are you doing this, my brothers? You are supposed to protect us," some people said, stretching their arms toward the policemen they knew very well.

"Would you let this happen if it was your brother who had died, or your child?" the older women pleaded. A group of men shielded those carrying the coffin, batons hitting their backs, so that the boy's body wouldn't fall out in the commotion. The policemen succeeded in pushing the burial procession to the side for the machines to go ahead. They even fired a few rounds in the air.

The mother of the boy let out a wail that was covered by the sounds of the machines roaring by. The women tried to console her, pulling her along when her feet were unable to hold up her body. She swung in their arms, allowing her feet to touch the ground every now and then as though to assure herself that she was still here on this earth.

The machines continued on, the men operating them in tears, helpless and filled with sadness. It was a day that already felt too long, and every hour made the world heavier. Men stood around hiding their faces because they couldn't do anything to help.

Later that same day, Wonde came to the funeral home with a bag of rice for the boy's family. He dropped it off in the yard from the back of his Toyota and left without greeting the mourners. The gesture made the equation clear: the company and the minister of mines felt that the lives of the people of Imperi were worth one bag of rice each. Sadder still, the family had no choice but to take the rice and use it. And Rogers, the father of the boy, soon afterward sought employment with the company as a general worker, and later as a driver of one of their trucks.

As usual, that night the bar in town was filled with the foreign workers and, also as usual, Wonde. The men from Imperi who worked for the company were all at the burial house, paying their respects. But the music from the bar and the boisterousness of the chatter drowned out the prayer being said for the boy. While Colonel and Miller watched, Sila came to the bar and pleaded with the owner to turn the music down, which he did. He then turned to the men: "Please, just for this night, could you bring your voices down for the burial house not far from here?"

But the men ignored him, and one of them told the bar owner that if he didn't turn the music back up, they would all leave. The men started shouting at him, "Turn it up, man, what is wrong with you, trying to stop our enjoyment?"

Their voices grew even more raucous than the music, so the owner turned up the music to appease them, the only small contribution he could make. One of the foreigners stood and pulled one of his hands up inside his shirt to mimic Sila's stump. No one could say where Ernest had come from, but suddenly he was there, shoving the man into tables, spilling beers, and breaking a chair. The foreigner staggered to his feet and was about to throw punches at Ernest when Sila stepped between them, as did the bar owner.

"The next round is on the house, gentlemen," he said and escorted Sila and Ernest outside. No words left Sila's lips, but before he started back for the burial house, he looked Ernest in the eyes. It was the first time. Ernest walked into the night toward the river where he usually went to sit on a rock, away from everyone.

"Wonde and his friends are very disrespectful. They are preventing God's ears from hearing the dead boy's mother and her prayers," Colonel told Miller, his eyes getting red with anger. He asked Miller to follow him to the shed he had built in the back of their house that contained things he collected for purposes that Miller found out as they went along. He handed a rubber hose and some jerry cans to Miller. They walked back toward the bar. As they got nearer, Colonel made sure that they remained unseen and crept closer to the vehicles parked outside. Moving from one vehicle to another, he opened the petrol tanks and, using the rubber hose, sucked the petrol into the jerry cans. They made several trips to store the petrol in buckets, and when they were done, he took a gallon or more of the petrol and walked toward the mining site.

Miller didn't ask where they were going; he just followed. Colonel knew where the electrical grid was that connected the power to the living quarters of the men at the bar. He also knew that the light for the bar was connected to that same grid. Why couldn't the mining company offer the same power to other houses in town, or to the schools, for example? Colonel instructed Miller to make several piles of dry grasses. These he carefully soaked with petrol and threw into the inner part of the fenced electrical grid. Then he struck a match.

Colonel and Miller ran rapidly away from the sparks that flew out and exploded the wires. Soon enough, darkness took over the hills where the quarters were, along with the bar and even some of the offices. When the men at the bar came out to get into their vehicles, they couldn't start them, and they had no way of reaching anyone, since the lights were out. They called on their radios for help, but it took hours before a bus could be found in the dark and dispatched to fetch them.

It took a week to get power back up and for the bar to be operational again. During that time, the town's nightly natural sounds slowly returned—the crickets, the laughter of older people staying up talking, the vigorous orchestra of the frogs, the call for prayer. Colonel, who still rarely slept, listened to all the sounds. No one knew how the power failure had come about, though Wonde suspected Miller, but he didn't know the boy's name or whose son he was. Some of the workers suspected Ernest but had no proof. He, too, was not the son of anyone working for the company—or of anyone alive, for that matter. Usually in such cases, Wonde would sack the father or threaten to do so to get the outcome he desired. As a result, he and some of the foreigners became a bit afraid, though they still took liberties, as a mind accustomed to arrogance has limited space for remembrance.

Once the company resumed operations, the sounds of mining once more drove away the natural sounds of Imperi and the town returned to its crooked road. The machines were everywhere again, especially the ones the locals called "belle woman," meaning "pregnant woman," which they indeed resembled. Many vehicles were getting pregnant from the land and all that comes from it. They gave birth at the docks where ships carried the benefits somewhere else—riches generated from their land, which they would never taste, to places the people of Imperi would never know. They settled for the immediate but temporary enticements. They no longer believed they had control over anything in their lives; desperation became their master. But desperation does not lay foundations. And the elders struggled, as their presence and importance faded, to find words that might reach the ears of whatever God or gods were in the hearts of those in charge.

Colonel and Miller, however, refused to grant control of their lives to the company and to those who had given the company the power to make people's lives cheap and disposable. They did what they could through methods they had acquired over time. Some might say their methods were violent. But what was more violent than making people disbelieve in the worth of their own lives? What was more violent than making them believe they deserved less and less every day?

The night that followed, the rooster started crowing at 9:00 p.m. for daybreak.

6

"GOOD MORNING. I am going to be as brief as possible."

It had been over a month since one of the students died on the electric cables on his way to school. Customarily people celebrated forty days after someone had passed away or at least spoke of him so he wasn't forgotten. So when the principal came to the assembly that morning with a melancholic face, the students thought he was going to say a few words about the boy. At school, everyone had avoided discussing what had happened and it wasn't because it was difficult. After all, they all knew death and had seen it closely during the war. But they didn't want to be reminded about what had happened because all of them, teachers and students, had to pass by the live wires every day on the way to school and that was enough.

The principal waited for a few announcements before it was his turn to speak. His mind was scattered in many places, so his attention faded in and out of what was unfolding that morning. Since the arrival of the mining company, he had given up trying to encourage his staff to inspire their students. The company's operations were now in full swing, and it was intent on luring brilliant young men to work using their strengths and not their minds. The other day he saw two former students, Vincent and Khalilou, who now wore hard hats, boots, and overalls, their young faces already becoming old with countenances that had accepted that this was the best possible outcome of their lives. The sight of their wasted youth bothered him. As he stood in front of the entire school now, and having said he would be brief, he wanted to tell them what he had seen, but he didn't think it was the appropriate time, and perhaps it never would be. Not everything about mining was bad; he had been educated on a scholarship from a mining company in another part of the country when he was a boy. But that was a long time ago, when those in power saw it as a service, not a business, and therefore opened their eyes to look ahead for their people. It was in the wake of independence. What happened to the pride and wisdom of that time?

The principal's face had become consumed with despair beyond his control. But he managed a quick smile and exhaled deeply, freeing his mind from the many places it had been. He wiped his forehead with his handkerchief, put on his glasses, and brought the leaflets he held behind him in front of his face. The assembly was too quiet.

"The board of education has decided to set standards of decency for schools. And to that end, yesterday I was provided with a list of new rules." He held a paper up above his head. The students and teachers sighed with relief that this wasn't a reminder of the boy who had died.

"I must make all of you abide by what I am to read, otherwise the school may be closed down permanently, especially if an inspector stops by unannounced."

His eyes surveyed the length of the paper and then he began at the top. " 'Henceforth, all students must wear white socks and black shoes. No sandals or open-toe shoes for boys or girls.' "

He looked away before continuing. " 'All students must come to school in uniform. The new uniform for boys will now be blue trousers and plain white short-sleeve shirts. Girls are to wear blue skirts and plain white long-sleeve shirts.'"

He paused again. The words he had spoken obviously bothered him. He cleared his throat to make his voice stronger for the next sentences. "We have two weeks to make the change. There are more new rules, but these are the most immediate ones. Please inform your parents at the end of the school day so that they can start making arrangements."

The principal removed his glasses and left without another word, quickly returning to his office. He knew this would create a problem for most of the students. Their parents were barely able to afford the school fees. Most of the audience now wished the principal had spoken about the boy's death instead, however difficult it would have been to manage the nightmares that came with it. What he had presented was a heavier burden to carry.

"Poverty is worse than nightmares. You can wake up from nightmares," Benjamin whispered to Bockarie, as the students slowly returned to their classrooms, the teachers—most of them parents, as well—lagging behind as they searched for the strength to walk into the day.

Bockarie was distraught. He could not think of a way he could acquire the money to buy his three school-aged children the new uniforms and shoes. Even extreme cuts in spending—reducing the amount of food cooked at home—would yield enough for only one child's outfit. How could he explain to the other two why they would have to stop going to school? How would he choose which of his children would receive the first uniform? There were no satisfactory answers to the questions in his mind.

He avoided everyone during lunch and sat behind one of the three school buildings. Looking out at the hills, he imagined a better life. Benjamin found him and sat quietly beside his friend before starting a conversation. "We may lose some of our students—not only here in school but also for our lessons."

"I know, man. Parents have to make some tough decisions."

Benjamin nodded and leaned upright against the wall. "I am somehow glad that both of my children are still in primary school. I fear, though, that this will happen there, too."

"What sort of 'improvement' is this that only increases the burden on parents? What difference will it make to have a uniform if your school has no materials, if your teachers don't receive proper salaries, if the quality of the teachers is poor because they haven't received training in years?" Bockarie had more to say, but he stopped.

Benjamin laughed. "This is the first time that I have seen you exasperated. Not bad, my man!" He threw his fist in the air. But Bockarie's mood didn't change, so Benjamin adopted a more serious tone. "We have idiots in charge, man. Everywhere. That is why the world is the way it is. Remember when we were in school? Those were the days, man! My first week of school, I arrived with no shirt and no shoes—only shorts with holes in them—and they accepted me in class. The teacher told everyone, 'Now, this exemplifies the strongest desire to learn. He walked six miles like this to come for learning.'"

Benjamin finally got Bockarie to laugh. The men slapped each other's hands, snapping their fingers at the end. He continued, "I had no idea what those words meant, but I liked how they sounded. The teacher and the class made me feel that I had done something good. And at the end of the day, the teacher sat me on the handlebars of his bicycle and took me home. He had a long conversation with my father and I started school full time. And every day after that, that teacher picked me up and brought me back home until I was old enough to walk the miles on my own."

The simple memories from the past made them both smile. "Do you want to know how I started school?" Bockarie asked.

"Why do you always ask before you speak?" Benjamin chided warmly. "Just say what you have to say, man."

"I was in the same condition as you, but I didn't have the courage to go into the classroom. So I found a mango tree by the school. I climbed it and from a comfortable position in the branches, I could hear the lessons and see the blackboard. The teacher saw me and he began to open the classroom window completely so that I could properly see." He chuckled.

"I did that for an entire month, reciting everything that I heard, over and over, and practicing writing the alphabet on the ground. One morning, the teacher was waiting for me under the mango tree, and he held my hand, and he took me into the classroom. Those were the days, indeed, when we had decent people in a decent environment and they could do such things."

The small wind from the past had made the day seem lighter, and they sat happily until the bell rang for class. Each clang of the bell drove away some of the joy until there was none left. They stood up and wiped the dust off their trousers.

Before they parted, Benjamin extended his hand to his friend for a shake. "I am strongly thinking about applying to work for the company," he said. "I want to keep on teaching, but with the irregular pay, and commodities getting increasingly expensive, I am not sure I can continue."

Bockarie said nothing. What could he say?

Not so long ago, Benjamin was throwing stones at the company cars. Now he was going to work for them.

Everyone dreaded what would happen when the school's new policy took effect. Teachers tried to move lessons quickly ahead to provide notes for those students who would miss school during the transition. The teachers all agreed that the only way they could help was by providing students with plenty of readings and assignments so that they could study at home while waiting for their parents to find the money to buy them uniforms or have them sewn by the tailor in town. The tailor was probably the only happy person around because he got more work than he could handle. He charged higher prices for his services and the people protested, but at the end of the day, they had to pay. His reasoning, as he explained to Mama Kadie, was this: "It will be a while before I get another job so I am making sure that I have enough income to last me for who knows however long."

The tailor did sew some uniforms for free—but he didn't let anyone know about it. The principal visited him a week before the new uniforms became mandatory. He came by foot, without his motorcycle and with no flashlight, and he told the tailor that he would pay for all the students whose parents could afford only a fraction of the payment, or nothing at all. He gave the tailor money to buy the cloth to start the work.

"This has been a Nicodemus visit and arrangement. You and I must take this secret to our graves." He shook the tailor's hand and held it tightly.

"But what if I rise from the dead like Lazarus, could I tell the secret then?" The tailor pulled his hand from the principal's grip.

"It will be the only secret that isn't resurrected if you return from the dead like Lazarus." With a half smile, the principal walked into the arms of the darkness, which quickly embraced him and hid him from all eyes. Even with all of the contributions, and there were others, some students couldn't afford to attend until weeks later. And even when they all had uniforms, there was the matter of black shoes. Black shoes were expensive, far more expensive than, say, sneakers.

Bockarie had managed to get uniforms for all of his children, even though he'd paid only for the one for Miata. He didn't understand the sudden generosity of the tailor, but he was grateful for it. The tailor praised him. "You are a good teacher—so teach our children how to get out of here." The tailor said he was joking; his tone suggested otherwise.

Even with the tailor's help, though, Bockarie had no money left to buy shoes for his second son. So Abu stayed home on the first day of the new rules. But Abu and his older brother, Manawah, had a plan. They had decided they would share the one pair. One day Manawah would wear them to class; the next, it would be Abu's turn. The shoes were certainly too big for Abu but not noticeably so, or so he convinced himself.

"So what do you think about our idea, Father?" Manawah asked quietly. When he spoke, his voice became like that of his father's. His calm behavior, as well.

"Maybe we could—" Abu, who was faster at doing things, even the way he spoke, was about to present another solution when their father said, "This is temporary. I will buy another pair of shoes for you, Abu, soon. Thank you boys for understanding." He pulled them close to him on either side and squeezed them. Then, to break the spell, he tickled them until they screamed with laughter.

What happened on the first day of the new uniforms was "necessary," the elders would later say. It was necessary to wake up the joyous muscles of the hearts of the teachers and students, if only for a day. And it was another kind of lesson to be learned: even horrible things can contribute in the creation of natural comedy. Even the most absurd situations can be punctured.

It was a wonderful sight at first. All the students—at least those with proper attire—in their brand-new blue-and-white uniforms and their white socks and black shoes, convening from the various parts of town and surrounding areas to walk together to school. It brought smiles to the faces of those they passed. In sharp contrast, the teachers walking alongside them looked shabby, which only served to remind the teachers of their condition. Anticipating this, Bockarie and many others left early. But when the students began arriving, sluggishly dragging their feet as they lined up for assembly, the teachers—the principal included—couldn't contain their laughter.

They looked at the students in their brand-new uniforms and their brand-new socks and shoes, and they laughed so hard that even the students joined in. For the whole forty-minute assembly they all laughed, and kept on laughing throughout the day.

Here is why. The mining company had begun digging a new site for its operations not far from the school. So there had been more trucks than ever that morning, maybe a dozen or more, one after the next, after the next. And there was no escaping the dust they raised. Red dust. All the white shirts were now the color of the dust, as was the students' hair. Their black shoes were unrecognizable. Standing together, they looked as if they had been washed and rolled in the dust. Even their eyelids were dusty. Some tried to beat it off themselves, but then the dust just rose from their bodies in clouds and sailed above their heads only to settle on other students. They struggled to keep the dust from staining their work. It would fall from their uniforms into their notebooks and onto the white pages covered with neat handwriting. However much they dusted, the uniforms stayed dirty. The more they tried to wipe the dust away with their soiled hands, the worse it got. And the teachers could do nothing. You couldn't send everybody home for untidiness!

In time, the students came up with a way around the problem. They would wrap their books in plastic; wrap their uniforms, shoes, and socks in plastic bags, too, and wear ordinary clothes to and from school, washing their feet and changing just before they reached school grounds. And they started arriving earlier, leaving their homes at 6:00 a.m. to avoid the stream of heavy dust. It was risky because they couldn't see the live electrical wires in the dark, and the passing vehicles, in the last remains of night, couldn't see them.

Abu was full of plans, none of which he discussed with his parents or his siblings. The goals of all of them were simple: to attend class every day no matter what.

On the first day of new uniforms, after his father and siblings had left for school, he helped his mother with chores around the house. She tried to explain that his father was really trying and he shouldn't feel too bad about missing school.

"You know, your father had to make a tough decision, as he wanted all of you to be in school. I can give you some homework to do if you want," she said as she packed her goods for the market.

"I know, Mother, I know it isn't easy, so don't worry too much." He smiled reassuringly and offered to help carry her baskets.

As soon as he returned home, he took his notebook and pen, and wearing ordinary clothes and walking barefoot to avoid ruining his white sneakers, he followed the forest path to the school compound. It was the shortest route, but it went through two swamps with mud up to one's waist; hence, it was not frequented by many people. Abu stripped off his clothes and made his way through the mud, stopping to wash off before climbing the hill that brought him to the back of the school grounds.

As he reached the clearing, he crawled to the windowsill of his classroom. The window was always open in the morning, after the teacher lifted the boards that prevented animals from climbing into classrooms at night.

Under the window, Abu sat and listened to the lessons, diligently taking notes. When the bell rang for lunch, he quickly ran, head down, into the bushes to avoid anyone laying eyes on him, and he waited there, studying his notes. When lunch ended and classes resumed, he crawled back to his spot.

At the end of the school day he made it back home, running faster, before his father, brother, and sister's return. They regaled him with the story of the uniforms, and they laughed together all evening. Their grandfather pensively suggested that perhaps the ministry of education should consult with each school and ask the teachers to prescribe appropriate attire for each region. He lay in his hammock and gently pushed on the earth with his walking stick to swing himself.

"We can help you swing, Grandfather," the little twins offered. "Next time," he said, "but you can come and sit with me." And Oumu and Thomas cuddled with the elder.

The next day, it was Abu's turn to wear the shared shoes to school. His father told him to be ready to walk earlier than usual to avoid the dust. Abu waited, all smiles, the next morning. He'd pushed extra socks in the toes of the shoes so that his feet didn't slide back and forth in them, but his family laughed when they started walking and suggested he take them off until they were near school grounds. This did indeed make the walk less strenuous. In school, Abu's friends made fun, calling him "canoe feet"—he literally looked as if he were standing in two miniature black canoes. But he didn't mind at all; he was just happy to be in school.

When Abu returned home that day, he had already devised another plan for the next day. He handed the shoes to Manawah, got his homework done, and then started working on his new plan. To avoid his family's suspicion, he made an excuse that he was going to a schoolmate's house to copy notes he'd missed during his absence. Instead, he threw his white sneakers into a plastic bag filled with black markers he'd found in a dustbin out back of the mining company's living quarters and ran to the edge of town, near the blacksmith's hut, and began working. Shaking the old markers for whatever ink they had left, he carefully painted his sneakers until every part of them looked seamlessly black. He let them stand in the last strong rays of the evening sun and then carefully wrapped them up. He ran home excitedly, tossed the sneakers through the window he had left open, then went to sit with his family on the veranda.

Kula was helping the young twins, Thomas and Oumu, with their homework. She had almost gotten her master's degree in nursing and education before the war interrupted. And she'd worked a few years as a nurse and had taught in the refugee camps they'd lived in for years of the war. One didn't get certifications for such things, but she liked using her mind, and now, when her husband was correcting papers and would pass each one to her for a final opinion, she found contentment.

"This is my favorite part of the day, when all my roles, my experiences and education, are put to use simultaneously," Kula told Bockarie, her weary face brightening, revealing the beauty that sometimes got lost in the relentless drive to keep a family together. She took the papers he handed her, made her comments with red ink, and passed them back. "I must check on the rice."

The evening students and Benjamin arrived for their lesson, and the family retired to the rear of the house. Later, as the students headed back to their homes, Benjamin told Bockarie he had applied at the company and was waiting for word. He said he would rather teach but could not do it anymore.

"If I get the job, I will instruct all the drivers to slow down and avoid dusting a lanky, pensive, and hungry-looking teacher on the road!" Benjamin joked.

"You'll save me soap money! Good luck with it, brother. I sure will miss your company and humor," Bockarie said.

"But I haven't gotten the job yet, so I will see you in the morning."

He shook hands with Bockarie and was about to depart when Colonel emerged from the dark cloak of the young night. Without a word, he handed the two teachers their fees for the lesson. He had wrapped the money in an old newspaper. As soon as he handed it to them, he turned to leave.

"You don't say much, young man," Benjamin said, snapping his fingers to get Colonel's attention.

"Let the young fellow be," Bockarie interjected.

"I am always quiet so that I know what to say when I must speak." Colonel's voice caught them by surprise.

"He is very smart, too. Why don't you go to school?" Benjamin turned to Bockarie, and by the time his eyes came back around, Colonel was gone.

"He is like a ghost—but he shows up to pay!" said Bockarie.

"An honest ghost. Not many around." Benjamin took his share of the money and gave the rest to his friend.

The next day, Bockarie, sixteen-year-old Miata, and seventeen-year-old Manawah left home for school, leaving—or so they thought—Abu behind. However, as they stood in assembly before entering classes, their eyes found him. He smiled at their confusion.

His father pulled him aside. Where, he asked, had he gotten these odd-looking black shoes?

"Creativity and determination are in my genes, Father," Abu said as he ran off to class. Bockarie laughed—he had said these words often at home, words that his son now spoke back to him. He couldn't believe what he had just heard but was thrilled by the resourcefulness of the boy, even as his mind tried to answer his own question. *Where did he get the money to buy a pair of black shoes?*

At the end of school that day, as they walked home, it began to rain. Everyone was happy even though they were getting soaked. They preferred the rain, because it would tame the dust for a while. Students and teachers protected their books with plastic bags and ran for cover. It was during the run that Bockarie saw what his son had done. The marker began to wash off Abu's sneakers, and soon they were white with spots of black here and there. While they huddled under a corrugated iron roof left behind by the mining company, Bockarie, Miata, and Manawah stared down at Abu's feet and laughed. And then they began to praise him.

"Creativity and determination, eh? Come here!" Bockarie hugged his son, wiping the rainwater off his face. Abu said nothing about the plan he already had in motion for the following day: he'd convinced another boy to lend him his shoes, since he was a better note-taker.

At the end of the school year, Abu was first in his class and so were his siblings. His father remained puzzled about Abu. But he was proud of the enthusiasm the boy had for learning. He was proud of all his children and the mature way they dealt with the conditions of their lives. He knew he had to do better for them.

7

KULA WAS HUMMING. Her spirit was still dancing from the happiness of the previous evening when she had sat with her family. She cherished those moments. They had become rare. And she had no childhood memories of family, only those as a mother.

"Shall we go to the river, my daughter?" She mimicked an English accent, making Miata laugh.

"How come you are always content with simple moments, Mother?" Miata asked as she tied her waistcloth and prepared to pick up the buckets, one filled with the dirty clothes that needed washing.

"I like them because they are pure," said Kula. "They come with no requirements or explanations, and they are meaningful, or at least they should be. Like life itself is supposed to be." She closed her eyes and turned her face toward the morning breeze. Miata sometimes didn't understand her mother, but she could feel the happiness emanating from and about her, and that was enough. Kula felt her daughter's confusion, but she just smiled and motioned for them to go. Kula went to the river every morning to bathe and to wash clothes so they didn't pile up. Bockarie called her the "incremental woman," as she wouldn't allow her work in any area to accumulate. Her daughter came with her at times, especially on weekends, when she wasn't leaving for school before dawn. On their way to the river that morning, Miata carrying the two buckets—one on her head, the other swinging in her arms—they came across Benjamin sitting on the path, rubbing his palms together to warm his fingers from the cold morning air.

"Good morning, ladies. How is your health and that of your family?"

"Everyone has their health, and good morning to you, as well, and how is your family?" Kula responded. "We are as well as life can allow us to be and we hope to continue that way."

Benjamin rose and picked up his bamboo fishing pole. "I am going fishing upriver and will mind my step so as not to dirty the water for all of you. My wife is at the river, too, so I want her to have the cleanest water. I make no promises, though, after she leaves!"

He smiled into their faces, resting on Miata. She was a quiet girl and Benjamin liked teasing her.

"Miss Miata, you are becoming more beautiful, even more than your mother, which is difficult to believe! We should have already started hiding you from all these boys in town. Oh, trouble for your quiet father!"

Miata smiled shyly and hid behind her mother.

"Leave my child alone and go about your fishing," Kula joked, tossing pebbles at Benjamin as he ran away, laughing loudly.

When Kula and Miata arrived at the river, things looked strange. The water was completely dirty and murky, and it smelled rusty. And it was high, as if a tide had come in. Water filled the banks and rushed downstream with uncommon speed. Other women gathered at the grassy edge of the river, their calm morning faces now lit with worry. They stared upstream to see what was going on.

"It wasn't like this when I first came to fetch water earlier today," Fatu told Kula. She said that the water had just now started rushing with this force, and that the women were thinking it would pass. "I lost my children's clothes that I had laid out on the washing stone there," one woman said.

"The river took my only bucket away. How am I going to fetch water now?" another said to no one in particular, with tears in her eyes.

"Perhaps we can find your bucket downstream later on," a younger woman said consolingly. "In the meantime, I will lend you mine when I am done bailing."

A woman with naturally beautiful wrinkles of age on her cheek-bones spoke next. "Where can the water be coming from at this time of year? I have never laid eyes on such a strange behavior of the river."

The women sighed in agreement. There was nothing to do but wait for the water to calm. The wait almost exhausted their patience. At the first sign of normalcy, they plunged into the river without paying much attention, so as to get on with their day as quickly as possible.

Kula and Miata returned home and hung the clothes out on the rope to dry, and they left a bucket of water in the yard. It would be used for cooking later on. Midday, when Miata went to turn the clothes over so the sun would dry them properly, she noticed there was rust on them and they smelled strange. There was none of that fragrance the sun usually left on the fabrics. She couldn't understand it; her mother had done this for years and had never carelessly washed anything. Miata called out to her, "Mother, could you please come out and see this."

Tying her waistcloth, Kula came out of the house to inspect. The whites, which were mostly the uniforms, were the worst. Rubbing the fabric, Kula could feel the rust on her fingers, and there was an oily substance that continued to stain each cloth she touched. She brought her nose closer and could smell something that made her wince. She touched it to her tongue and instantly felt an acidic sensation. Saliva filled her mouth, and she spat it out.

"This must be from the water. What has happened to the river?" she murmured.

Taking one of the white shirts from the line, she began walking toward the neighbor's. *I must see how their clothes look*, she thought. She paused at the bucket of water in the yard. Miata joined her, and crouching down they could see that it was clear on the top but below the surface was a layer of rusty murk.

"Make sure none of your brothers or your sister drinks this water. I will be back," she said and hastily walked to the neighbor's house, where, sure enough, the garments on the clothesline were rusty and smelled.

"What do you think?" Kula asked.

"It is the water from this morning," her neighbor said.

Together, the women began going from house to house, examining one another's ruined washed clothes and the sediment settling at the bottom of their buckets and drums.

Their gathering got the attention of the men, whose immediate reactions were deep sighs, as it was plain they would now have to buy new uniforms for their children, especially if the river remained this way.

"We should have the men find out what has caused this," Fatu said loudly enough so that the men lurking about heard. They nodded in agreement.

A few, including Bockarie, volunteered to walk along the river to explore the banks. Miller was among them, there to gather information for Colonel. It wasn't long before they found the source of the problem. Several artificial dams had been created for the mining of rutile, but the dams were overflowing, spilling into and destroying the roads the company needed for its vehicles. So the company had begun draining excess water directly into the river, thereby contaminating it.

"The river was our only source of clean, drinkable water," said the men. "Why did they not direct the water somewhere else?"

The farmers among them were livid. Their lands for planting next season had been dug up and flooded without any consultation. "This means that our rice fields have also been contaminated," one of the farmers added, as he dipped a hand in the water and smelled it.

Among the gathering were men who had laid the very pipes that now spilled dirty mining water into their collective river. They had operated the very machines that dug up the land and flooded it. But they said nothing. Though they were ashamed and realized what their work had done, they had needed the job.

All the men began walking back to town, but Miller lagged behind to inspect whether there was a way to prevent the spillage. He knew Colonel would ask him about that.

He could see it would be impossible to fix quickly just using human hands. He ran after the men.

From that day on, clean, drinkable water became a highly sought-after commodity in town. Pipes bearing good water passed through Imperi directly to the mining company's living quarters, but nothing was done to provide some of that water to the townspeople. It would have been a simple matter of laying a few more pipes, but it was not done.

On their way back to town to report what they had found, the men encountered Benjamin. He jumped at the sight of so many men on the path and stopped in his tracks.

"There is a problem with the river," Bockarie said to his friend.

"I know," said Benjamin. "Look at these fish I caught." Benjamin opened his fishing sack.

"Ya ya ya ya, you have to show this to everybody." Bockarie's reaction brought all the men to peer in the sack.

Benjamin put the fish on the ground for proper view. The men gasped in unison when they saw what he'd caught. One fish had only one eye. Others had one fin or no tail.

No one had ever seen such deformities on fish. The men refused to believe what their eyes saw, and they kept staring as if doing so would eventually lead them to realize their eyes hadn't deceived them. Benjamin gave three of the worst ones to the men to take with them to the town meeting that was now being called. He ran home to give his wife the other fish that were in slightly better condition to fry for his lunch. He had nothing else to eat and thought the hot oil should be able to kill whatever bacteria the fish contained.

Most of the townspeople gathered at the town hall, an open building covered with an old tin roof held up by four iron pillars. Miller had fed the ears of Colonel with what he heard and saw, and they were present, sitting within earshot in the nearby guava tree.

The elders—Mama Kadie, Pa Kainesi, and Pa Moiwa—explained to the crowd what the women had experienced at the river and what the men had found. And then they added their own wisdom.

"When I was a boy, my father told me that there are three important things one's heart must be satisfied with before choosing the location of a village—now a town, but this still applies," Pa Kainesi said, his voice trembling terribly. It had been a while since he had spoken in public. He had been quiet since Wonde had humiliated them. "There must be a good source of water, good land for growing crops, and a suitable place for burying the dead. We are losing the first two, and this is tormenting my old spirit." He ended there.

There were murmurs in the crowd. Then arguments began to burst out. Some argued that matters should be taken up with the paramount chief, who likely did not know what was taking place. Others, who knew what would happen to their jobs if the company's work were threatened, cautioned that perhaps everyone was overreacting.

"The water may finish draining by the end of the day, and there may be no need to make a problem out of it," one man said, still holding his work helmet.

Some nodded in agreement; others took issue, with shouts directed at the fellow. "You heard what the elders said, we are losing what makes us people of this land. What is next after our water source has been destroyed?"

"You are a fool to think something will happen," another shouted. "Accept what is going to always be."

One man threw a punch. Another followed. But the fight didn't escalate, because Mama Kadie's voice rang out above the commotion.

"My children, why do we fight among ourselves over what someone else has done to us? Have you all lost every ounce of your natural intelligence? We the elders have decided to take the case to the paramount chief early tomorrow morning. We will need some young boys or men to carry the buckets of water and the fish to show the chief. Offer to use your strength for a purpose other than fighting."

The gathering was quiet. The children were amazed at Mama Kadie's ability to keep an entire town silent. Most had never witnessed a woman do such a thing. Colonel, too, was impressed and signaled with his eyes that Miller and Ernest should volunteer to carry the load. They raised their hands and the elders called them over to whisper in their ears where they would meet the following morning. Murmurs started rising again in the crowd when the elders said with these two boys, they had enough for the task.

Mama Kadie stilled the crowd by letting them know she was as angry as any of them. "My feet are already on the road as my heart remains on fire and I would like to cool it down." She ended the gathering. She hadn't accompanied the men last time they went to see the paramount chief. She hoped that this time, having the ears and eyes of another woman would make them more successful—that she would be able to make the paramount chief hear the past and therefore be able to have eyes for the future.

As people were dispersing, Benjamin's wife, Fatu, entered the gathering holding a cooking pot. "Look. I tried frying the fish that my husband brought, the ones that were in good condition. This is what happened." All that remained in the pot were bones lying in cooking oil. The flesh of the fish had completely dissolved.

One by one people lined up to look in Fatu's pot, their minds and countenances burdened by what they had seen. Those who had money bought bottled water to drink that night; the rest—the majority—boiled the rusty water and cooled it before drinking it or cooking with it.

"If whatever bacteria that is in this water can survive after that boiling, then it deserves to infect me," Bockarie joked to his family. His father sat on the veranda talking to himself, asking questions into the darkness as though there were answers within its crevasses, or at least a breeze that might calm the anxious blood flowing in his old veins. Eventually, the night found the appropriate air that seduced his old eyes with sleep.

They left early in the morning while night was handing over the troubles of the living to day. They walked on paths that were now interrupted by the wide roads that had been cut deep into the backbone of the earth. Hazardous trucks with tires higher than humans sped down the road at all times. They had to watch both ways before crossing and on the other side had to search for where the path continued. Whenever they arrived at a crossing, Ernest and Miller would walk ahead, remove the loads from their heads, and stand facing opposite directions. They would survey the distance, and when they were sure that no truck was in sight, they would signal for the elders to come across.

"My side is clear, and yours?" Miller would say to Ernest.

"Nothing here," he would say, but they would keep watch and repeatedly check in with each other. When they'd safely gotten the elders across, they would return to pick up the loads and follow behind.

Before the sun finished its negotiations with the clouds and took over the sky, they had reached the village of the paramount chief. As they made their way along the potholed street leading to the chief's compound, people came out of their houses to wave to them and greet them. Gradually, as if they'd been told why the elders had come, they followed, and soon there was a crowd accompanying them. The chief knew about their arrival, too, and even before they had the chance to sit down had made it clear she had eyes and ears everywhere in the chiefdom.

Nothing had changed in the paramount chief's village except that her house had just been painted bright green and it had a new tin roof. The surrounding dwindling and decaying houses now looked even sadder in comparison. And its unnaturally green color seemed to make the trees turn their backs away from the village and dance to the wind in a different direction. The chief, however, seemed quite pleased with it, and she offered her guests cold water in bottles, which they drank thirstily. After they set the bottles down, the chief offered them soft drinks, which could have come only from the coffers of the mining company.

Mama Kadie would not permit such a ploy to distract them. She took the hand of the chief. "We thank you for the water and these other offerings, but we must now employ your ears and heart, and tell of occurrences that are breaking the spine of our town—" Before Mama Kadie could finish, the chief's mobile phone rang: *the city is getting hot and the youth dem ah get so co oh oh old* . . .

The ringtone was the chorus from a popular reggae song that one would expect on the phone of someone younger. A young person had probably set it up for her and she had no idea what the song was. Such things happened these days.

She removed her hand from Mama Kadie's, flipped opened the phone, and brought it to her ear. After a series of *yes, okay, yes,* she snapped it shut, turned her eyes to the visitors, and spoke.

"I heard you, but we must wait for the police to get here before we can start this meeting."

"Why do we need the police to discuss matters of our land?" Mama Kadie asked, a bit confused and irritated.

"You must tell me what has happened in front of them and they must take the names of those who saw these occurrences that you speak of," the paramount chief said.

"We didn't come here to report those people who saw what happened. We came to discuss what you, as our representative to the government, can do to stop what is happening to this land, to make decisions that benefit how this land and its people are treated." Mama Kadie, now clearly exasperated, her face rigid with disbelief, her hands shaking, tried to find calm in her tone.

"Kadie, let us show her what we have brought with us." Pa Kainesi called on Miller and Ernest to bring forward the bucket of water, the rusty clothes, and the deformed fish.

"Please wipe away whatever cloth has been set on your eyes and look at these things," Pa Moiwa implored.

The crowd that had gathered around the chief's compound began to murmur of similar things occurring even in this village and how they had tried but failed to get an audience with the chief. Finally, Mama Kadie could no longer take it, so she told her friends they must depart. She directed the boys to pour the water into an empty bucket in the chief's compound and to place the fish and clothes on the ground next to it.

Without saying goodbye or performing the traditional rituals for leave-taking, they began to quietly make their way out of the village, when they heard vehicles approaching. From where the elders stood, they could see the dust rising in the distance. Most of the crowd ran away and the visitors seemed a bit confused. A talkative little girl who was standing near the wall of a mud-brick house told the elders that some people had been beaten by the police for raising concerns about their land. When their eyes could finally make out the vehicles, they were all the mining company's Toyota Hiluxes, and they were filled with policemen with guns and armed security guards. They surrounded the visitors and commanded them to return to the chief's compound.

Ernest and Miller, heaving with anger, reached into their pockets, possibly for knives. Mama Kadie laid her hands on their shoulders and her eyes told them to calm down. They removed their hands from their pockets but still carefully watched the armed men, who shoved the elders, Ernest, and Miller back to the compound. There, the elders were asked to repeat their concerns so that the police could take their statements.

Once more, Mama Kadie spoke for the group. "We came here this morning to have the ears of our chief and not to report anything to men with guns. We have done what we came here to do even though not to our heart's satisfaction. We have nothing to say to you. The chief has our report, and if she wants to tell it to you, then she would at least be performing a duty for her people for a change."

"Mother, you have to tell it to us again." The chief of police tried to hold her hand while begging.

She pushed his hand away. "Don't let your tongue falsely call me Mother. Would you use guns to get your mother to speak to you? I am done here and I am leaving." She rose from her bench, and Pa Kainesi, Pa Moiwa, Ernest, and Miller followed her.

"You cannot leave here without telling your lies against the company to the police!" shouted the paramount chief. It was behavior that people with such roles are not supposed to exhibit in public. "Tell them about the water you and your people have mixed with rust and the fish you have deformed just to start problems! Can't you see the company is helping provide jobs for our people?"

"Well, there you have your statement with our chief's interpretation." Mama Kadie sighed and continued, addressing the chief by her first name. "Hawa, this is your land, too, and I am sure that fragments of the wisdom of our ancestors remain within you. Your eyes tell me that you do not believe what you say. We do want our people to have jobs that provide better lives for them and their children. We want improvements—but not ones that destroy our spirits, our traditions, and literally kill us while we are still alive. Goodbye now."

As Mama Kadie turned to walk away, one of the private security guards tried to lay hands on her, pointing his gun at her as a deterrent. To the surprise of everyone, including the security fellow, a young police officer standing next to him released some blows to his head, knocking the security fellow to the ground. The police officer was quickly contained with gun butt strikes to his head. His bleeding head landed on the dusty ground, but his face seemed content as he watched the elders walk away. No clouds moved in the sky. The wind had nothing to speak of. Only the sounds of the visitors' feet could be heard. They left with tears in all of their eyes, especially the elders.

If only it was during the war. We would have solved this situation rightly, as we, too, would have had weapons. Ernest and Miller looked at each other with eyes of kinship that spoke the quiet language of their thoughts.

Back in Imperi, the crowd waited for news. When the elders emerged from the path through the old town, they said nothing at first. Their faces silenced the crowd and people knew that the wind of happiness had not danced their way today. Mama Kadie went home, leaving the explanations to Pa Moiwa and Pa Kainesi. They told the crowd what had passed in few words, their tongues gripped with sorrow and helplessness. The next day, all the men who worked for the company who had participated in finding the source of the river's disruption were sacked without reason or pay. They came home with only the smells of their labor on their bodies. The only thing they could do was sell their work boots, overalls, and hats to other workers whose clothes had been stolen.

A week after the men were fired, a good number of them were sent to jail. They had gone at night to the parked machines at the clearing sights and with rubber hoses sucked petrol out of the machines into plastic gallons to sell in order to feed their families.

They were caught and badly beaten by the private security guards, then dragged into the backs of trucks that took them to the police station. The police didn't take reports or question why the men were bleeding. They locked them up for a few days, then transferred them to another prison somewhere in the country without telling their families.

When Ernest and Miller first returned, Colonel had not been able to sit with them to hear in full detail what had happened because their firewood business was in great demand. Finally, at the end of that week, after the last meal of the day, Colonel was ready. "Tell me all that happened during the visit to the paramount chief. Tell me everything—even what you don't think is important," Colonel commanded, and the others left the three of them sitting together deep into the night as Colonel listened intently to Ernest and Miller, his body erect and his face stern, allowing no emotions to pass over it.

8

THE EVENINGS NOW BEGAN with truckloads of men returning from work. Most, if not all, went straight to the bar, where they would be joined shortly by the men who lived in company quarters. Their conversations made no sense—they shouted one another down midsentence—and the noise took over the evening serenity of the town.

Here in Imperi, nights used to be welcomed with the warmest of handshakes. There were visits with friends, and stories told by elders later in the night were a way for the heart to cleanse itself for whatever the following day might bring. But gentle people could no longer enjoy the arrival of evening. That sweetness had been soured by the behavior of drunkards in their midst. It was as though the workers, foreign and local, came to the bar to cure their torments by releasing their anger on the unfortunate townspeople. At the beginning of the evening, they sat on the open veranda of the bar, facing the road that divided the old and new parts of town. As the alcohol diluted their blood and falsely strengthened their belief that they could get away with anything, they began letting loose their unwanted natures, calling out to women and girls who walked by on their way to buy kerosene, fetch water, or perform some other function for their families.

"Woman, here is money, I will pay you to spend the night with me," a local man said.

"I am married, and even if I wasn't, you are out of line and must use your tongue properly if you are ever going to get a woman," the woman passing by said. The response didn't deter the fellow, and his friends egged him on. He took a gulp of his beer, wiped his mouth in the palm of his hands, and headed after the woman. "I will pay your husband, too, to loan you to me for the night." He pulled more money from his pocket and displayed it in the open.

Such behaviors would go on for a while, and as the men got drunker, they began walking out of the bar to physically touch women in places that one must ask and be granted permission to touch. The men got so aggressive that they even pulled down the wrappers of the women. The first time this happened, the woman ran home and brought her husband, brothers, and uncles, and they attacked the fellow who had misbehaved. His drunken friends came to his aid and a big fight started that ended with several wounded men. That was the first incident, and the police didn't come to arrest anyone then. But more and more of these situations occurred, and the fights got more violent, and bystanders began getting hurt from bottles flying out from the fracas. That's when the police started coming. But they arrested only the local people, especially those who didn't work for the company. The men responsible were simply sent to their living quarters, being reminded they had work the next morning.

During one such fight, Sila and his children had been walking by when a foreigner let fly a bottle he had broken against a table. It hit Maada and slashed the little boy across his forehead. Sila ran toward the fellow and head-butted him so hard that the man fainted. At that moment, the police vehicle was heard from afar on its way toward Imperi. Someone with a walkie-talkie or mobile phone must have called them.

Ernest, who had been nearby, stepped up to Sila. "Take your child home so you don't have to go to jail," he said. Sila hesitated, perhaps deciding whether to trust the boy who had amputated them. But he decided to do as Ernest advised, as his son's wound needed tending to. Sila pulled his children along while looking back to see what Ernest was going to do, but his eyes lost him in the crowd.

Ernest gathered some big rocks, stepped in the middle of the road, and sat down on his heels so that the light from any incoming vehicle would not reveal his face. As the police vehicle neared, he threw a few of the rocks with such precision and force that he broke the windshield and side mirrors. Then he stood up and ran, under the cover of darkness. The police chased after him, forgetting about the foreigner who had recovered but with a bloody nose. The police couldn't catch Ernest, and no one told who he was. And the foreigner was embarrassed because a man with just one hand had knocked him down, so he refused to speak to the police.

Sila learned what Ernest had done and wanted to thank him. But he still needed time to be able to shake Ernest's hands.

After months of fights at the bar and men being jailed without their families knowing where they were, wives and daughters, without means and desperate, began to take money from foreigners at first, and eventually from anyone, in exchange for their bodies. And soon enough, young women arrived from other parts of the country to do the same, and prostitution became a booming business in Imperi, and the elders could do nothing about it. And since they were powerless, they withdrew themselves from such sights.

One weekend, a group of men—two foreigners and two locals—forcibly took a young woman who was returning from the river carrying a bucket of water. They slowed down their vehicle and offered her a ride into town. She refused, so they grabbed her, threw her in the back, and drove her up the hill to their quarters. Her name was Yinka, and she was not from Imperi, but she could have been anyone's daughter. The next morning, she was found on the side of the road by the bar, her pelvis broken. Unable to stand, she had dragged herself toward her house but could not get that far. The women came with clothes and covered her bloody and naked body. They carried her home and tended to her, but she didn't want to be in this world any longer. No one knew where she was from and no one came to claim her body. She was buried and people cried for her because she was someone's daughter and this could have happened to any other young girl or woman in town. The police did nothing, even when people went to the station to give the names of the four men.

"We know who they are and you do nothing about it! This means you encourage them to do more of such things," a neighbor of Yinka's shouted from among the people who had come to the station to demand an investigation. The police threw tear gas into the crowd.

This town—where not so long ago, even after the war, one allowed one's daughter to play under the moonlight with other children; where, even though things weren't even close to perfect, a mother and father didn't stand barefoot in a pot of hot oil each time their daughter left the house to fetch a bucket of water—this town . . . what was it now and what would become of its people?

Soon there were rapes that no one spoke of, not only because the women were ashamed but also because the families felt helpless and the only dignity left was silence. Sometimes, the growing belly of a young girl shattered that falsehood and the child she gave birth to had the color of and resembled one of the workers, white or black. Nothing was said about such things. The child became part of Imperi's forgotten population.

For the moment, there was some laughter coming through the wind. So life still lived here, after all.

One night, a loud explosion silenced all conversations—even at the bar. People came outside, looking all around for a sign of smoke, but there was nothing, so they returned to what they had been doing. The next morning, there was no water at the mining site or the company quarters, and it took a week before the problem could be found. Someone had dynamited the main water pipe up in the hills under the bushes. The company fixed it, but the water that then came through the faucets and out of the showerheads was contaminated with petrol and rusty murk. For two weeks, it went on like this, then stopped.

That's when Colonel and Miller ran out of the petrol they had siphoned from the company machines and got tired of bailing the dam water at night. They had fed the dirty dam water and petrol into the water pipe through a hole they had drilled. Miller laughed as they did it; Colonel showed no emotion.

Colonel never showed any emotion—except once. One evening Salimatu came home, her face swollen and her dress torn into pieces; she was almost naked. Colonel pressed her to tell him who the men were who had done this. She did, and though his demeanor didn't change much, it was the first time that tears came to his eyes, and his entire body trembled with anger. He boiled some water and tended to Salimatu. Then, while she rested, he put his bayonet in his pocket and headed for the bar, stopping at a shop to buy a small can of red paint.

Before going on, he passed by Bockarie's house and gave Bockarie all of his savings. It was for the others, he said; it was their school fees for the coming year. Then he bought a box of matches from Bockarie's stand.

"Are you okay, man?" Bockarie sensed something was angering the young man.

"Of course. You know, I learned something during the war."

Colonel moved away from the light of the lamp. "I learned that you are not free until you stop others from making you feel worthless. Because if you do not, you will eventually accept that you are worthless."

He was gone before Bockarie could find words to respond.

Arriving near the bar, Colonel observed the area carefully. He saw the four men—the two foreigners and two locals, the same men who had assaulted Yinka and now Salimatu and possibly many others. He crouched near their vehicles and with an old cloth he wrote RAPIST in capital letters on their cars with the paint. The men were still drinking, laughing, and harassing women who walked by. He waited in the dark where he knew each of them was bound to come when the beer no longer had space to settle in them.

Sure enough, one of the foreigners came to urinate. Colonel attacked with several blows to the man's temple that made him faint. Colonel dragged the foreigner to the back of the bar, undressed him, and tied his penis with a rope that he attached to the branch of a mango tree. He tore the fellow's shirt and trousers and used the strips to bind his hands and legs, and gag his mouth. The fellow came to after Colonel was done, and each time he moved, the rope tightened, elongating his privates. His eyes watered but his voice couldn't go anywhere.

Colonel did the same to two others, tying them to the same tree. But the last man, a local, stayed in the bar longer than Colonel expected. Finally, watching him inside the brightly lit bar from where he stood in the darkness, Colonel's anger got the best of him. He needed to finish this before people saw the three men. So he took his bayonet from his pocket and held it tightly behind his back. He went into the bar and sat next to the fellow.

"Did you happen to run into a young woman today who has some tribal marks here and is quite beautiful?" he asked, touching both sides of his cheeks to indicate where the marks were on Salimatu.

"So what if I did? I run into girls and women all the time. Are you the police, small boy?" The man rose up from his chair and stood over Colonel.

"She is my sister, and I am better than the police." Colonel pressed the bayonet against the man's side, not wounding him but letting him know he would, and he asked the man to walk outside. The man thought about refusing, but he changed his mind as he felt the knife about to enter his flesh.

He was treated the same way as the others.

Colonel had a parcel of sugar that he sprinkled all over them. Then he took the keys from their pockets and left.

They weren't aware at first of what he had done, but they soon found out, as killer ants started arriving and climbing all over their naked bodies, biting them everywhere, until their bodies became red, swollen, and numb. Meanwhile, using their keys, which bore the names of their quarters and room numbers, Colonel crept into their living spaces and set their rooms on fire, burning everything in them.

The men weren't discovered until morning. People gathered around them until the police came with some armed guards and an ambulance. The local fellow described the boy who had done this, and people were forced to give the name of Colonel. But who was Colonel? Few knew his real name and he was nowhere to be found. And those who did know his name said nothing. As for where he was, only Miller knew, and he certainly told no one.

The rapes ceased and men stopped staying too long at the bar. They also looked around before using unnecessary words to women and girls who walked by.

9

THE END OF THE YEAR was approaching and all the teachers were desperate. They hadn't received their "every three months" salaries that they had gotten used to and adjusted their lives around. It was now almost six months without pay, and they were going into the Christmas holiday—and of course nothing could be earned while on holiday. This caused panic among the teachers. They already had to miraculously make their current salaries work, and such miracles lose their effectiveness if stretched out too much. Simultaneously, while the nerves of teachers who had preached the relevance of education to their students were being tightened by burdensome circumstances, the mining company was advertising job openings for clerks, processing operators, mechanics, and security guards.

The teachers decided to hold a meeting with the principal, who was also affected by the lack of salaries. He could no longer afford petrol for his motorcycle, and some days he pushed the thing onto the school grounds sweating right through his suit. Sometimes, the students helped push the motorcycle with him sitting on top. The boys thought it was fun, and since there were many of them they didn't mind, and the principal would give them a few leones every now and then for lunch. He called the boys his "hybrid engine."

The meeting ended very quickly, and whatever good spirits had been retained by the teachers were dispelled in an instant. The principal didn't know when the next pay would be coming, and he tried to plead with his teachers not to abandon their jobs, "which are more than just earning a salary," he said. But his plea, though genuine, fell on ears that desperation now controlled and that now were able to hear only unpleasantries. Everyone was suspicious of the principal, especially as another secondary school in the nearby district had received salaries before the holiday. What is more, he was finishing a cement house in town that had become the envy of everyone whose eyes saw this simple four-bedroom house.

For the first time, Bockarie started seriously thinking about working for the mining company. He could not see any other way to take care of his family. When he told Benjamin what he was thinking, Benjamin told Bockarie he'd already gotten an interview and hoped to be hired soon. Benjamin also told his friend about something he had been planning and wanted to accomplish before he stopped teaching.

"I am going to steal the principal's ledger and use it against him, sort of force him to do some good things for the school," Benjamin said. He wasn't joking around, as he usually did. He was serious.

"How are you going to do that? Can I help?" After he said that, Bockarie hesitated. He wasn't sure he should have offered. The thought tormented him, but it also made sense. And, Bockarie thought, perhaps there was a way he could personally benefit from Benjamin's plan. Perhaps the demands could include using the nonexistent teachers' salaries to pay for the school fees for all his children. He didn't mention this to his friend.

"As a matter of fact, I do need your help—for lookout and distraction, if needed, and for some work that we will have to do after. I have studied the principal's movements and know exactly when to strike. We strike tomorrow at lunchtime."

He abruptly switched the topic. "Wait for me after school today so we can stop by the company's site, where you can pick up an application." He forced a smile, but it quickly departed, as though his face wanted only what was pure from within.

After school, Bockarie told Manawah and Miata to head home without him, that he would see them later on. While Bockarie waited for Benjamin, the principal came by, two boys pushing his motorcycle. He waved to Bockarie with a smile that showed he enjoyed what was happening. The boys took turns making the engine sound of the motorcycle, and the taller of the two honked at Bockarie when the principal waved. Bockarie waved back and smiled at the ability of these young boys to find joy in such a laborious and ridiculous activity.

Why does he bring his motorcycle to school if he has no petrol? he asked himself, as he had so many times before.

"Sorry, man. I was getting these." Benjamin's voice reached Bockarie's ears. He was slightly in the distance, jogging lightly, grasping two ledgers under his arm. Bockarie surveyed the area, looking worried. "Relax, man, these are blank." Benjamin laughed. He said that he had stolen them, one at a time, from the storage room a few weeks back. He went on to explain that the following day, he planned to swap one of these in the principal's bag for the real ledger. That way, the bag would weigh the same and the principal wouldn't notice the ledger was gone. Then, throughout the night, with Bockarie's help, Benjamin would copy the contents of the entire ledger into the second blank one. And then, on the next day, the original would be returned with a note attached, reading, "We have the original and here are our demands!"

"So, some plans have changed. I will need you, close to the end of school tomorrow, to snatch the ledger, as this will guarantee that the principal won't notice overnight, and we can do the swap first thing the next morning during assembly when he is speaking." Benjamin was quite proud of his plan.

"What if he notices that the real ledger is missing before he goes home?"

"We would still have the ledger. And we would find a way of leaving our demands in his office. I am going to make sure he knows it is me—especially after I get the job at the company."

Slowly, they approached the site of the mining company, stopping at the entrance to speak to a fellow they knew by the name of Ojuku.

"The teacher men, teachers of knowledge! What brings you to my humble post?" Ojuku asked, even though he suspected why they were there. They shook hands.

"My man Ojuku, we are here to pick up an application," Bockarie said.

"That is right, and we know you are the man in charge!" Benjamin slapped the hand of Ojuku with another handshake.

"There are no applications for now," Ojuku said with a laugh, a short laugh that suggested the suspension, from here on, of whatever friendship was between them.

"The applications are right there, man, on the shelf. We can see them." Benjamin pointed to the papers.

"Those papers are papers. I say they are applications only when I want to. For now they are just papers, plain!" Ojuku played with the baton at his side and held the gate open for a fellow dressed in overalls.

"So give us the plain paper, then," Bockarie said.

"Those plain papers are under my watch and they are company property. They are not free." Ojuku went inside the gate, closed it behind him, and spoke to the teachers from the other side. "Those plain papers won't last long, though. For some reason people love them and shake my hand with notes that make me see the papers aren't so plain."

"You know that the applications are free, and yet you still make trouble for your own people." Bockarie raised his voice a bit.

"I say what is free around here. Can't you see I am in charge, man?" Ojuku refused to give Bockarie the application for free even though it was free. Bockarie knew it was futile to continue arguing, so he gave him some money and took the papers angrily from Ojuku's fingers.

"You were right, my brother. They are applications! I was blind but now I see applications and *hmmm*." Ojuku smelled the notes and laughed again. He told Bockarie that he must remember that they would see each other again when he returned with the completed application. He rubbed his thumb and index finger together as a warning that Bockarie should behave or he would have to pay more money upon his return.

That evening before nightfall, Bockarie paced up and down in confusion on his veranda holding a pen and the application form. He had asked Kula about applying to work for the company.

"If you think it would help the family, then try it, and you can always quit if the work breaks your heart too much." Her response assured him that she would stand by him no matter what, but he still felt that this wasn't right. Realistically, though, it was what had to be done. He asked his father, Pa Kainesi, who said nothing for a while, perhaps because he had hidden his voice within him for some time now. Then after a long sigh, which was even more tormenting to hear than his piercing silence, he spoke.

"Yes and No are the same these days in this land of ours. Good luck, my son." He fell quiet again and left for a walk to see his friends, whom he sat with to observe the goings and comings of the towns-people. Bockarie didn't understand what his father meant. He decided to fill out the application before night fully embraced the clear blue sky.

It will be temporary and I may not even get the job, he said to himself, his hands shaking as he began by writing his name on the application. He filled it out carefully, thinking about each word before he wrote it. He had only the one copy and he knew if he made a mistake, he would have to give Ojuku more money. He barely had enough money to get Ojuku to receive the completed application and put it in the box where it would be picked up and looked at. He couldn't afford another.

Meanwhile, that night, as during many others, the police and armed guards showed up in town looking for Colonel. They even questioned Salimatu about his whereabouts but nothing about what had happened to her. Miller and Ernest took over the wood selling business in the absence of Colonel, and Kula began cooking for them full time, something that apparently Colonel had discussed with her. Salimatu was looked after by Kula, Mama Kadie, Miata, and especially Mahawa, who became a close friend. The two young women were always together everywhere, giggling and taking turns carrying Tornya. Sometimes one couldn't tell who was the real mother of the child.

For a week, Bockarie and Benjamin tried unsuccessfully to snatch the principal's ledger. And every day, after another failed attempt, they would pass by the notice board at the mining site to see if the list of new employees had been posted.

It was a Wednesday, and they were going to check the notice board once again, not hopeful at all. It was just a new routine to delay going home and to play with the possibility of something, anything, happening. A conversation began between them about what would happen if they got employment at the mining company. They spoke about the impact that it would have on the students who wouldn't have teachers for however long it would take to find their replacements. They also knew that no one was seeking an unpaid teacher's position and that one of their colleagues would likely be manipulated by the principal to take their places. They were unsettled by the ramifications of their decisions. They got even sadder when they thought about the brilliance of some of their students and the enthusiasm for learning the children had under all sorts of difficult conditions.

Bockarie thought specifically about a boy and a girl who walked eight miles one way every day from the nearby chiefdom to attend school and scored one hundred percent on every subject. The students had told him that they took turns reading their notes aloud to the other while they walked to and from their village. It was the only way they could have ample time to study, as by the time they got home they were too exhausted to study for long. The girl and boy had also convinced the teachers to give them lessons on weekends, when they should be resting from the long walks.

"I think we should still continue to give lessons even when we are no longer teachers," Bockarie said.

"I agree. Could we still charge, or is it going to be for free?"

"We have to charge. You know our people. If it is local and free they think it is not good. And some students will slack off." Bockarie's response made both of them feel slightly better about leaving the school.

"Look—I wasn't expecting this to happen today." Benjamin pointed ahead of them and they hastened, nearly running. A crowd of men and young boys—boys whose youthfulness struggled to cling to their desperate faces—stood around the empty notice board. There were more than fifty men and twenty boys, most of them new to the area.

As Bockarie and Benjamin came closer, they could hear the low voices of men wishing one another good luck, their utterances filled with anxiety. Ojuku, they learned, would soon bring the list containing the names of those whom the gods had blessed and cursed at the same time.

While they waited, they chose to look at this possibility of employment as a blessing. It was really a short wait but it felt longer, and Ojuku played with the emotions of the crowd, showing them the small power he had over them. He stood behind the wire fence and pretended to have a phone call while scanning the list of names and raising his head up to survey the faces in the crowd. Having exhausted mocking the crowd, and worried about his foreign bosses catching him in the act, he finally came out of the gate.

The crowd surged around him, their huddled weight pushing him quicker to the board where he pinned the list of twenty names. The crowd, no longer recognizing Ojuku's importance, almost trampled him on their way to get a look at the list.

Benjamin and Bockarie waited behind the crowd, watching, and slowly, men and boys who had run forward with enthusiasm started dispersing, disappointment in every part of their bodies. It could be seen in the way their arms refused to swing, stiffly tucked by their sides, resisting their natural rhythm. It could be heard by the way their feet stamped deeper into the dusty ground, as if wanting to bury the bodies they carried. After those many miserable men and boys (who would rekindle their spirits somehow and return here again to apply) had departed, a few jubilant faces congratulated one another, forging instant friendships, especially if their job placements were the same.

Benjamin moved ahead of Bockarie toward the list and, turning around, he picked up his friend and raised him in the air before setting him down closer to the notice board. They had both been employed. They had work that would pay. Benjamin would be a processing operator and a mechanic, and Bockarie a clerk and a lab technician.

"Do you have any idea what these jobs titles mean or what they require of us?" Benjamin asked.

"I am at a loss—but we are employed!"

The remainder of their walk home didn't feel as unbearable as usual. Their new jobs would start soon, though on different days—Benjamin first and then Bockarie. So they needed to write their letters of resignation before the end of the week. But most important, they needed to take the ledger from the principal.

"We have to take the ledger from him tomorrow if we want to have time to copy its contents and hand in our resignation letters on Friday," said Benjamin.

"I agree, and we can return the ledger that very morning." Bockarie's response was quicker than usual, and that made Benjamin raise his head to meet his friend's eyes. With another handshake they parted ways and went home in moods that most men in town were envious of. Benjamin was going to bring his family over to Bockarie's home that evening so they could all celebrate together.

"I know you have good news when that handsome face of yours is this bright," Kula said when she laid eyes on her husband. She wrapped her arms around him, pressing every part of her body closer.

"The children are watching," he warned as he kissed her.

Bockarie asked his wife to make chicken stew for the family and to cook extra rice to celebrate his employment. He sent his oldest son, Manawah, to buy soft drinks for everyone and some batteries for the cassette player. Pa Kainesi looked at his son with warning eyes. Still, the old man could not resist when Manawah brought the batteries back and Bockarie played Salia Koroma, an old favorite musician of his father's. The musician, accompanied by his accordion, sang parables of the old ways, and the songs made Pa Kainesi get up and start singing and dancing. He sent his granddaughter Miata to invite Pa Moiwa and Mama Kadie over. They arrived with reluctance but soon livened up and danced around, singing and remembering those days of their youth.

Benjamin, Fatu, and their children, Bundu and Rugiatu, came by. Fatu had prepared food that she brought in a basket. She handed it to Kula, who pulled her away for a private conversation. They giggled as they dished out the food they had cooked, preparing one large plate for the boys and men, and a separate one for the women and girls. Then they all sat together on the veranda and ate. At the end of the meal the music resumed and the small party went on for hours.

Mama Kadie gathered the children. "A man arrived at the river with a goat, cassava leaves, and a lion. He needed to cross and could only do so with one of the items at a time. The lion would eat the goat if left alone with it, and the goat would eat the cassava leaves as well. How would the man cross the river?"

Such banter was exchanged into the night.

At some point, Thomas and Oumu flanked their father while delighting in the cold bottle of Fanta they shared. Each child would take a sip, then pass the bottle to the other with excitement.

"Father." Thomas got Bockarie's attention—and everyone else's.

"We"—the little boy pointed to his sister Oumu, and Benjamin's children, Bundu and Rugiatu—"we want you and Uncle Benjamin to get a new job every day. We love the party, especially the Fanta!" The other children clapped for Thomas, and for their parents, and for their siblings, and for their friends . . . and the night went on toward daylight, as it must be.

At school the next day, Benjamin went to see the principal. He knocked on the half-opened door and the principal sprang up and walked quickly to him.

"How can I help you?" he asked with nervous irritation.

"Could I print some flyers for our after-school lessons closer to the end of the school day?" Benjamin stood in the doorway, but the principal wasn't letting him in.

"Why closer to the end of the school day?" The principal dabbed his forehead with his handkerchief.

"It is the only free time I have and I don't want to use class time to do this task," Benjamin said. "Do you want me to?" He broadened his eyes at the principal, who became quiet for a while.

"Of course you mustn't use class time. And I made a promise to help you and your nice, quiet friend. You, on the other hand, are a rebel." The principal looked at Benjamin with strong eyes that were meant to intimidate but didn't succeed.

"I didn't come here for insults, but if that is what you want, I will be glad to exchange as many as needed with you, sir."

"You don't like to be a subordinate, eh? Okay, enough of this unnecessary chatter. Come by my office when you are ready. I will be here," the principal said, and continued, "There is very little petrol left in the generator and it will not last more than five minutes. We must finish it, anyway. Anything to help my students and dedicated teachers!"

Benjamin nodded with a wry smile. The principal remained standing in the doorway watching the fast and confident gait of Benjamin as he walked away.

Later on, during the printing, which lasted for three minutes before the generator started coughing, Bockarie came by and asked to speak with the principal privately. Before they stepped outside, leaving the task of watching the printer to Benjamin, the principal sized up Benjamin with a look that reiterated that he didn't like him at all.

Benjamin ignored him, and as soon as the principal turned his back, Benjamin resumed his bent-down posture by the printer, collecting the papers and laying them in his open bag on top of the ledger so that the ledger ceased to be visible.

"So what is this private matter you would like to discuss with me?" the principal asked Bockarie while looking back to the office at Benjamin.

"I love teaching, sir, but I am having a difficult time doing it with the same enthusiasm I used to have." Bockarie got the principal's attention back to him. He was about to continue when the generator made a funny sound and everything went off.

"I shall talk to you another time," the principal said as he began walking back into his office. He used the excuse of needing to make sure that Benjamin had printed enough flyers to get out of a conversation he didn't want to have. Bockarie nodded in agreement. In his office, the principal eyed Benjamin, who showed him the inside of his bag with the pages sticking out.

"Well, that should do for a while." The principal managed a smile and picked up his own bag to go home. Outside his office, he shook hands with Bockarie and Benjamin again before pushing his motorcycle, which he climbed on at the top of the slope for the ride downhill. They walked home quietly; Benjamin never asked what Bockarie had said to the principal and Bockarie didn't inquire as to how Benjamin had taken the ledger.

That night, they stayed up until almost morning. They collected all the kerosene lamps and flashlights in both households and took turns providing light while the other copied the ledger down to the very last detail.

Then they penned their terse resignation letters, both of which ended with the promise that they would "continue to contribute to their students' growth through their after-school lessons." And they composed the final demands, which guaranteed the secrecy of the principal's ledger, in exchange for . . . for . . . for what, exactly?

"We must make demands that we can monitor," Bockarie said.

"I want to make sure that he keeps the school open no matter what, and that all students—especially those who are brilliant and cannot afford school fees—are supported by some of the money he is embezzling," said Benjamin with a yawn.

Bockarie added kindling to the glowing coals in the fireplace, to restart the fire to boil water for tea. With his back turned to Benjamin, he said, "I think that we have to be specific. Keeping the school open, that he can do to some extent without us forcing his hand. Regarding the students, we have to name the ones we want him to pay for, and it has to be a reasonable number."

"I hope you are not feeling sorry for this fellow. If I had children in that school, I would include them in the terms. Hence, I am not sure why you haven't brought that up."

Benjamin's comment, though it surprised Bockarie, freed him from the burden of having to sound selfish. "Let's make that part of the terms, then," he said quickly, with a smile that came about in time to beat the yawn that wanted to possess his jaws. They also agreed to add the names of all Colonel's siblings—Amadu, Salimatu, Victor, Ernest, and Miller.

"Where do you think Man in Charge is, anyway?" Bockarie asked.

"I do not know, but I am not worried about that boy. He knows how to take care of himself better than you and I!" Sipping their hot tea, they finished writing their demands, which included getting supplies for teachers, paying school fees for all of Bockarie's children and fifteen other students, providing chalk for the after-school lessons, and making sure that school remained open no matter what. Roughly calculating the cost of all these things, they realized it would be half of the nonexistent teachers' salaries that the principal had on the payroll.

"He will still be able to buy petrol for his motorcycle when we are finally paid, though he won't be smiling half as much," Benjamin said with a little laugh.

They didn't sleep that night and their walk to school the next morning was sluggish and slow. But the miles and the heat gradually wiped the sleep off their faces even if their bodies remembered they had been starved of a night's rest. Nearer to campus, Benjamin got into a much happier mood than his friend. Bockarie was still anxious and would remain so until they had returned the duplicate ledger. He started worrying less, though, when Benjamin disappeared while the students were sorting themselves out for assembly. And when Benjamin returned, he was smiling even more than before.

When assembly finally commenced, the principal made his way to the front of the gathering, holding the ledger under his arm. This was very unusual, him carrying it openly, and Bockarie was especially relieved they had returned the thing earlier. After the principal finished his announcements and stepped back for the singing of the school song and the national anthem, he began leafing through the ledger. Bockarie's and Benjamin's eyes were on him as he pulled out the paper that contained their terms. His jaws tightened as he read, and he immediately looked toward Bockarie when he was done. Bockarie averted his gaze. The principal folded the paper and pushed it into his right pocket while his eyes surveyed the teachers to see who was responsible. He ruled Bockarie out of the equation because of the explicit mention of his children's school fees in the terms. But when the principal's eyes finally met Benjamin's, he gave him a wry smile and a mocking half salute.

The principal walked to the back of the assembly and stood next to Benjamin. Underneath the voices of the students singing, he said, "So you are behind this madness, my friend? Do you have any idea what problems I can give you?"

"You mean you can sack me. That is the only problem you are capable of giving me right now."

"Not only will I sack you but I will make sure you cannot teach anywhere in this country."

"In that case I will make it easy for you. Here is my resignation letter effective today. Sir." Benjamin handed the principal the paper.

The principal knew he had no more grip on Benjamin, but he had to say something that didn't completely reveal the defeat he now felt. "I am not done with you. You are under me for today and I am going to make it hell for you."

The principal walked away, crumpling the resignation letter but not throwing it on the ground. Benjamin wanted to respond that "you can only threaten someone with hell if they have never had hell," but he let it go. Throughout the day, during his lessons, the principal passed by the window of his classroom, distracting him and his students. He had Benjamin step outside and spoke to him in whispers. "I want to see you at the end of the school day," he demanded.

"There is nothing to discuss. You have my terms," Benjamin said, starting back to class.

"Who else is involved in this? And how do I know that you won't continue with more demands?" The principal stepped gently in front of Benjamin and turned to the side so the students would not see this as a confrontation.

"No one else is involved. I have your secret in a safe place and the terms will remain the same. Also, you are in no position to negotiate anything, so stop bothering me." Benjamin brushed past the principal and returned to his classroom.

Benjamin didn't tell his students that it was his last day. But they were used to the impermanent nature of things and could instinctively tell when circumstances were about to change. They needed no explanations. Therefore, at the end of class, some students came to their teacher one at a time, shook his hand, and walked out. Those who didn't like the idea of goodbyes just left, avoiding eye contact. Benjamin felt slightly sad that he was abandoning them. He sat in the empty classroom and remembered all that had passed in there.

"Everything comes to an end, like life itself," he mumbled to comfort himself before getting up to depart.

Bockarie waited for Benjamin to perform their routine of walking home together. It was their last walk as teachers.

"I have to pick up my work supplies, so come along, my friend," Benjamin said.

"How did it go with the big man today?"

"He tried to threaten me and to find out who else was part of the plot. But he got nothing!"

"You think he suspects that I am part of it?"

"He has nothing, and he is afraid of finding out if you are a part of it or anyone else. So do not worry. You will start work soon, anyway." Benjamin nudged his friend. They were by the tiny fishing ponds that the company had created as one of the measures to rehabilitate the land.

"How many ponds do you see here?" Benjamin asked, pointing

to the murky water and the weary fish that swam from one end to the other with unnatural movements of their fins, a clear indication that they wanted out.

"No more than five."

"Have you ever had fish from this pond?"

"No, and I do not know of anyone who has."

"They say these ponds are to grow fish for the people whose rivers they have destroyed, but these fishes aren't even enough to feed a child for a day." Benjamin laughed.

"Why grow barracuda in a country that has more of that fish than it can eat? And you will be working for these people?" Bockarie's sarcasm made his friend smile.

"Yes! And so will you. And we must hurry before the supply store closes."

When Benjamin returned ten minutes later, he carried a duffel bag of his new work materials, and his new ID card dangled around his neck. Bockarie patted his friend on the shoulder to congratulate him. They then sat by the wire fence and Benjamin went through the bag, showing Bockarie his blue overall uniform, yellow hard hat, and black boots that were heavier than any shoes either of them had ever worn. The company insignia with the head of a lion, in a distorted form, was on the hat and the bag. Benjamin put his hat on as they embarked on the last miles home. People smiled at him when they passed. They encountered an old man who said, "You are teacher no more. Will that hat protect your head?" The old man laughed sarcastically.

They parted to their various homes. Bockarie briefly told his family about Benjamin's news and he settled near his kerosene lamp to correct papers and prepare the lessons for the next day. For the first time, he felt a strong distaste for what he was doing and had to struggle through it. He couldn't stop thinking about starting work for the mining company. Even though he didn't know what the work entailed, the prospect of additional and steady income was enough to forgo teaching. Kula sensed the change in her husband's mood. She took most of the papers from under his hand and corrected them herself.

When she was done, she handed him the papers and walked slowly to make sure that his eyes found the enticing qualities of her body. "You are still a teacher, and you will be for your children always. Never try to write it off. I am going to the bedroom now and need your instructions, teacher Bockarie!" He followed her.

Meanwhile, Benjamin and Fatu had just put their children to bed and were happily discussing what they would do with the additional money. They agreed to save and build a house. Benjamin insisted that Fatu should re-enroll in the nursing studies that she had abandoned because they had no money.

It was a night filled with dreams of what was to come. Dreams were still possible here even though the paths to attain them weren't necessarily the best ones. But who can ever know what path to walk on when all of them are either crooked or broken? One just has to walk.

10

BENJAMIN WAS AWAKE BEFORE 5:00 A.M., the time the alarm was set to go off. He switched on his flashlight and looked through his old notes and lesson plans while in bed, not wanting to get out just yet; wanting to avoid waking Fatu. He read:

"During this lesson, teach them how to absorb knowledge as opposed to just memorizing. Teach them to become individual thinkers and not part of the majority that agrees with what is popular—afraid to stand alone in their thinking." He chuckled at the optimism he had had, at his certainty of the positive impact he could have on his students. He still believed in those words but no longer had faith in how to teach them to others, especially here in Imperi . . . in his country . . . on earth, in general. Fatu rolled in her sleep and Benjamin turned off the flashlight and didn't move. She fell back to sleep. He resumed reading his notes until it was time for Fatu to rise. She went to the fireplace and boiled water, cooled it down to the right temperature, and called on her husband to wash up. Afterward, she sat with him, caressing his face as he ate the chicken stew and rice that she had specially made the night before and had warmed up while Benjamin was washing. Some of the neighbors who didn't sleep well and were wondering about how to keep their families alive for yet another day found the smell of the stew tormenting. They rolled around in their beds, covering their noses with bedclothes that didn't smell of any sort of promise. That was a good place to start the day: where the dosages of disappointments were in abundance.

When he was fully dressed in his new overalls, hard hat, boots, and socks, Benjamin practiced walking, going forward and backward in front of his wife, whose smile competed with the brightness of the flames from the fire. After he had allowed his feet to grow familiar enough with the new socks and boots, the shiny black body of the boots that signified a worker for the mining company, he remarked, "Well, I think I have made a dent in them and they know who I am now."

Benjamin smiled at Fatu. His expression told that he was ready for work, whatever it entailed.

"Let me go and say goodbye to the children." He walked into the room where they slept.

"Don't wake them," Fatu whispered. Benjamin sat on his heels and placed his palms on the foreheads of his children, pulled the cloth properly over their little bodies, and walked outside.

Fatu was ready with a bucket in one arm and she held her husband's hand in the other. They walked to the junction where the other men waited to be picked up for work. As soon as they saw the couple, the men began laughing because they, too, remembered their first day of work and the anticipated joy that was within them.

"You smell fresh, my man! One always smells fresh of everything on the first day," Rogers greeted Benjamin.

Benjamin was surprised to see Rogers. After his son had stepped on the live wire that the company had left exposed, Rogers had withdrawn himself from social gatherings.

"Good to see you, sir," said Benjamin and shook Rogers's hand.

Fatu hugged her husband and went on her way to the river. The truck arrived and the men jumped in the back. The benches were as hard as the bed of the truck and Benjamin's new overalls had already started getting dirty. He tried wiping his boots and parts of his overalls with his handkerchief. The men laughed.

"Don't waste your time," Rogers said. "As soon as you get into this vehicle, all that was shiny becomes dusty and dirty. Soon you will only smell of chemicals."

As the truck sped down the road, the dust and stones chasing it and eventually catching up with it, Benjamin began to realize why the overalls and the hard hats were needed even before getting to work.

The vehicle didn't go to the mining site. It went past it, weaving its way through endless dams, which got bigger and bigger in size, and the earth got redder, exposing its wounds, and the men got quieter. Their laughter grew forced as they accepted the final banter of the morning. The truck halted at a large clearing in the middle of the dams that could be seen miles and miles in the distance. Once there had been forests here. Now the forests had been pushed back to the green mountains afar. Other vehicles were unloading. The men greeted one another and soon the clearing was filled with chatter.

"Which is the dredge and which is the plant?" Benjamin asked a fellow standing next to him. He pointed at the plant that looked like an iron house with several floors floating on the water, and the dredge, a similar structure, but one that also resembled Caterpillar machinery, as it had zigzagged teeth in the front of it for digging.

I wonder which one I will be going to, Benjamin thought. The white workers arrived shortly in their white Toyotas, and the lively conversation stopped abruptly. The locals who were supervisors abandoned the men they had been chatting with and took on an air of superiority as they approached the foreign bosses.

"Form lines here and here—now," one of the supervisors shouted at his companions, who filed in, foreigners in the front, local supervisors behind them, followed by the rest of the workers. Benjamin picked one of the lines, his mind anxious about what waited for him with this work.

Two low-lying barges approached the banks of the dam so loaded with men that if any of them dropped his hands to his sides, they would drag in the water. One barge was from the plant connected to the dredge with a row of iron buckets that spun around. The other came from the dredge. The men, some with faces darker than their real skin, dismounted the barges and filled the empty vehicles, which took off.

The foreigners got on the barges and a local supervisor directed the rest of the workers to one barge or the next. Benjamin was told to board the barge headed for the dredge. On the boat were some of his former students. They nodded in his direction. Once, he had lectured them about the importance of getting an education. Now he felt slightly ashamed, but he brushed that feeling away.

The engine halted and the body of the boat smacked the side of the dredge. One after the other and as quickly as possible the men climbed the iron steps to the main deck. The white men immediately went to offices outfitted with two-way mirrors overlooking the entire operations, leaving the supervisors to take charge. Benjamin looked around. Everywhere were warning signs that read DANGER. They were so plentiful he knew right away he must be on his guard at all times. Some signs were wordless: they just showed a skeleton imposed on a red stop sign.

The noise was too much. One of Benjamin's students handed him little things and indicated that they were to be pushed into his ears. He did, and the noise got slightly better.

"You are new, yes?" one of the supervisors shouted.

Before Benjamin could answer, he shouted again, "Come with me." Benjamin followed and was stationed near some pipes to observe the iron buckets that carried the soaked minerals and, if they were out of place, to align them.

"Your training starts. Focus, my good man." The supervisor snapped his fingers to get Benjamin's full attention. "Tell me, Mr. Teacher, where can you find work in this country that pays you while in training?" He patted Benjamin on the shoulder and left.

Benjamin wanted to ask questions but the supervisor was already gone, walking through the iron steps, on the pipes through the moving parts of the dredge with so much ease it was as though he was on land.

"Here. Take this and I will supervise you for a bit. It is my break, so don't worry." Another of Benjamin's former students handed him clear goggles and leaned against one of the iron posts that held a ladder.

"Any pointers for a novice?" Benjamin asked.

"Always make sure to wear your goggles and gloves. Also, carefully pay attention to where you lean or what you hold on to because a good number of these pipes and metals are hot. I mean really hot. So hot that if you touch them the only thing they won't burn are your bones. They will leave marks on them, though."

"Does most of the work require standing for most of the eight hours or more?"

"Yes, Teacher. You only rest during short breaks and lunch, but you will get used to it. It gets easier if you work near a fellow who likes to tell stories and jokes!" The young man wiped sweat off his forehead. He followed the distracted eyes of his teacher and saw that he was looking at two men praying. Both recited the Islamic prayer first, the Al-Fatiha, facing where the sun rose. They followed with the Lord's Prayer. They hesitated and then entered a work area where flames leapt out.

"What was that about?" Benjamin asked his student.

"Some people do that before they go into the most dangerous work areas. We say around here that it is so dangerous you have to do two or more prayers—because hopefully, at least one of them will get God's attention!"

He laughed. And just as he did a loud and painful sound ripped the air. It came from the place the two men had just entered. One emerged, his overalls partially on fire, his flesh severely burnt on one side from his armpit all the way down to his waist. His hands and face looked as though the fire had sucked flesh from his bones. Men laid him on a cold pipe and rubbed wet sand on his burnt skin, the areas that still had skin. Someone shut off whatever gave the flames life, and all the men, including Benjamin and his student, rubbed their heads together as they huddled to see what had happened. There was blood in the small area and the corpse of the other man. His right hand was still caught in the zigzag teeth of the machine that continued spinning his body around and around. The supervisor's radio went off and he held it to his ears. "Yes, sir," he said, looking up toward the offices covered with mirrors.

"Back to work, everybody. Now," he shouted, and the men dispersed back to their workstations. The former student who had kept Benjamin company patted him on the back and they went their separate ways. It wasn't lunchtime yet and Benjamin wondered what else the day would bring—perhaps something good to make up for having already claimed a life.

At school, Bockarie was daydreaming about starting work. He wondered what Benjamin was doing. He envied him, the freedom from the boredom Bockarie now felt. The mood on campus was getting stiffer. The one man who always managed a smile, the principal, had been in a bad mood lately and no longer gave his motivational speeches.

As Bockarie's students quietly worked on their essays, he reached inside his new-employee bag and felt the overalls, the boots, the hard hat. Their brand-new smell filled his nose. He would start work in three days and couldn't wait.

That evening, Bockarie canceled the lessons on his veranda because a musician was coming to town. Kula, Benjamin, Fatu, and Bockarie had arranged to go dancing. As he sat on his veranda quickly correcting papers so he could get ready for the night out, Bockarie looked up and saw Benjamin returning from his first day of work. Benjamin's overalls and face were completely blackened.

Beaming, Bockarie leapt up and gave his friend a handshake. "So how was it, man?"

Benjamin wanted to tell his friend about what had happened at work but Bockarie seemed too happy. So he responded instead with a question. "Has there been a funeral in town today?"

Benjamin's question didn't make sense to Bockarie. "No. What are you talking about?"

Benjamin blanketed his face with a smile that was weak underneath. "Work was exhausting but great, man. I am getting paid while in training for the work that I will be doing!"

"I cannot wait to start, man. So we dance tonight!" Bockarie hit his friend's shoulder and began walking backward to his veranda, giving his friend time to go see his family.

Benjamin waved him off, still smiling but consumed with thoughts about what had happened to the body of the man who had died at work. Why does no one know about it? What would happen to the man's family?

He walked home maintaining a smile on his face, for his wife and children. *I am lucky to have a job that pays me a little more*, he thought, forcing the smile to become even wider as he saw Fatu waiting for him on the veranda. She had plaited and oiled her hair and made herself quite beautiful for him. She wore a green embroidered dress with palm tree patterns at the hem, and the children stood by their mother with clean and shiny skin from the Vaseline lotion, in traditional outfits of light cotton with patterns of African heroes.

"Welcome home, dear. I am so happy, and how was your first day of work?" She pulled a chair for her husband to settle down.

"Welcome home, Father! We wish you a pleasant evening and thank you for your hard work!" The children had rehearsed this all afternoon. Giggling, they hugged their father and ran off to do their homework.

"It was nothing a former teacher couldn't handle. We are blessed." He smiled even harder to make sure the pretend happiness on his face didn't fade.

"We are going to celebrate tonight, so you must wash up. Leave the overalls there and I will rinse them." Fatu went to the fireplace to prepare the hot water for him.

"Thank you, my dear, but you mustn't worry yourself about the overalls. They will only get dirty again tomorrow. They must only be washed when my nose cannot tolerate the smell!" He laughed and she shook her head at how funny her husband always was.

At the back of the house, he couldn't enjoy throwing calabashes full of hot water on his head and body. The soap stayed on his skin longer and his hands forgot what to do, his second-nature motions intruded on by thoughts of what had happened at work. How could he bring this up when all his fellow workers kept quiet? On the way back to Imperi, everyone had gone about his banter as if nothing had happened. He seemed to be the only one tormented. Perhaps such things had become common occurrences for them? The dust that chased the truck on the way back from work now seemed to have a brutality about it. The stones that flew up with such determination now seemed to Benjamin to want to hit the workers.

On the truck, another worker came over and told him, "If you take everything to heart like this you won't last. Trust me, brother, there has been worse, way worse." And then he'd sat back down, his body dancing to the rhythm of the galloping vehicle.

"This is the longest washing you have ever done. What must you be doing there?" Fatu's voice woke Benjamin from his torment. He hurriedly finished so that he could eat and get ready to meet Bockarie and the others for the disco that night.

Everyone—Benjamin and Fatu, Bockarie and Kula, and several others from town—was in high spirits as they walked to the secondary school field that had been shielded by sticks and thatch to make a dancing hall under the stars. A long cloth hung over the entrance to keep away the eyes of those who couldn't afford this simple luxury. Still, young boys and girls hung about outside, enjoying the music, even if every so often the shouts of excitement coming from inside made them detest their youthfulness, which meant pennilessness, which meant they couldn't go into the dance space. Inside, Benjamin, Fatu, Bockarie, Kula, and most of the people from Imperi and surrounding areas danced like there was no tomorrow. The intoxicating music, the good company, and the local brew that flowed in abundance slowly overshadowed Benjamin's torment.

Of all the dancers, Sila was the best, and he danced by himself to every song. Sweat soaked and dried on his body and he didn't care. Benjamin and Bockarie spotted Colonel at some point during the night. He wore a red baseball hat, the brim disguising his face, and was dressed quite well, better than how they remembered him. He wore a plain white untucked long-sleeve shirt with a tie hanging loosely on his neck. He came close to Kula, and with his back facing her, he said, "Thank you for taking care of the others. They tell me they have never eaten food as sweet as yours."

"You are welcome. Who are you?" Kula said, knowing well that it could be several people telling her those words. Colonel started dancing and used a move to turn around and raise the brim of his hat for a quick reveal.

"I thought I saw a smile there. Did I, young man?" She turned briefly to her husband to tell him, and by the time she turned back, Colonel, as usual, had disappeared.

He went that night to see Mama Kadie to tell her she could count on him for anything she needed.

"Thank you, Kpoyeh, or Nestor. Which one do you like these days?" she said with a smile, and he responded, "Whichever it is that you choose, I accept."

He spoke calmly. *Kpoyeh* means "salt water," and he was given that name because salt water doesn't allow anything to stay inside it, it would throw it out. And Nestor because the registrar of his birth name couldn't pronounce or write his original name and he had looked up Nestor and loved the meanings behind it.

Close to 5:00 a.m. the gates were let open so that all could pour in and see the musician who had come from the capital. Everyone knew his songs, and one in particular called "Yesterday Betteh Pass Tiday" (Yesterday Was Better than Today) caused an uproar of excitement. People came alive perhaps for the truth in the song that they knew of so intimately but could never find the right words to communicate to themselves. They danced and shook the earth from its core so that even disturbed ghosts became merrier.

The last song spoke to all the men, women, and youngsters who struggled every day to make something of their lives. The song was called "Fen Am" (Find It) and it encouraged people to rise up every day and go look for opportunities. Even though they were tired of going around all day, and mostly for nothing, they shouldn't give up. The lyrics went on:

> *There is no hand of food for an idler*
> *I will not do anything bad but I will try and make it*

And later, the song went on cautioning that one shouldn't envy what others have, whether wealth or possession, because you do not know how they acquired such things.

The night prolonged its last muscles of darkness as the song blared on, sung with equal vigor by the musician and the crowd that hung on to every word of it. The nostalgia of that night had already settled within them as they walked home crooning the words of "Yesterday Was Better than Today."

"I am coming with you to work today, man. I start today! I will see you at the junction soon," Bockarie told his friend and pulled his wife's exhausted body home. Benjamin just conjured a laugh and patted his friend's shoulder, knowing full well he couldn't say anything.

Bockarie was the happiest fellow that morning in the vehicle and with the cleanest overalls. He was dropped off at the mining site and waved off Benjamin, who was carried to the dredge.

Bockarie was being trained how to test soil samples and determine what minerals were in them. While he was learning to test the samples, one of his coworkers pulled out some interesting-looking stones, really big, from the soil samples. The bosses who monitored them on camera announced, through the speakers, that he should come to their office and bring with him the stones and soil samples. He never returned. No one ever saw him again or knew what happened to him. After searching for him unsuccessfully for many months, his wife and child left Imperi. The only thing Bockarie remembered was that shortly after the man was called out of the sampling area, a truck with armed guards came by, something was quickly loaded in the back, the doors slammed shut, and the vehicle departed. From that day on, when Bockarie and Benjamin returned from work they didn't say much about what they did. The only gratitude they expressed, and they did so to please their wives, was that they would make a little more money than they had, and that thought was enough to hold the forced smiles on their faces longer than their hearts wanted.

The elders were not happy.

They wanted Benjamin and Bockarie to return to teaching because they felt the mining company would take their strength and dull their spirits. For a while, the two men did still teach some lessons, but their zeal dwindled, and the students, sensing the tiredness and disinterest of their teachers, stopped coming. The households of Benjamin and Bockarie got quieter as the number of days they worked for the company increased. Each of them only wanted to be left alone after work.

"Father, how come you don't read anymore and those big and tall boys don't come here with their books?" Thomas asked his father one evening while Bockarie sat alone on the veranda concealing with the darkness whatever emotions had taken hold of his face.

"Go back inside and do your homework." Bockarie's response used to be an invitation to sit near him, and he would explain things to his youngest son and read to him. Now, the boy dragged his feet inside, and his mother knew what had happened. Oumu, Thomas's precocious twin sister, always remedied such situations. She went out on the veranda, wrapped her little arms around her father, and climbed on his lap.

"Father, Mother said you are the best teacher ever. So I want you to be my only teacher when I am in secondary school. You have to promise. And Grandfather said you are losing your strength for others. But I think you will have some to teach me when I am big . . ." She went on until her father finally smiled, and it was not a false one. He promised to teach her. She ran back inside to tell everyone, and they could hear Bockarie laughing on the veranda while Oumu recounted what he had agreed to. He stood by the door, watching his family, then turned to join his father, who always sat outside waiting for the cool breeze that came in abundance when the night was much quieter.

"My son the teacher, mining worker. Sit with your father and share the breeze." Pa Kainesi knocked on the wooden bench next to him.

"In every person's life you acquire lots of titles for the things you do. Yours so far are 'teacher' and 'mining worker.' However many you acquire, there is one that always fits you best because it brings sweetness to your spirit. You seem troubled these days, my son."

"Everything is all right, Father. Work isn't what I thought, but the money is slightly better and comes on time."

"Your eyes, your movements do not say things are all right. Perhaps we mustn't pry. Just be sure not to lose yourself completely to this hand-to-mouth business." The old man held his son's hands and they chatted into the night. Their laughter drifted into the house and made Kula and the children happy. Pa Kainesi's face glowed, and his cheeks, which had tensed, relaxed. At some point, Bockarie took his father's hand and placed it on his cheeks. He had loved the feel and warmth of his father's hands when he was a child, before life's worries came along, before the war.

Bockarie decided to walk home one evening after his shift ended. He had been missing the walk that he made when he was a teacher. It had allowed him to see and greet others more than he did nowadays. Though he was exhausted, and the dust was particularly heavy, he slowly made his way home along the road.

A few minutes into the walk he heard someone running up behind him. "Teacher, Teacher, why art thou so pensive? Are you lecturing to the road or perhaps to the dust?" The giggling belonged to Benjamin, who put his right arm around his friend's shoulders. They made jokes about the principal, who was still angry with Benjamin and looking for ways to get his ledger back.

"I swear, one time he wanted to run me over with his motorcycle at the junction. I think it was only because some other people showed up that he changed direction." Benjamin hummed with disbelief.

"Where is that ledger, anyway?"

"I think I lost the thing, man! I was moving it from place to place because I was worried about someone else finding it. But the principal doesn't know that," Benjamin said. They made way for the truck that carried the rutile mineral to the docks. The driver waved to them.

"That's Rogers! So he's a driver now? That explains why I haven't seen him at work in a while." Benjamin turned to Bockarie and was about to ask a question when they heard a loud sound followed by the wailing of a woman. They ran toward the cry.

A woman sat on the earth holding the body of a little boy in her arms. He had been trying to run across the street to his mother, and because of the height of the truck, Rogers hadn't seen him. The left front tire had knocked the boy down, dragging his body under, and the double right back tire had flattened him to the ground. The truck had galloped a bit as it went over the boy, so Rogers had stopped to see what had happened. He stepped down, shaking. His eyes saw what had occurred. Some of the boy's bones had ripped through his skin. The mother's face was instantly rugged with sorrow. Rogers was on the radio calling for help. Somehow the boy was still breathing. The voice from the radio instructed him to get in the truck and drive to his destination; someone would be there soon to take care of the boy.

"I will not do that. I will stay here until help arrives," Rogers said to the voice.

"Then consider yourself suspended until further notice," the voice responded, and the radio went silent. In a matter of minutes, a Toyota with tinted glass arrived and another employee took the radio from Rogers, got into the truck, and drove it away from the scene of the accident. The back tires, soaked with blood and bits of dirt, painted the already disturbed earth with the boy's life. The vehicle that had dropped off the new driver sped back toward the mining site, near where the hospital was, leaving the boy in the arms of his mother. Rogers told the mother they should carry the child to the hospital. He knew that help wasn't coming—the vehicle that was supposed to take them hadn't. The mother stood up with her son, and that was when life completely departed him. She laid the boy down carefully and sprang on Rogers, hitting him everywhere until she was exhausted. He threw his arms around her and embraced her, weeping.

"He was my only child left. I lost everyone in the war and now am alone," she said, sobbing as she removed herself from the embrace of Rogers and picked up her son. Benjamin and Bockarie tried to help, but she wanted to carry her child herself. She walked toward the mining site. Rogers followed, not knowing what he could do.

"I wonder where she's going," Bockarie said.

"And Rogers, that poor fellow. Just when he was regaining himself from the death of his son," Benjamin said. They watched the woman walking far into the middle of the road, so cars had to swerve to avoid her.

When she reached the gate at the mining site, she called for who was in charge to come out and see what they had done to her child. The security guards received orders to escort her out of the area.

No one anticipated what happened next. The woman ran with her child in her arms toward one of the electric security fences and leaned against it, electrocuting herself. A crow cried sharply nearby and the silence deepened. Something had torn in the fabric of that day. Rogers ran from the crowd toward Imperi. He didn't go home but into the bushes, tearing off his clothes until he was naked. He never came back, but he was sighted every now and then eating raw food and roots at the edge of town. Had he gone mad, or was he punishing himself for the accident? No one knew, not even his wife, as he didn't speak to anyone and appeared to have forgotten even his family, friends, and workmates.

As for the woman and her child, they were removed from the fence at night after the armed guards dispersed the crowd. No one knew who removed the bodies or where they were buried. There was nothing about them reported anywhere. It was as though they had never existed.

11

LESS THAN A WEEK AFTER THE INCIDENT, there were white men all
over town, aided by some locals who carried their equipment. They
began marking houses, trees, and the ground with paint: red, white,
and yellow. Rumor had it they were geologists (those who speak to
the earth to find out what it chooses to give to the living—this was
the closest translation for the elders) who had determined that there
were large mineral deposits under the ground of Imperi. People
knew what this meant: soon their town would be bulldozed to
extract the minerals. But they refused to believe it. What did the
colors mean? Where were they going to go? These questions took
hold of every gathering in town and even intruded on private whispers. As the confusion increased, the geologists moved into the cemetery and started marking gravestones and cutting trees.

The elders, about eight of them, decided to confront the white
men, waking up early and waiting patiently at the end of the road
where the path into the cemetery began. A few hours later, four
white men got out of their vehicles and rubbed something on their

arms, faces, and necks; they put on hats and started talking among themselves while the locals offloaded their equipment.

The elders cleared their throats. "You there, young white fellows. We have been told that you are supposed to listen to the earth and learn from it. But what you are doing is different and against those whose role is to listen to the earth," an elder with grace and wisdom in every part of his being said to the foreigners.

"We have permission to mine anywhere we find rutile in this chiefdom," one of the geologists said.

"Who gave you that permission?" another elder asked.

"Your government. Our company has it for ninety-nine years."

"Even if that is the case, would you dig up your own grandfather's or grandmother's grave to find some minerals?" Pa Moiwa asked. The white men ignored the question.

The elders couldn't get any more answers. They had a quick meeting standing at the entrance of the cemetery and agreed to send someone to plead with the paramount chief. They couldn't believe that someone would lease their land for ninety-nine years with impunity and no monitoring whatsoever; they couldn't comprehend that someone chosen as a minister or president of a country could make such a decision. Even local chiefs didn't do that to people they knew and grew up with. However idiotic it was, a solution must be found, and there was no need to give up yet on the one who was supposed to represent them. Surely she would rail against the decision to mine where their ancestors were buried.

The paramount chief sent word back the next day that she would come to town for a meeting in two days and that until then all work on the cemetery and around town would stop. The work did stop. There was some relief in the air: finally, someone was listening.

On the day she arrived, everyone brought whatever hope and strength was left in them to the football field. It was the only space big enough to accommodate the crowd. Some men from the government came, too—their dark sunglasses and fancy cars gave them away. And of course there were the white men in charge of the company, escorted by their armed guards and police.

"Finally, we can have a discussion together about this land," someone shouted, and the people clapped and chanted old slogans about solidarity.

The paramount chief took the megaphone and the chanting died down. "We have had meetings with your section chiefs and they will tell you the details, but here is what we've decided: this town will be relocated. Your houses will be rebuilt elsewhere and you will be paid surface rent for your farms and properties. You must cooperate and cause no trouble for these men." She put the megaphone down and shook hands with the government officials and the foreigners. They all seemed pleased with themselves, smiling as though they had performed a remarkable service for the many hardened faces before them.

The crowd started shouting: "We own this land! No one consulted us!" The officials, shielded from the people by their armed guards and police, got into their vehicles and left the townspeople to their quarrels. Pa Moiwa fainted and had to be carried home. That evening, the usual layered clouds that summoned night to cloak the sky were broken into many pieces and struggled to make their call. Thus the night, too, arrived at a defeated pace that deepened the gloominess of the town. Even the birds didn't chant; they just went quietly into their nests, as if they knew that they would soon have to find new homes.

As though the company felt that if it waited, the people would find a way to stop them, men started tearing down the cemetery a few days later.

No one knew how the machines came to the cemetery, but they were there one morning, ready to further wound the shattered backbone of the community. The armed guards and police were there as well, in full riot gear, standing by a barrier that had been made with sticks and pointing their guns at anyone who came too close or looked too hard.

The machines' engines bellowed, releasing smoke that rose toward the morning sky and tormented the rising sun. The blades of the machines dug into the graves, pulling out bodies, skulls, and some bones still wrapped in old cotton clothes; they were all deposited in a big hole the machines had dug. People cried and shouted in vain. They apologized to the ancestors. No one had ever witnessed an entire cemetery destroyed like this.

Some people refused to believe that this was actually happening. They thought they were having a nightmare that would pass. It seemed the sun had told the moon what it had seen, because the moon refused to come out that night. There was a silence that made the dark last longer, longer than it had even during the war. The next morning, hesitantly, one after another, the townspeople went to the cemetery. The place was now a deep hole with all the graves gone and no indication that they had ever existed. The big hole where all the dead had been piled up was covered. The people left offerings there, prayed, and cried.

Pa Moiwa got sicker. His friends told him he mustn't die of heartbreak.

"There is no place to bury you, to join the others. So you have to live," Mama Kadie pleaded with him.

"I must go and tell them that we tried to stop these things, that they must try and be with us another way," he told his friends as they walked home. The elders took off their shoes to feel the earth, but it felt different: abrupt and bitter.

There were flames by the cemetery that night and an explosion that killed two unarmed local security guards. Someone had set fire to the machines. But it was only a small setback—the destruction soon continued, and more armed guards were deployed everywhere. News of such things did not make it to the papers or radios of

nearby cities, let alone the capital of the country. The mining company's annual brochures were filled with colorful stories of community building, stories of new schools and libraries. There were no
mentions of the destruction of towns and cemeteries, the pollution
of water sources, the loss of human life, or the children who now
frequently drowned in the many dams.

Pa Moiwa died a few weeks later and so did many other elderly
people. They were buried near the old cemetery with the hope that
their spirits would join those who had gone ahead. But the area,
along with the mass grave near it, was soon flooded.

The town was in the midst of a relocation to a barren land. The
new houses were smaller, with weaker foundations. They were made
of mud brick, not cement or clay. As a result, they sometimes collapsed on families, killing everyone inside. Of course, the police reports blamed the inhabitants for not maintaining the houses the
mining company had had built for them. The new town also had no
trees, no proper land to farm on, and no streams for water. Every
morning, a truck carrying a tank would come to distribute water to
the people. Everyone, even women and children, fought one another
just to get a bucket or two, even though the water smelled impure
and had rust in it. The schools that had been destroyed hadn't been
rebuilt, so everyone had to go to the town where the secondary school
was. This meant long walks on roads with big trucks passing frequently. When your child left you for school, you waited anxiously
to see if he or she would return alive. Accidents were common. The
vehicles didn't stop when they hit someone; the company took no
responsibility whatsoever.

Benjamin and Bockarie still worked for the company and Rogers had completely disappeared. The older people waited in what
gradually became the carcass of Imperi. Everyone moved out except
some of the orphans. When the foreigners came to count the number of houses they had to pay for or rebuild, they didn't count any

households occupied by the youngsters, the orphans, the former child soldiers. Some adults tried to assume ownership of the houses so the children could be compensated—their parents had, after all, owned the buildings—but such efforts were to no avail. Families took in as many of the orphans as possible, but their numbers were too great. At Kula's insistence, Bockarie took in Colonel's group, with the exception of Ernest, whom Mama Kadie had grown fond of.

Mama Kadie purposefully gave tasks to Ernest that would bring him in contact with Sila. Sila had started speaking to the boy, uttering words in his direction without looking at him. He'd started after Ernest had defended his children from some bullies without using violence. One bully had thrown a stone and Ernest stepped in front of it with his back to it. Then he growled at the bully, who ran away, and winced from the pain. But as soon as Maada's and Hawa's eyes caught his, he smiled, and they did, too. Sila had seen it all from a distance.

"Thank you, Ernest," he said, lowering himself to hug his children. Ernest walked off, still feeling that he hadn't done enough or could never do enough for them.

But now wasn't the time for mending broken connections. It was the time for teaching the heart to relocate to another land, to hold the memories of the land that would soon be abandoned, to embalm the image of what had existed so it wouldn't decay with time, so it could live on vibrantly in the stories.

How do you pack up to leave your town for mining? It was easier to run during the war—you knew that no matter what, if you stayed alive, you would be able to return home and stand on your land. Now the land would be flooded; it would disappear.

It was the last day of the life of the real town of Imperi, before its name became something new, something that the tongues of its inhabitants had to try to get used to. Mama Kadie and Pa Kainesi had asked everyone to spend Saturday there one last time. The sky had washed its face and its tears had soaked the dirt road, so the dust seemed unable to rise. Even the trees now rejoiced, shaking their leaves lightly with the passing wind, relieved from the burden of carrying dust.

The elders slowly found their footsteps on the road, their bare feet leaving marks on the ground that the earth embraced with familiarity. The houses looked lonely now. After every few paces, the elders raised their heads toward the sky. They sent a boy to run around town asking everyone to gather at the field after the rain. They sat on Pa Kainesi's veranda and waited. As soon as the boy finished the announcements, it started to rain again, this time with such vigor that each raindrop left a deep mark on the ground.

Pa Kainesi cleared his throat. "Ah, my friends, we are alive yet another day to collect memories. My blood is full with so many memories. So I must stand and stretch to make more space before we start talking." He stood and paced up and down the veranda, slowly moving his shoulders and lifting his knees.

"Kainesi, if you awaken your bones any more than you have, those old things will break. So please sit. You've made enough space for new memories today," Mama Kadie said with a chuckle.

"Look at the rains, how they fall these days. There is no lightning. The thunder is afraid to announce its arrival." He stood up again and walked to the edge of the veranda, holding his hand under the rain. He rubbed the cold rain on his rough face and continued. "When I was a boy, my grandmother told me that lightning occurs because God sends the ancestors to take photographs of the land and its people. We do not have lightning anymore. The last sets of lightning happened during the years when guns spoke. My heart fills with fire when I think of these things." He returned to his bamboo chair.

"It has also been raining more than usual. It is as if the earth wants to cleanse itself." Mama Kadie hummed a tune that begged the rain to cease, but nothing changed.

"If the last time God sent the ancestors to take photographs of this land was during the years of bloodshed, then we must find a way to invite more lightning. We need newer pictures of this land. Not all of it was lost," Pa Kainesi said.

"I have been sending my voice to the world beyond our eyes, but I haven't received anything," Mama Kadie said with a low voice. The other elders only listened. As though it had been eavesdropping, the rain abruptly stopped. No one said anything for a while. They knew it was time to make their way to the field for Mama Kadie to speak to everyone one last time.

When their feet had reached the last bit of earth on the old part of town, they stood near the main road. It took days of rain to soak the dust on this road. They looked both ways for the cars and trucks that sped through town with no regard for people crossing. As they were about to carry their old bones across, they heard the bellow of an engine that sounded like a wounded cow. A white Toyota Hilux, its windows rolled up, sped past them, sending dust and small stones into the air. The dust rose to their wrinkled faces, getting on their lips and in their noses, causing them to spit and cough.

"My mind has never understood why these white men drive so fast through this town. You have to hold your breath to reach any-place around here," Pa Kainesi said, coughing and wiping the dust off his forehead. "And why do they have white vehicles only to drive on such dusty, muddy roads?"

The field was packed with people, and lively pockets of conversations were breaking out all over. The few young people in town hung about, some in trees so they could see the gathering properly. Colonel was there, too, standing away from everyone with the intention of stopping any intruders. This would be the last time he was in Imperi.

"How has the world greeted you today?" Pa Kainesi asked everyone.

"The world greeted us kindly this morning by waking us with life. However, we are troubled," someone shouted above the voices of the crowd. Some people laughed and others agreed by humming.

Pa Kainesi motioned for Mama Kadie to step forward and take over. She stood quietly for a while to invite the silence that brought spirits among the living. She began:

"We used to sit around in a circle to tell many stories. Nowadays in our circles, when we manage to have them, there are mostly elders and adults. There aren't many children to receive the stories. We, the elders, our hearts cry, because we worry that we may lose our connection to the different moons to come, to the moons that have passed, and to the sun today. The sun will set without our whispers. The ears and voices of those gone will be closed to us. Our grandchildren will have weak backbones and they won't have the ears to understand the knowledge that lies within them, that holds them firm on this earth. A simple wind of despair will easily break them. What must we do, my friends?" All the faces in the crowd became serious. "We must live in the radiance of tomorrow, as our ancestors have suggested in their tales. For what is yet to come tomorrow has possibilities, and we must think of it, the simplest glimpse of that possibility of goodness. That will be our strength. That has always been our strength. This is all I wanted to say." She turned away from the crowd.

Gradually, people began to sing and dance and joke around with one another. The smiles that had dulled brightened again. This wasn't a place for illusions; the reality here was the genuine happiness that came about from the natural magic of standing next to someone and being consumed by the fortitude in his or her humanity. This was what started the dancing and singing and brought out the sun. It was the last day of the life of the real town of Imperi. The name moved on to the new town, but the new town would never be able to hold the stories.

Three months later, you wouldn't know that a town had existed where Imperi had been: an artificial dam now occupied much of the land, the top of the water shimmering with the reflections of the minerals underneath. The dredge was in full swing, digging the rutile or, as the older people referred to it, "the colorful and shiny excrement of the earth that shows that it is still healthy." Most days, though, people wished that the excrements of their land were like all others, undesirable, and that their earth didn't carry within it beautiful things that brought them misery.

The new town didn't have the magic of Imperi. The birds didn't come, as there were no trees for them to build their nests in. The roosters that were brought along crowed at the wrong hours.

Bockarie was at work one day when his mobile phone rang. He never got calls during the day, and when he did, people would only "flash" him—call him and hang up, expecting a call back, as they had no credit on their phones. Today, however, his phone rang persistently and he answered it.

"It is your brother, Benjamin. How are you, man?" His voice was shaking.

Bockarie frowned. "Aren't you at work? And why are you crying? You are a grown man."

"I am calling to say goodbye, brother. Take care of my family and return them to my homeland for me."

Bockarie's heart started racing. He could feel Benjamin's pain through the phone and tried not to believe it. "Please stop joking. This isn't funny, man."

"I know I joke around a lot, but this is serious. The dredge fell and I am stuck under one of its huge iron buckets with five others. Three have already died and it is just a matter of time," Benjamin said, the fear no longer in his voice.

While he spoke, Bockarie had decided to run home so Benjamin would at least be able to speak to his wife and children on the phone. He got up from his desk and started heading out of the lab where they tested soil samples.

His supervisor said, "Bockarie, sit back down at your work-station or you will be sacked."

His heart and entire body was filled with so much pain that his ears didn't take in what any of his bosses shouted at him. He pushed them out of the way and ran to town while listening to the last words of his friend. Since he had his company attire and ID, he got a lift, the phone glued to his ear, listening to Benjamin. The men in the back of the truck discussed the fallen dredge and said they heard no one was harmed.

Bockarie jumped off the vehicle before it stopped and got to Benjamin's house, handing the phone to Fatu. She tried not to cry in front of the children. She said nothing, but she dropped the things she was holding and stood in one place, as though her feet had grown roots. Her beautiful shiny face was twisted and lost its glow, tears coming out slowly, her tongue unable to utter a sound. After what felt like a long time, she removed the phone from her ear and handed it back to Bockarie, her eyes telling him to stay with her children. She ran to the back of the house, vomited, and began to wail, her belly convulsing.

Meanwhile, Bockarie was with Bundu and Rugiatu, who weren't old enough to understand the situation. They were fascinated that they could hear their father's voice in the phone. "See you soon, Father, when you come out of this machine," Rugiatu said, and she and her brother chuckled. Bockarie took the phone from them. He could hear only his friend's heavy breathing now, and the voices of the other men trapped with him discussing how to get the phone from his hands. Bockarie ran back to the junction to board one of the company vehicles, which he assumed would be headed to the dredge. He was told that no one was allowed there at the moment. He pleaded with the driver.

"I am on the phone with my friend and he is trapped there, dying with others."

"Haven't you heard that no one was harmed? The dredge just fell and everyone working at that time is safe," the driver told him. Bockarie sat on the ground and cried, the only thing he could do to honor his friend. He couldn't go to the police and he had no way of spreading the truth—no money to pay for a radio announcement or a notice in the newspapers. He and the families of the other men couldn't even recover the bodies—the company stuck by its story, which was that no one had died. They hung a printed roster of the names of those who were at work with check marks opposite all their names indicating that they had been accounted for. Benjamin's name wasn't there, nor were those of the others who had died.

The dredge was lifted and operations resumed. The incident reminded people of the war, when they'd suffered the same emotional and psychological toll, burying people without their bodies or graveyards.

Bockarie returned to work, placed his badge on his boss's desk, and left before he could be formally sacked.

That night the families of Benjamin and Bockarie and the elders sat together on the veranda. They swung between sadness and happiness. They couldn't talk about what had happened or cry in front of Benjamin's children. The older children knew, and they were careful not to say anything. Even with these precautions, there were moments when Bundu and Rugiatu unknowingly made everyone's eyes fill with tears, and the adults closed their mouths so their jaws wouldn't shake with sorrow.

"I want to tell a story that Father told me yesterday," Bundu said at one point and went on telling the story, mimicking his father's voice.

"I wish Father was here to tell the other story he had promised us," Rugiatu said, stretching and looking toward her mother with a smile. Later that night, when all the children had gone to sleep, Benjamin, his father, Kula, Fatu, and Mama Kadie sat quietly in the darkness. Kula was next to Fatu, consoling her by rubbing her back so her convulsing stomach wouldn't make her vomit.

"I promised him over the phone I would take his family back to his home in Kono," Bockarie said. "I have to make plans to do it as soon as possible, as things are so fragile here." He stood up and walked off the veranda into the night without saying anything to anyone. No one asked.

The days that followed were difficult. They couldn't mourn for Benjamin because the mining company refused to admit that he had been killed, and some of the workers refused also. The children still asked Bockarie when their father was going to come out of that machine from which he had spoken to them. Their mother pressed her lips together so she wouldn't sob in front of the children. She wasn't sure how long she could carry on. Kula helped take care of the children while Fatu was in mourning. Bockarie waited for a week just in case Benjamin's body was recovered, but nothing was found. No one had been granted access to the area of the accident. Armed men guarded the place day and night until the company cleaned up and reerected the dredge.

12

"WE CANNOT WAIT ANY LONGER. We must leave Imperi tomorrow," Bockarie said to Fatu one afternoon at the end of the week. They were returning from a stroll down the road away from town. There was a tree there that she would hold on to and shout into the wind, releasing her pain. She would then dry her eyes with her waistcloth and return to her children, wiping all the sadness from her face.

"You are right. Staying here isn't helping me. I will get ready tonight." Fatu's voice was weak from crying.

That evening, as she packed her things, she decided to leave her husband's clothes behind. It was too painful to pack them. She held some of his shirts against her and brought them to her nose to remember his smell. She needed to bury him somehow, and leaving his belongings was a way to start. Kula washed and dressed the children and packed some food for them. When they asked why their father wasn't coming, she told them, "This is a special vacation for you to see your grandparents." They grinned and ran to tell their mother. She smiled at their innocence but said nothing; since her husband had passed away, she had been quieter than usual. She had started thinking about returning to nursing at any hospital or clinic she could find; even a pharmacy would do.

She and the children got in the transport vehicle for Kono. Behind them was Bockarie, who waved to his family as he climbed in and banged on its body to signal for the driver to take off. He was going away for a week. He and Benjamin had sometimes discussed the possibility of moving to Kono to try their luck at diamonds. Imperi was no longer suitable for him, so he was thinking about giving Kono a try. He had never been there.

On the road to Koidu, one of the main towns in Kono, you would never think you were going to a place rich in diamonds. You held on for dear life and hoped your vehicle didn't flip over, lose its tires, or just fall apart.

The car they were in was like no model Bockarie had ever seen; it was a mixture of parts, doors, and tires from many vehicles that had probably died on this road. Bockarie asked about it.

"You have never heard of this model. It is called 'Get You There,'" the driver said. He laughed, but Bockarie didn't. He wanted to be sure that Benjamin's family got home safely, but this was the only quick and affordable way for them. This was the only way to travel for ordinary people, the majority of the country's population.

All day the driver would avoid holes by zigzagging, going from one side of the road to the other to catch the potholes that weren't as deep as others. He wiped his face each time he managed to successfully avoid a hole, and he would push his whole body in the direction he intended to turn the steering wheel.

Sometimes the driver would get out of the car and look around before deciding to force it through the bushes away from the road to avoid areas that were too damaged. He would find the road again only to halt at another obstacle—a small river in the road, a tree that had fallen. Those used to traveling on such roads went on with lively conversations as if nothing dangerous was going on outside. When the vehicle sped closer to the bushes, a branch slapped a man who was about to bite into his bread and he lost his meal to the road. People laughed—not at the man but at the situation. Bockarie was quiet, even though the fellow sitting next to him tried to bring him into many conversations. The eyes of the children swung between Fatu and Bockarie throughout the journey, and they were met with smiles and funny faces from Bockarie. They would giggle and then hold on to the waistcloth of their mother.

At one point all the passengers had to step out so the vehicle could climb a hill on its own. While they walked behind it, doused in smoke from its dying engine, a man in a white robe with a cross dangling from his neck offered to pray for them. He went on without the passengers' consent, and when he was done he asked for donations. Everyone refused.

"Perhaps if you had prayed for a new vehicle—and it had arrived—you would have had better luck getting contributions," someone said.

"No, that isn't it," said another. "I think it's because he wasn't planning on sharing the money he would have made with God, whom he is asking to keep us safe. God does all the work and yet this man keeps the money. I wouldn't go in for such a partnership, and I am very sure that God is smarter than I am." Even the man in the white robe had to laugh at that.

When Bockarie, Fatu, and the children finally arrived in Koidu, they decided to walk to a nearby restaurant to settle down and drink some cold water before heading to Benjamin's family home. At the entrance to Koidu stood the corpse of a United Nations tank. It had become an accepted part of the decoration at the roundabout; children even played on it, chasing one another around it, climbing inside, swinging on the machine-gun frame. Their bright faces made Bockarie and Fatu forget that they were looking at an instrument made to claim lives. Bundu and Rugiatu saw it only as a plaything and wanted to join in, but their mother's face had an answer that made them keep their desire to themselves.

It wasn't just the tank. Bullet-ridden buildings, still missing walls and roofs, had also been accepted as normal. It was remarkable to see what human beings could get used to. It seemed no one had tried to fix things or remove the scars of the recent past here, at least visually. The only houses in excellent condition were those of the diamond buyers and sellers. They all had signs that read WE BUY AND SELL DIAMONDS, and they were surrounded by iron gates, cement walls, and concertina wire. Fatu searched for clinics, hospitals, or pharmacies; she knew where a few used to be, but they might no longer exist, and these days one was better off pretending the things you once knew about were gone.

Inside the restaurant, a well-dressed black fellow and a white man were discussing business. Looking at the amount of food and drink on their table, Bockarie could tell they were well off and showy, so he eavesdropped on their conversation. A poor man with no prospects sometimes needs to live vicariously through others' proclamations of wealth or seeming happiness to remind him he may still have some luck left in the universe besides the luck of being alive.

"This is a wretched place with beautiful things in the soil. I have spent hundreds of thousands of dollars just to set up my operations," the white man said.

"You will make back your money in no time. Don't worry," the black fellow responded. "We all know that a businessman is only going to spend that kind of money, even in a 'wretched place,' if he knows he is going to make way more than he spends." He laughed.

"I love this land. That's why I spent that much money."

"Really?"

"Of course not. But people buy that story about loving this land and wanting to invest in its development and future!" The white man toasted the black man. They drank deeply, with great satisfaction. They went back to tasting the various dishes they had in front of them.

Bockarie thought, *It is indeed part of the larger truth. This is a place with beautiful things, not only in the soil but outside as well. Yet*

that beauty causes the wretchedness of this place. The wretched land
with beautiful things and people with indescribable strength . . . Has it
always been like this? Will it change?

The waitress brought cold water and mango juice and they
drank quietly before leaving for Benjamin's house. Fatu and Bockarie prolonged the short walk by starting unnecessary conversations
with every person they passed. It has always been difficult to bring
the news of death, but it was even more so these days after the war,
when some had convinced themselves that having survived the past
ordeals, they might at least have some years' pardon from death.

Alas, Fatu, her children, and Bockarie had come all this way, and
no matter how much they stalled, the destination brought itself nearer
to them. Finally, they saw the house, its veranda and yard animated by
the activities that anticipated the arrival of evening. The men sat on
wooden benches and in hammocks; the women finished their cooking, some hovering over boiling pots of food, others fanning rice or
pounding something in a mortar. The younger girls were braiding one
another's hair, and some were returning from wherever the source of
water was, carrying buckets on their heads. Nearby, the boys juggled a
football, stopping only when they were called upon to run errands
such as going to the market to buy an ingredient or chop firewood.

Benjamin's mother was sitting against the guava tree in the yard
and she was the first to see them coming. After her heart did its
initial welcoming dance, she started to cry: she saw that her grandchildren were without their father. A mother has instincts on such
matters.

"Why are you crying, Grandmother?" Rugiatu asked.

"If you miss Father, don't worry, he is in that small machine that
Uncle Bockarie has," Bundu said. Their grandfather, who had left
the company of his friends to greet everyone and console his wife,
decided to take the children for a walk so Bockarie and Fatu could
explain what had happened.

On the veranda that evening, Bockarie told Benjamin's parents,

Mr. Matturi and Sia, how wonderful their son was, how he had made it easier to cope with life's difficulties through the humor and determination he had about everything.

"He left here after the war because most of his friends died in the diamond pits trying to make quick money. I made him leave to find a safe job somewhere else. I suggested he teach again, as that seemed a safer job," Mr. Matturi said. "Perhaps he was right that he could have made it here in the diamond business without setting foot inside the pit. Now he is gone." Bockarie knew then that Benjamin hadn't told his parents about working for the mining company.

"We were hoping to leave this place and go to your part of the country," Mr. Matturi went on. Bockarie wanted to ask why they would want to do such a thing when he was looking to leave his own hometown. *There is nothing there to improve one's life and the things that used to make it feel like home are destroyed every day,* he wanted to say, but he kept his thoughts to himself and listened to them talk about how difficult life was and about the desperation, especially among young people who were looking for opportunities. You could see them everywhere in town, waiting in vain for something. After they had waited for so long, anything, even the devil, became an opportunity—they found themselves in holes digging diamonds, holes that collapsed on them. Mr. Matturi spoke until deep into the night, his voice becoming heavier and adding solemnity to the sigh of the darkness.

A cock had crowed around midnight and Mr. Matturi thought it was very strange. Bockarie had remembered that such a thing had happened in Imperi before things got worse.

Sleep didn't come to Bockarie that night. His mind kept replaying Benjamin's last breaths, which he'd heard over the phone. It felt as though it were happening again, as if Benjamin were in the room or breathing through the phone. Sometimes Bockarie picked up his phone and put it to his ear. The breathing seemed to get louder as the night aged.

Since his spirit was unable to entertain sleep, he rose early and went for a walk around town. As his body released its sluggishness, he saw young boys and men with shovels and pickaxes heading to diamond pits, hoping to find one stone that would make them rich. Some of them held their heads in their hands with a heaviness that came only from going through the night hungry over and over again while having other problems on your mind. Bockarie couldn't take these sights anymore. He had been hoping to find something in the new morning that was pure, that hadn't yet been bruised by the world.

He returned to see Fatu and the children around ten in the morning. Nearer to the house, he saw police trucks and policemen armed with batons and rifles. They were banging on doors and demanding that people come out and depart the area immediately.

"Let's go, people," the commander shouted in his megaphone.

"Quickly."

"Off your lazy buttocks."

Men came out shirtless and picked up their littlest children, the others trailing behind, and ran toward the center of town. Women who were already up followed their families with whatever food they could grab during the commotion. Young children were everywhere, but their faces told that they had done this a lot. It wasn't like the panic of war, of something unknown, but nonetheless, Bockarie found it disturbing. He tried to ask what was going on, but he got surly looks. *Should I know what this is?* he thought. He ran toward the house to find Fatu and the children. The sound of a siren came through the wind and more people ran out of their homes. Bockarie saw Benjamin's father.

"Let's go, man. I will explain later," Mr. Matturi said, jogging as fast as his old bones allowed him. He passed Bockarie with Sia behind him; Bockarie picked up Rugiatu and Bundu from the veranda and made sure Fatu was with them. The children were trembling with fear from the chaos; they had frozen on the veranda. Fatu wasn't afraid, and something about her slowness showed that she didn't care what happened to her. They ran behind the crowd.

People kept running even as they were struck by the rocks, which came with such speed that Bockarie guessed it wasn't a human being throwing them. A boulder hit two boys and their father, hurling them into a tree, where they were left unconscious. No one was going to stop now to check on them. An explosive sound erupted and the earth trembled. All the buildings wobbled and some began to come apart, shedding corrugated tin, thatch, or bamboo roofing.

Everyone sat on mats and waited for a few hours. The explosions went on and stones were seen flying in the distance.

Someone should explain something to me, Bockarie thought, and as though Mr. Matturi had heard him, he spoke: "This blasting happens here every day, and the times vary. So we have to be ready to run away from the blasting perimeter at any time. The sirens don't give us enough time."

"So you mean you are displaced every day?" Bockarie tried to understand.

"I haven't thought about it that way, but that is correct." He pondered something for a bit and then continued. "They say they have nets over the blasting holes to prevent the stones from flying and wounding people. But you saw for yourself what the truth is. Sometimes the police come and force us to leave our homes. You saw that, too." He shook his head.

"The wounded people, do they go to the diamond company's hospital? I saw a hospital on my walk this morning that looked sophisticated," Bockarie said.

"That should be the case, shouldn't it? But no, my son, if you are wounded or killed, that is your problem or your family's." Mr. Matturi sat by his wife and held her to comfort her. Their son's death had somehow been brought up within her during the run. She hadn't cried so much the night before, but now she saw the opportunity.

"Is Grandmother crying because of the stones flying?" Rugiatu asked.

"They can come with us back to Imperi. There are no stones flying there and Father is still there," Bundu said. He went to his grandmother and touched her face, trying to wipe her tears with his little hands.

They returned home several hours later. Some houses had been damaged, their windows shattered by rocks, and the old tin roofs had collapsed. There was debris everywhere. The women and girls took brooms and started sweeping. The men and boys began repairing the damage, and soon people went about their lives as though nothing had happened. The youngsters who had school in the afternoon put on their uniforms and left to learn.

Bockarie had abandoned any thought of moving his family to this town. At the same time, Imperi wouldn't do. He had to go somewhere else in the country. He decided to speak with Mr. Matturi so that Fatu and the children could come along if they wanted.

When Bockarie brought it up, Mr. Matturi agreed to speak with Fatu and said he had already made plans to move with Fatu, Sia, and his grandchildren to the capital city, Freetown. He had a cousin whose home they could stay in until they found a firm footing. Bockarie said he would speak with his wife about it.

"My cousin can help you find a place or provide you one. You are family. I hope you know that. I see the same curiosity in you that my son had in his eyes. It will be good to see you often," Mr. Matturi said, putting his arm around Bockarie's shoulder.

That evening they had a small ceremony for Benjamin. The pastor said a prayer and the imam recited another. People ate and spoke of Benjamin. Sia and Fatu took the children aside and found the words to tell them the truth about what had happened to their father. Bundu and Rugiatu still didn't understand that their father was gone and never coming back.

"Why didn't he come and say goodbye, then, before he left forever?" Rugiatu asked her mother. Her brother ran and forced himself between Bockarie's legs, his little eyes searching for his attention. When he got it, he asked, "Uncle Bockarie, can I say goodbye to Father through that small machine?"

"He will not answer, but he will hear you. Okay?" Bockarie handed him the mobile phone. He placed it on his ear and said, "Goodbye, Father. We are visiting with Grandfather and Grandmother. Hold on for Rugiatu." Bundu ran to his sister and gave her the phone.

"Father, don't go away just yet. You said you would tell me the end of that story you had started." She waited for a response. The wind howled about her and the phone slipped out of her hand onto the earth.

Bockarie dreamed of Benjamin, who thanked him with no expression on his face. As the dream tossed him around in bed, the siren went on again. He knew the drill. He put on his trousers and went to the other room, where he picked up the sleeping bodies of Bundu and Rugiatu. Fatu gave him the only half smile she could muster and they all left the house. They ran past pots of food that had been left unattended, that would surely spoil.

When the family got to the safe area, Bockarie heard crying from a group of women gathered in a circle. Another woman, younger, was lying on the ground, blood trailing on her legs and underneath her. The tremor from the blasting had caused a miscarriage. The woman had been asleep in bed and couldn't move away fast enough. The young woman's husband sat away, leaning his head against a tree, his hands folded into fists.

"How are the police here with such matters?" Bockarie asked Mr. Matturi.

"They are in the pockets of the diamond miners. Everyone is in their pockets except those who really need to be," Mr. Matturi said. "Children have been killed here in their sleep with rocks. Older people as well. No one hears about it. We have some human rights fellows who have tried to get these stories on the local radio, but they are small in number and no one believes them. The companies do their best to hush them with bribes to the local station." Mr. Matturi looked around and went on, his eyes worn-out from the sight of so much suffering. "Even though miracles have been exhausted here, we are still alive, son, so cheer up! Look at the sun coming out. We have tomorrow." He elbowed Bockarie, his eyes changing his face and shedding what had made them look deprived of vitality.

But the day wasn't over. Another accident occurred at the diamond site that cost the lives of six people. The townspeople accused the company, called KHoldings, and the accident gained national attention in a day. The vice president of the country came to town while Bockarie was still around. But when he arrived, he went to a meeting with the company and then met his people afterward, gathered and awaiting his arrival. All hope died when he began speaking.

"Everybody sit down on the ground. Sit so you can see me, only me," he shouted, even as the older chiefs struggled to bend to the ground. The gathering protested a bit with murmurs, and the vice president said, "I will use my law to punish you," he shouted, referring to the law of Lion Mountain as his. "If you all do not sit on the ground and keep quiet, I will show you my power. You'll wish your mother hadn't given birth to you."

That was the end of the discussion. Bockarie walked away, refusing to sit on the ground.

He stayed for another day and left for Imperi the following morning, earlier than he had planned. He hoped to move to the capital city and to see Benjamin's family again. Rugiatu and Bundu cried as he left.

Bockarie sighed with relief and coughed out the dust and smoke he had inhaled on the road when he got to Imperi. As the vehicle pulled away, it revealed the welcoming faces of his family. The littlest children ran across the road and jumped into his arms, followed by hugs from the others and then a kiss and a much-needed caress from Kula. She whispered something to him that made him smile. At home, his father's first words were news that the dredge had fallen again. More people were missing.

"That dredge is cursed because it is operating on burial grounds," he concluded. The foreigners said otherwise. They called it mechanical failure due to the incompetence of the workers.

While the family sat on the veranda in the interlude of the afternoon, Bockarie described his plan to move away.

"There is nothing here to do for me, for us. We will only become like those who have accepted that this is the best outcome of their lives." He returned to his pensive mood.

"I was thinking of discussing this with you, my husband. I agree that we must leave this place that is barely home these days, for the sake of our children," Kula said. But Bockarie's father said he would stay behind.

"This is my land and I must witness whatever happens to it. Someone must stay around to witness this part of our history. It is the only way to pass it on orally; we must experience it to make the telling meaningful and effective. Kadie and I have decided to do that." He warned Bockarie to be careful in the city, where he had once been; he saw it as a place where people no longer heard the whispers of the past in their hearts, where people did not sleep well enough to dream of stories.

Mama Kadie came by while Pa Kainesi was speaking and added her voice to the warnings. A young man had come here from the city to attend his father's funeral. The young man had on dark sunglasses throughout the funeral, even when stories about his father were told. "How can the spirit of his people find him if he covers his eyes at the funeral? How will the elders know what stories to tell him if they cannot find his eyes, which tell what he needs?"

She sighed. "We must not forget everything of the past. Take care of your traditions and guard the useful ones when you are out there." She turned to Bockarie and held Kula's hand.

Two weeks later, Bockarie, Kula, and their children, after gathering some money and selling whatever they thought they wouldn't need in the city, departed. The children were on holiday break, so they would start the next school year in the city. Other than close family members, Bockarie and Kula had cautioned their children not to speak of their departure to anyone. Sometimes people's bad thoughts interrupted or placed a barrier on new beginnings. The only people who knew were Mahawa, Sila and his children, and of course Colonel's group, even though they didn't come to say goodbye. They didn't like such things. Mahawa and Sila and his children did come, though, to say their goodbyes.

"Actually, I came by to have one of your meals one last time so I at least have a memory of how good food should taste," Sila said, laughing along with everyone. Kula hugged him and his children, who had tears in their eyes. Mahawa was sobbing, her lips shaking. She held Miata's hand, both of them sitting on a mat on the ground outside. Tornya was asleep on the mat.

"Please don't forget us," Mahawa finally managed to say.

"I will not, my sister." Miata squeezed her hands.

"Oumu, my child, come sit here with me for a bit." Mama Kadie extended her hand. Oumu went to sit on the bench next to the elder and soon the two of them were so deeply engaged in a conversation it was as if the others present didn't exist.

"I have a last story to tell you and you will know when you need to tell it," Mama Kadie said, and for five minutes or more she whispered earnestly into Oumu's ear. The little girl stared straight ahead into the night until gradually, as the story came to an end, a smile emerged. She then turned her eyes to Mama Kadie's face and thanked her without words. She laid her head on the old woman's lap and let her tears run onto the elder's wrapper.

"There shouldn't be sadness in our parting, my child. You have my words within your spirit and so we will always be together." She touched Oumu's cheeks and waited until her tears had passed before she released her and spoke to the rest of the family.

All the ceremonial goodbyes were done at night so that in the morning no one would see such deliberations and suspect what was happening. Mama Kadie and Pa Kainesi touched the heads of everyone, passing on their blessings before they went to pretend to sleep. When those you love were leaving you, even for good reasons, sometimes sleep would not visit.

On the morning of their departure, it rained, just sprinkles. They waited in the last blanket of darkness for the transport vehicle to arrive, which showed up even later than the normally expected lateness. But things mostly happen at the appointed time, even when we think they do not.

13

THE ROAD TO THE CITY was still covered with the residue of night when the Bedford truck left Imperi. It was slightly better than the "Get You There" that Bockarie had taken to Kono. The Bedford wound its way through the dams, the driver honking every so often to alert other drivers to the presence of his vehicle, as its headlights were barely as bright as an old flashlight.

About ten minutes into the journey, they nearly had two accidents. The first came about because a sharp turn had been constructed the night before and the sign to turn left came into view only when the driver was faced with a pile of iron pipes and machines parked at the edge of the dam. He applied the brakes, which grumbled with a terrible sound, to slow down enough to just make the turn. The passengers fell on one another this way and that. Everyone was now properly awake.

"This road changes so often that I am never sure where I will end up," the driver said, laughing. Turning back to the passengers, he went on, "Now that you are all awake, I will collect the fare while we are all still alive." He signaled for his apprentice, who went around and collected the money.

"Why the rush, and what good will the cash be in your pocket if we don't make it?" an old man asked, carefully separating his money so that he gave the most wrinkled notes to the apprentice. "These are almost dead. They need to be used perhaps one last time." He smiled at the young fellow, who carefully smoothed and folded them. "Answer my question, Mr. Driver." The old man turned his body sideways toward the front of the vehicle.

"This way," said the driver, "I will die with money in my pocket, and I may be able to bribe some angels to let me into heaven for a bit. If you pay now, I may be able to afford an hour or several days in heaven!" The driver laughed and honked. The passengers laughed as well.

As soon as Bockarie handed over the money for his entire family, the vehicle swerved and its back tire got stuck in the dam. A truck with one headlight almost crashed into them. The driver couldn't tell where the rest of the truck's body was on the road. The passengers got off and helped push it back on track.

"Driver, you should pay us for helping you push your vehicle," someone said.

"I just saved your lives by avoiding that accident, so consider *that* your payment." He jumped in and restarted the engine.

The journey was long. Whenever they went down a hill, the driver would turn off the engine to save petrol. The children's favorite parts were the stops where people would crowd the vehicle on both sides, shouting out what they were selling. *Perched groundnut. Bread. Soft drinks. Biscuits. Cold water* . . . Their father bought them a few sweets at such stops. As they left the interior of the country and came closer to the capital, the road got better in the sense that the driver could at least drive on his side of the road for a period of time. Also, there were now more vehicles and some had white people in them and insignias that proclaimed they were SAVING PEOPLE IN THIS LAND. These vehicles with only three people in most of them overtook the crowded passenger ones with overwhelming speed.

"Please tell them to slow down and save some of us from this wretched vehicle. Then again, at that speed, they may not reach whoever they are going to save!" the old man who had spoken earlier said to Bockarie.

"I have never seen these organizations in my part of the country," Bockarie said, scratching his head.

"Let me guess. You have no good roads that lead to your town and no electricity." The old man nodded, clearly indicating that Bockarie needn't answer such an obvious question.

"You must only save those you can get to with some comfort. I am an old man so the truth doesn't sit inside me anymore!" He howled with laughter, and just then another one of those vehicles zoomed by.

Small kiosks selling all sorts of items began appearing on the sides of the road. On the pavement, especially wherever there was some light, a horde of young people sat with their feet on the tar road. Some stood around, others ran up and down the street looking for something that wasn't obvious. It was approaching evening and Thomas and Oumu were getting exhausted.

"We are almost there, Kula," Bockarie said to his wife, whose eyes had posed the question. None of them, except Bockarie, had been to the capital city. Manawah was excited, though a bit nervous about how he would fit in with all those city boys. He was looking forward to all he could discover without the restrictions of a small town where everyone knew you. His younger siblings, Miata and Abu, felt the same about the freedom. Miata, however, was worried about whether her old dresses and skirts would attract the young men, but of even greater concern was that her parents might relegate her to house chores and looking after Thomas and Oumu, as they both planned to seek employment. Abu had no worries, only a plan

to search for the nearest football pitch to play every evening. He
thought perhaps he'd join a junior football league, too. The parents
and three older siblings harbored their anxieties, as well. Bockarie at
some point had the thought that he and his family might be too late
to find any luck in the city. It seemed if there was good fortune to be
had, it would have been grabbed long ago by one of these people
walking on the road with determined faces.

The vehicle began to slow down and it turned off the main road
into a smaller dirt drive that had more potholes than the countryside. For an instant Kula thought they had returned to the roads
that led to Imperi. The driver turned off the engine and a cloud of
smoke shot out, making all the passengers cough. The driver ran to
the front with a jerry can of water, opened the hood, and poured the
water in the engine.

"We are here. This is the last stop," the driver shouted, his head
under the hood. The apprentice went through the loads that had
been tied on top of the truck and found Bockarie's, tossing the bags,
one after the other. More vehicles began arriving at the park, from
various parts of the country.

Bockarie and his family stood by and waited for Benjamin's
uncle, who was supposed to meet them. The place was so crowded it
was hard to know where to look. People were going about their business; traders were selling their commodities. Thomas and Oumu
came awake with the energy emanating from the boisterous crowd.

"Mother, can we buy some balloons?" Thomas pointed to the
fellow who was blowing them up and making figures.

"Another time, children," she said, holding tightly to the hands
of her small ones. Bockarie paced around their luggage, thinking
this might have been a mistake. What if the man they were supposed to meet didn't show up? He, Bockarie, had no other plans.

Oumu saw someone across the street who looked like Colonel.
She rubbed her eyes to be sure. He smiled and put his hands on his
lips for her not to say anything to her parents, whose attention she

was trying to get. Colonel put his hat back on and disappeared in the crowd. He didn't go far. He was near enough to watch the family; he wanted to know where they would be staying. Oumu's eyes searched for him, but she gave up after a while.

"Mister, don't look so nervous. Have a seat here with your family." One of the traders offered Bockarie and his family a bench. He called a young boy to bring them bottles of cold water and Coca-Cola for the children. Bockarie wanted to say that he didn't have money for these things, but the man, as if reading Bockarie's mind, said, "You are my guest until whoever you are waiting for arrives. Do not worry. And don't thank me; this is what decent people should do for one another. This is how we are and how we all used to be." He smiled and went back to his business bargaining with a customer.

The family drank quietly, observing the unceasing movement of people. A man went by carrying six bags of rice, fifty kilograms each, stacked on top of one another. "How can his neck withstand that?" Kula asked out loud, as the man stopped a few stalls from them and added even more bags on top of what he was carrying. Their eyes left him at the junction, where he turned off and a group of young women emerged, walking with an ease that was contrary to the rhythm of the crowd at this vehicle stop. A young fellow who was passing the group retraced his steps and tried talking to one of the young women. Their exchange caught the attention of Manawah and Miata more than everyone else. They wanted to immediately start learning the young parlance of the city.

The man said, "Baby girl, ah lek u bo. Ah want for tell you sontin wae ah nor want for leh no wan yeri" (Young woman, I like you and I want to tell you something that I do not want anyone else to hear).

The girl smiled while pretending to ignore him. She was coming from a school function with her friends, and they proudly wore hats from one of the popular secondary schools for girls.

"I don't have time for idle boys." She deliberately responded in English either to intimidate or to discourage the young man. She continued on with her friends. The fellow walked faster and slowed down next to her.

"I am a man of words myself and right now my words are looking to please your ears if you will grant me that pleasure, sweet rose of my day." He managed to impress her with the sentence—but it wasn't enough.

"You are not M3 material so I don't want you," she told the young man, who was now trying to hold her hand. Her friends laughed, smacking their lips with bubble gum. The young man was ashamed but not defeated; something in his eyes said he would try again. He walked backward, and each time any of the girls turned around, he would wave to them.

"In the old days, all you needed was a ripe washed mango to court a girl. Nowadays, they want M3—mobile, money, and motor vehicle. You have to have at least one of these, or the appearance of it, to be eligible for a longer conversation with most girls and women." The man who spoke, as the family sat laughing, introduced himself as Mr. Saquee, Benjamin's uncle. He was tall with a face that was constantly jovial, almost beyond his control.

"Welcome to Freetown! It isn't as free as it used to be, but it is our freedom land nonetheless!" He took a packet of mints and handed some notes to the kind trader.

"Thank you, Mamadou," he said as he received his change. He then shook hands with Bockarie and acknowledged everyone before offering to carry a bag or two. Abu took the hands of Thomas and Oumu, and the rest of the family carried the remaining bags. They didn't have much in them; it was a hopeful gesture to arrive with big empty suitcases. "One has to be hopeful in every aspect of your life—your stride, your smile, and laugh when you can find it, even in your breath, to be able to live in Freetown." These were the last words Bockarie's father had whispered to him. Bockarie still felt his warm morning breath in his ears.

They followed Mr. Saquee, all of their eyes glued to him so they wouldn't lose him. Maybe it was a family trait, as he walked as fast as Benjamin had, even with his age. Kula was next to him and Bockarie kept up the rear, with the children in between. Colonel followed at a good enough distance that even Oumu couldn't detect him.

There were many things their eyes wanted to feast on, but Mr. Saquee's pace denied them most of it as they hurried between the rows of houses made entirely out of corrugated iron, not just the roofs. There was a remarkable liveliness among these congested houses. It seemed that wherever possible, men and women, girls and boys, returned every night to celebrate whatever little the day had given them. They did so with the vigor of music blaring from their unlivable homes, in passionate conversations about football matches and, inevitably, about politics.

This isn't Imperi. There may be possibilities here, Bockarie thought to himself.

They arrived at a cement house that stood at the edge of the town of tin shack houses—*pan bodi*, as they're called—and the rest of the city. Mr. Saquee showed them the single room he would offer them for free for a month. Other arrangements would be made after the month had passed. His wife brought them some food and water, and after the meal, the children and their mother went to sleep. She took the only bed in the room; the two girls, Miata and Oumu, slept on a mat at the foot of the bed in the small space between the bed and the wall. Manawah, Abu, and Thomas also slept on the floor near the door, which had to be opened carefully at night to avoid hitting the head of whoever lay closest to it.

Their father went to sit on the veranda with Mr. Saquee to thank him for welcoming them and also to get directions for the appointment he had the next day for an interview to teach summer school. He had gotten a contact from one of his old teacher friends at Imperi and had called ahead of time.

"When will Mr. Matturi, Fatu, and family arrive?" Bockarie asked during their conversation.

"He called to tell me to take care of you. He will arrive with everyone when the time fits and said to tell you not to worry." Mr. Saquee
gave a reassuring nod. In that moment, they heard a commotion
down the road. A young man came flying past with a group of young
men shouting after him, "Catch that thief! Thief man!"

"Well, welcome!" Mr. Saquee said with a laugh. "That should be
a way to close the night. Let's hope they do not catch him."

Bockarie wanted to ask why Mr. Saquee hoped that a thief
would get away, but he didn't. He was new to Freetown and would
discover many things that at first did not make sense.

"Good evening, sirs," a young fellow greeted them, standing
under the stoop of the veranda. They answered with suspicion.

"My name is Pastor Stevens and I am going to pray for your financial success this evening, to ask the lord to open your financial
gate." The man began to pray. When he finished, he put out his
hand, asking Bockarie and Mr. Saquee for some money.

"Young man, you should have prayed for your own financial
gate to be opened first. Ours has just closed. Thank you, though,
and God bless you, too!" Mr. Saquee tried to suppress his laugher.
The fellow turned on his heel and walked into the night, leaving
them two flyers. The first read, "Come to the national stadium and
learn how to invest in next world (life after death)." The second,
"Put u money na bank to Jesus" (Put your money in the bank of
Jesus).

"Everyone is trying to believe in something these days, and they
forget that miracles happen every day when we truly acknowledge
the humanity of another or just have a simple, pure conversation
with someone else." Mama Kadie would have said this truth, Bockarie
thought, and he knew that his family's safe arrival in Freetown was
nothing short of a miracle, a blessing.

As he slowly dragged his feet toward the room to search for sleep,
Bockarie's mind was consumed with what the following day would

bring. There were questions about life in the city with his family; about his father, whom he had left behind. He wondered how Benjamin's family was faring. He leaned his back against the door and stared into the dark night with strong eyes, as though wanting to leave his burden outside, then he gave the door a powerful shove. He nearly fell into the room. He heard a thud, followed by groan, a hissing, then a sniffle. He waited a bit to see which of his children he had hit, but the room was too dark to see Manawah, clutching his head and clenching his teeth. In pain, but not wanting his father to feel badly, the boy quietly moved his body closer to his brothers and away from the door, as Bockarie shut it and tiptoed around the children, his hands stretched in front of him to find the bed.

Manawah couldn't sleep that night. Rolling around on the cold cement floor, he searched for a spot to lay the side of his head that pulsated so badly, but the cool of the floor did nothing to stop the swelling. Tears leaked from the corners of his eyes. He tightened his lips to hold the crying back, but it made him cough.

Bockarie was sleeping lightly and heard his son's restlessness. "Are you okay my son?" he whispered, as he got up to open the window to let some air into the hot room. Manawah pretended to sleep, and not hearing any more movements, Bockarie went back to bed.

However, they both lay awake, waiting to hear the other, and as they did they saw in the darkness a long stick making its way into the room from the outside. The stick hooked the handles of the bag that contained the little cash they had. Carefully, the stick started retreating through the window it had come in. Bockarie leapt up, grabbing the bag and pulling the stick as well. He heard someone fall by the window and the person's heavy footsteps take off into the night. He shut the window, went back to bed, and eventually fell asleep. The next morning the family woke to see that the window had been opened again and a bag of Bockarie's clothes was missing.

"They call it fishing—that is what the thieves call that technique of lifting things from rooms. You shouldn't open your window at night. If you must, though, make sure things are far away from the window area."

Mr. Saquee shook hands with Bockarie to complete their morning greetings. While the men spoke, Manawah rose and his father spied his swollen head. "I am sorry, my son. Why didn't you tell me last night?" Bockarie held his son's head gently and examined the wound on his forehead.

"Don't ever hide something like this from me." He looked into his child's eyes with a pleading stare.

"I wanted you to sleep, Father, because of your meeting. This will go away." Manawah lightly tapped the swelling and went to fetch water at the only pump in the neighborhood. There, the line was so long that people would leave their buckets and jerry cans and go about their morning activities, then return hours later just when it was their turn. This technique unknown to Manawah on the first morning, he stood in line for hours and each time he thought he would be next, as no other person was around, whoever's bucket was next in line arrived just in time. When he told the story later, deeply frustrated, they found it funny. Manawah didn't get easily frustrated.

Kula took the cassavas out of the rice bag that they were wrapped in and began peeling them. She had brought some from up-country. She cut them into pieces and hummed a quiet tune as she washed and tossed the pieces in a pot of boiling water. Soon enough she called on everyone to assemble and eat the boiled cassavas she had prepared. Mr. Saquee and his wife shared the meal, and he was ecstatic.

"It has been a while since I tasted fresh cassavas. It makes me miss my village. Thank you, Kula, *hmmm*." His eyes were closed and the children giggled at how much joy this man expressed for a piece of cassava. They knew their mother was an excellent cook, but this was incredibly funny. Bockarie ate his meal quickly and headed to his meeting, leaving Kula to supervise the family as they unpacked and familiarized themselves with their new environment.

14

BOCKARIE LEFT EARLY IN ORDER TO SAVE MONEY by walking the several miles to his meeting on the other side of the city center. He clenched and opened his fists, took short breaths and clenched his jaw, and whispered repeatedly, "Grant me luck today." He looked toward the sky.

He stepped into the main street, and as soon as he started his stroll he realized he had made the right decision not only to save money but to walk as well. The queues for passenger vehicles were so long that he would have been standing there way past his appointment time. However, he had to return home to change into a T-shirt. When he entered the room, Kula froze with the thought that this was not a good sign. She was the only one home, arranging their belongings so they would all fit in the small room. She also had a newspaper on the table and in between folding things was underlining ads for work.

"Is it already over?"

"I just came back because I need a T-shirt so that I don't sweat in my interview shirt. You are worrying too much." He patted her shoulder to calm her anxiety. He changed and neatly folded his dress shirt and undershirt. He then placed them gently in a black plastic bag that he carried under his arm as he readied to go out again.

"Did they all run away already?" He kissed his wife and lowered himself on the bed for a bit.

"The boys went to fetch water and Miata took the twins with her to the market and to walk around the neighborhood a bit. They wanted to do all their chores early so that they could 'discover the city,' as they put it." She stopped her work and sat next to her husband.

"Do you think we made the right decision to come here?" he asked her, his head in his hands.

"We have not yet started living here and you are already giving up. Now go out there and see what share we can have of whatever luck is left." She smiled at him while broadening her eyes for him to move on. He kissed her again and left the house in a more enthusiastic mood than when he'd headed out before. She waved him off with her newspaper. Bockarie started sweating profusely as soon as he set foot on the main road again, but he kept a positive attitude to attract hope and luck his way, determination in his every stride.

There were so many people on the street where the cars were supposed to be that he had to fix himself firmly on the ground so that he was able to walk in his chosen direction. Otherwise the melee would carry him somewhere else. He saw this happen a minute before to a man who lost his son in the crowd. When a car approached the crowded street, the driver honked relentlessly, revving the engine, threatening to run people over. It was only then that the crowd opened up with just enough space for the car to pass, then filled up the open spaces, engulfing the car. Some people grumbled and shouted at the driver, "You want to kill us?"

They banged on the body of the car. "Stop blowing your horn so much."

When another car came by whose driver didn't honk or rev its engine, the driver was berated for not alerting the crowd. A brand-new Mercedes-Benz came into view, and as the crowd parted to let it through, some children with dirty palm-oil-laden hands and Coca-Cola bottle tops first wiped their greasy hands on the vehicle and then etched jagged lines on it with the sharp little disks as they jogged alongside. The driver got angry and jumped out, but by then the children were gone, and he was peppered with insults because his opened door impeded the flow of foot traffic.

Were the children deliberately looking to destroy cars? No. They saw them as things to play with, things to lay hands on and mark while they passed by. The motion felt good to them, and they did it to any car except police, military, presidential, and ministerial vehicles. Of course, those vehicles went by so fast they would kill you before you had a chance to lay your hands on them. And even if they slowed down, the children knew enough that they didn't dare.

After thirty uncomfortable minutes of minding every part of his body in the crowd, Bockarie finally extricated himself from the madness. There were still a lot of people on the road as he left the city center, especially young boys and men hanging about—most of them dressed quite nicely but still just sitting around on the pavement, on packed vehicles, on anything, waiting. He passed an interestingly dressed young man who walked with so much confidence that it seemed he owned the very street he walked on. He had on nicely fitted jeans and a blue long-sleeve shirt, tucked in. On top of the blue shirt, he wore his undershirt, rather than below. This gave him a very sophisticated look, however, and his expression told anyone he passed that he was proud of this new style. *Using what you have to the best of your ability*, Bockarie thought.

The young man also reminded him that he had to change his T-shirt, which he did quickly on the side of the street, wiping his sweat with the shirt he'd been wearing. He walked the next few steps to a restaurant that sold local food, not the one that had white people's food and was always crowded by foreigners and those who could afford to pay for green things on plates with names and portions that insulted the money in a poor man's pocket. This was where he was supposed to meet a certain Mr. Kaifala.

At home Kula had marked enough employment ads in the flimsy newspapers whose pages tore as she turned them. She started calling the numbers to inquire about the jobs and hopefully make an appointment for an interview. Her first choices were nursing jobs at hospitals or clinics. Most of the numbers for these jobs had been disconnected, and the ones she managed to reach hung up on her as soon as she said that she had just arrived in the city from up-country. She wondered if coming from the interior automatically implied inexperience or unworthiness of everything in the city. No matter what the explanation was, she decided that on her next calls she would say nothing about it. Still, no one had any openings for her, or so they said, even though the ads just came out in the papers that morning. Sometimes secretaries would put her on hold and go on about their personal lives for minutes that were costly for her before retrieving the phone only to tell her that the person she needed to speak with wasn't around.

"But you didn't even check. I heard you on the phone talking the whole time," she'd responded to one of them.

"I said no one is here and I know how to do my job." The person hung up on her. Kula wanted to tell her that if she was going to waste her minutes to at least tell some interesting story about her personal life.

Manawah and Abu had returned from bathing after finishing their chores of fetching enough water for the day. They came inside to change their clothes. Kula left the room and stood by the door outside. She inhaled and exhaled deeply, trying to calm her nerves. While she waited for the boys, Miata, Oumu, and Thomas returned from the market and their wanderings. Oumu had again seen Colonel and wanted to speak to him, but he'd made a hand gesture indicating not when Miata and Thomas were around. She wanted to tell her mother but then thought if Colonel wanted her parents to know he was around, he would have made it known.

"Something on your mind, my child?" Kula asked Oumu, studying her little girl's clearly bothered face.

"No, Mother. Just remembering the things I have seen since we arrived." Oumu managed a smile, and her mother stroked her cheek tenderly, trying to assure her that she could tell her mother anything.

Kula took the ingredients that Miata had bought. She had to prepare the meal so she could get back to her job search.

The boys asked for permission to investigate their new neighborhood and were off before the answer came out of their mother's mouth. "Make sure to look after your brother, Manawah." She sent her voice after them.

Miata looked at her mother with questioning eyes about why she had granted permission to her brothers so easily and hadn't given them the responsibility of taking their littlest siblings with them.

"You don't have to take them with you now, either," Kula said, pointing at Thomas and Oumu. "You can go up to the college and see if you can take some classes this summer, later on. That will be your excursion." Kula motioned for her daughter to go.

"Ex . . . cur . . . sion. What does that mean?" Oumu asked her mother.

"I'll tell you later." She didn't want to deal with Oumu then. Oumu's questions were unending these days. Once you answered one question, there was another at its heels.

What Kula could not know was that Oumu was looking for any opportunity to go out alone so that she could run into Colonel. So she sat next to her mother as Kula went through what they had brought from the market.

"Your sister forgot to buy the Maggi," Kula said.

"I can go get it at the shop just over there," Oumu volunteered.

"Okay, take this and come right back," Kula said, looking suspiciously at Oumu—the little girl had been too quick to offer to do a chore.

As soon as Oumu left the house, her eyes went in search of Colonel. He was already standing behind her. He joked, "You have to have better eyes to look for me."

Oumu turned around, smiling.

"Did you follow us to the city?" she asked Colonel. He didn't answer but just walked with her to buy the maggi.

"You must promise me that you won't tell anyone that I am here. Not yet. Okay?" He broadened his eyes at her.

"Okay."

"Your father went to town to look for work, I am guessing."

"I don't know. But he did go to town."

"You have to go back before your mother comes looking, for she will have eyes to find you," Colonel said.

"You are probably right."

"But you can always find me there if you need to, okay?" He pointed at the small kiosk that sold cigarettes.

She waved to him as he disappeared among the *pan bodi* houses.

Bockarie sat near the window where the breeze from the sea visited intermittently. The waitress didn't pay him much attention and he quite liked that because he wanted to save the little money he had. He observed the young men across the street standing by the entrance of the fancy restaurant. Their eyes resented everything that showed even the slightest comfort that they didn't have. When someone came out of the restaurant with a bottle of cold water, they sighed with indignation.

The eyes of a struggling person see the smallest comfort, in the way another walks, laughs, sits, and even breathes, Bockarie said loudly in his mind. He was surprised by his ability to clearly express himself and decided then that he must write down some of his observations. But he had neither a pen nor a sheet of paper.

He did have an inner dialogue, though. *If I buy a mango juice, the waitress will certainly bring me a napkin. I could then ask to borrow a pen and write on that napkin.*

"Miss, mango juice, please." He raised his hand. Twenty minutes later, she still hadn't brought him the juice. He remembered Mr. Saquee explaining to him that in the city, he had to be forceful and not always polite to be heard, especially when he wanted to be served at shops and restaurants. Otherwise he would wait for hours.

"Hey, you. Mango juice—*now*," he commanded, raising his voice at the young woman and eyeing her hard. She reacted, though with reluctance in her movements and irritation in her eyes. She brought the juice with a napkin and asked Bockarie to pay before setting the bottle down on the table in front of him.

"Could I borrow your pen?" He took the pen from her fingers before she responded. He paid, she took his money and left him. He quickly removed the napkin wrapped around the cold juice bottle so that it wouldn't get saturated and started writing his observations.

The veins on the young man's forehead and the look in his eyes show that he has lost faith in the possibility of something good today, so he sits on the ground, leans his head on the 4×4 car, and allows his heart to breathe, as his spirit has been holding its breath all day.

The young man sits on the ground in a crowded city where he has come to look for hope. So many like him are searching for hope that it has become afraid here and is on the run. Whenever it shows itself—hope, that is—hands from the crowded streets reach for it with such violent urgency because of the fear that they may never see it again. They do so without knowing that their desperation frightens hope away. Hope also doesn't know that it is its scarcity that causes the crowd to lunge at it, shredding its robe. And as it struggles to escape, the fabric scraps land in the hands of some but last only for hours, a day, days, a week, weeks, depending on how much fabric each hand is able to catch.

"I need my pen back, sir." The waitress took the pen out of Bockarie's grip and placed it in her pocket, returning to stand by the counter and chat with her coworkers. They whispered to one another and laughed at the fact that Bockarie had bought only mango juice since he sat there. He ignored them, folded the napkin, put it inside his front pocket, and turned his attention to the young men outside. Just then a group of foreigners arrived in the area, headed to the mobile phone store down the street. One of the young men went in their direction and greeted them.

"Hello! You do not need to buy a new phone. I can help unlock the ones you have and you only need to buy a SIM card then. You'll be saving lots of money. So what do you say, my good people?" He spoke quickly, as the distance to the mobile phone store was quite short. The foreigners seemed hesitant, looking at one another.

"Please, give me yours and I will open it for free." He put out his hand to a young woman the same age as him, nineteen years old. She apprehensively gave him her phone. He first took out the battery and restarted the thing, then quickly typed in a few numbers and letters, pressed Enter and then another set of numbers and letters. The young woman, a bit intrigued, tried to see what he was doing. She moved closer and he turned toward her so that she could see his hands more clearly.

"I will do a test with my SIM card," he said, turning the phone off again and placing the card in it before turning it back on.

"Awolowo, call me phone, ya," he called out, setting his voice above traffic, to one of his friends who sat on the pavement of the street while handing the phone back to the young woman. Awolowo pulled out his mobile phone and dialed. The phone rang and the young woman answered. Awolowo said something that made her laugh.

"Man, nor mess wit me business oh," he warned Awolowo, who hung up and waved to the woman. Bockarie watched in amazement as the young man now unlocked the phones of all the foreigners, sent his friend Awolowo to buy SIM cards for all of them, and made sure everything worked. He charged them, and the foreigners were so impressed that they paid more than he had asked. One of them decided to give him an extra hundred-dollar bill. After the foreigners left, the young man showed the money to his friend Awolowo.

"I hate 1996, man," he said, handing the bill to Awolowo who looked at the 1996 series of the hundred-dollar bill.

"You won't get much for this." Awolowo gave it back to him. Hundred-dollar bills as old as 1996 were rarely accepted here, and when they were, the exchange rate was very low. You needed bills that were more recent than 2000. "You know, I have always wondered who came up with this rule that the 1996 series isn't good. We do choose some interesting standards, man, for people who have no money." He laughed. "Isn't it a law that money is legal tender?"

"Awolowo, you have too much time on your hands today, man. The law is different here on the street. You know that. And for the 1996 bills, the idea came about because people found out they were easiest to fake."

"Doesn't it mean, though, that those making fake 1996s would have moved on to making other notes?" Awolowo looked at the bill.

"Man, keep quiet and go find business there!" His friend pointed to another group of foreigners.

"Amazing, isn't it?" The voice of someone reached the ears of Bockarie. He looked up at the man who sat across from him. He hadn't noticed when he entered the restaurant.

"Amazing," he repeated and continued. "That young man has technology and business skills. But he only uses them to survive. Imagine if someone gave him an opportunity to use his talents to live well, not just to make small change on the street. He will be successful."

The man looked at Bockarie's face, his strong and intimidating stare piercing into Bockarie.

"I am here on behalf of Mr. Kaifala. He cannot meet you today, so he asked me to tell you to come to this address tomorrow for the meeting." He handed a piece of carefully wrapped paper to Bockarie. Opening it, Bockarie saw that the location of the next meeting was in Aberdeen, another part of the city, farther. He surely would have to take one of those transportation vehicles. The man did not tell Bockarie his name.

"Mr. Kaifala also instructed me to buy you a meal and give you some money to pay your way back home."

Bockarie wanted to ask the man to give him the money instead of buying the meal, but he was ashamed. So he ordered and ate food that his wife cooked better. After the quiet meal, during which the nameless fellow just observed Bockarie, he gave him the money for transportation. As he took the money, they both saw a boy no more than eight years old writing the alphabet in crayon on the body of a brand-new car. He used every inch of the vehicle's body. When the owner returned, he asked the boy in anger and amazement why he would do such a thing.

"My father has no money to buy me a notebook," the boy replied. The owner just shook his head, not knowing what to do.

The man and Bockarie, too, shook their heads. Bockarie left him at the table in the restaurant and pretended to catch a taxi while he was looking. As soon as he was out of sight of the man, he started walking home, keeping the transportation money in his pocket. En route he witnessed some bizarre things that, he mused, possibly only occur here.

He was at a very busy intersection where a traffic policeman was exasperatedly waving his hands to regulate cars whose drivers ignored his authority. The traffic was coming from four directions, all of them two-way streets. Suddenly, the policeman took off running as fast as he could. The drivers and pedestrians were at first confused, frowning as they searched for what had caused the sudden departure. And there it was: coming down the hill of one of the streets, behind the policeman, was a taxi, its driver not only out of his seat but also in front of the car, trying to use his body weight to slow it down. Inside the taxi were people seated comfortably, as though nothing was going on. Knowing that he couldn't stop the car, the driver shouted to the passengers to jump out. Then he stepped away, and the vehicle sped even faster down the hill, hitting a BMW that was coming from the other direction. The passengers, though screaming, weren't hurt, nor were those in the BMW. But the driver couldn't afford to pay for the damage so he took to his heels and disappeared among the houses, leaving his taxi behind. This provided laughter for everyone and eased their frustration with the traffic for a few minutes before they started blowing their horns and shouting at the policeman, who had returned to his unenviable post.

Shaking his head and wishing he had a pen and paper to write what just happened, Bockarie continued on. As he climbed a small hill toward the main college in Freetown, he saw the most wretched vehicle, a taxi, he had ever seen. The car had been welded together, but not properly. The areas that couldn't be welded because the metal was too rusty had been tied with wires. It was a car with a nervous condition because everything shook as its tires rolled under its dilapidated body. The taxi made a sharp turn around the corner— and the driver fell out, with the door! He wore no seat belt and the car kept on going, with its passengers, until luckily it slowed itself down without crashing into streetlamps, walls, or another vehicle. It was a blessing after all that the engine had no strength.

The driver staggered up, carrying the door with him, and ran after his vehicle. When he caught up with the car, panting with relief, he demanded that the frightened passengers pay him the fare. They cursed him and yelled for him to let them out; they couldn't open the doors on their own.

Bockarie left them arguing and increased his pace home to see his family.

Kula and the children waited for Bockarie on Mr. Saquee's veranda. As soon as he appeared in the short distance, Thomas and Oumu ran to greet him.

"Welcome back, Father!" they said together and pulled the plastic bag from his hands thinking it might have sweets or something of that sort. Learning that it was just his shirt, they quickly and excitedly explained to him all that they had seen during their wanderings to discover their new neighborhood—the buildings, the cars, so many people, and they also got sweets and ice cream!

"Please wait until I sit down so that the whole family can hear your stories," Bockarie pleaded with the twins, but they were too impatient.

"Father, have you ever seen a Chinese person like in the karate films?" Thomas asked. He went on before his father had a chance to respond. "We saw so many of them walking around and some even selling medicines in the market. Hawa and Maada will never believe me." He finished with brushstrokes of wonder on his face.

"We also saw people without arms like Sila, and they had children, too, like Hawa and Maada. Why were they begging, Mother? Sila didn't beg with his children," Oumu asked.

"This is a different place, my daughter. I am sure if they didn't have to they wouldn't." Kula pulled Oumu closer.

Thomas broke in eagerly. "We walked all the way to PZ, you know that is the main center of the city. Then we watched a Barcelona–versus–Real Madrid match, the last twenty minutes, from a big, big television in one of the Lebanese stores," Abu looked to his older brother for a continuation of the story.

"The Lebanese didn't let us inside so we watched from the street, and when the game ended we sat on the pavement and watched people. There was a group of four boys who just went up and down the road trying to steal things from people. One or two of them would walk in front of someone they had spotted and the others behind. One would distract their victim while the others pickpocketed or snatched his or her bag and ran away. Sometimes they would show people a fake bottle of perfume or a gold necklace as part of their distraction. They just went up and down the street the whole time."

Manawah still didn't understand why the boys spent so much time just to snatch something from passersby. Why couldn't they use that time for something more constructive? Perhaps they had tried their best and this was what they had been left with?

"What was your experience, Miss Quiet?" Bockarie asked Miata. She smiled a bit and started by saying that she made a new friend who was a student at Fourah Bay College, where she had gone on the instruction of her mother to find out about preparatory college classes during the holidays. Kula and Bockarie wanted Manawah and Miata to be prepared for school when it reopened and not feel intimidated by their classmates in the city.

"The campus is on top of the hill, way up there, and the view is so beautiful but it is difficult to get up there by transportation. On the way down my new friend and I decided to walk since we couldn't get a vehicle quicker. All these cars with tinted glass kept slowing down and asking if we wanted a lift. My friend told me we must not get in them. Her name is Isatu, and she kept telling all of them off including the boys who whistled at us." She ended.

"I would like to meet Isatu. She sounds like a good friend to have and a strong young woman." Kula looked at her husband, indicating that it was his turn. Bockarie told them all about his walk and the amazing, bizarre, and funny things he had witnessed and that he would have to go to town again the next day.

"I should come with you next time. Your day was more enjoyable than mine," Kula laughingly told her husband. She was about to recount the stories of her search for work when Mr. Saquee arrived and joined the family on the veranda. He told Bockarie that a friend of his, a pharmacist, had agreed to treat Manawah's forehead for free. It was then that even Manawah remembered that his forehead was still swollen. The excitement of the city had completely occupied him.

"Have the boys sleep in my parlor so you don't have to wound one of them every night, man!"

Kula then told her story about the rude secretaries she had dealt with all day on the phone. "It seemed to me that they didn't want anyone to get employed where they worked," she concluded with frustration.

"You are doing it the wrong way, my dear. You have to go to these places in person or try to know someone there, otherwise you are wasting your money making all these calls." Mr. Saquee cracked his knuckles thoughtfully. "Would you like to look at the possibility of working at a hotel? I think they have some openings for receptionist positions. I can call the manager who used to sleep here—on the ground, in that parlor. Don't bring that up when you see him!" His jovial face once again lit up with a smile. He pulled out his mobile phone and made a call, walking away from them to have his conversation. He returned shortly.

"You will go to Aberdeen tomorrow to the Inamutnib Hotel and ask for Pascal. He said no promises, but what have you got to lose? I will write his number for you and give you directions. It is something to occupy you and of course provide money while you search for what you'd really like to do."

"Thank you, Mr. Saquee! I will make you cassavas tomorrow!" Kula said.

"You know I will do anything for the way you cook cassavas. I feel as though you are giving me my childhood back when I eat it." Mr. Saquee laughed, and the silence that ensued invited the beginning of night.

There was a commotion growing, and the young men causing it soon came into view with a thief they had captured. The fellow, the same age (twenty-two) as his capturers, begged them to take him to the police station, but they refused and started beating him mercilessly. He cried out, "Please take me to be locked up in jail instead. That is the law isn't it? Why don't you want to abide by it?"

The young men didn't listen. The thief made a break. Limping but running as fast as he could, he escaped with a bloodied body and possibly broken ribs. Mr. Saquee called over one of the young men who had captured the thief.

"Come here, Almamy, and tell us what just happened."

Almamy explained to Mr. Saquee and Bockarie and his family that they had captured that same fellow the other day and taken him to the police station, but he had been released because he was in cahoots with the police. Whenever they took thieves to the station, he said, the police would ask them for a detailed list of items or the amount of money that had been stolen. All this, so that they made sure to get their fair share from the thieves they had sent out. In addition, they demanded money from whoever brought a thief to the station for feeding, lodging, and to buy pen and paper to write down the statement.

"So now when we catch a thief we just beat him up badly, as taking him to the police station will cost money," Almamy finished.

"There was a discussion on the radio about this the other day," Mr. Saquee said. "Should people take justice in their own hands when their system of law does not function?" He pondered but gave no response, just instructing Almamy to help start the generator so that they could watch the national television station for the news before the Manchester United–Arsenal match. Almamy happily went to the back of the house and soon the evening was greeted everywhere with the sounds of generators that covered the night noises of crickets. However, that night, when it fully came in, was darker as the lights from the generators were too dim to push back the darkness a bit toward the sky. The stars and moon came out later and won over the darkness. They shone brighter than the lightbulbs, and this was an assurance that God and gods still paid some attention to things here, this and the sun, its heat that remained as hot as it had always been.

"Light don cam" (Light has come), a boy called out from the other house and there was a small clamor as people who had electricity ran home to charge their mobile phones and turn on their fridges and anything else that needed electricity, as quickly as possible before the power went away again. The generators were switched off and the proper silence of night arrived. The power was, however, weaker and the lights were like the eyes of a sleep-possessed person who tried to stay awake. The bulbs dulled and then brightened repeatedly, but even when they were at their brightest, a flashlight had better vigor. Before the excitement of the arrival of electricity was finished, the power was gone.

"Almamy, please start the generator again," Mr. Saquee called out. "We are not lucky enough in this part of town. You see up the hill where the lights are now? There is always electricity there because one of the ministers has a mistress in that neighborhood. So whenever we have a new government, we pray that someone in it has a home in our neighborhood or will find a girlfriend in our part of town!" Mr. Saquee said. Bockarie thought about Principal Fofanah in Imperi and his conversations with Benjamin when they were teachers.

The quietness of night was driven away again when all the area generators came on. Bockarie sat with his family and Mr. Saquee's in the parlor and watched the local news, which was mostly about praising the work that the current government was doing. They claimed the government had brought electricity to the country and boasted of its natural beauty, as though the government were responsible for that, too. The president came on to brag about what his administration was doing.

"We have brought electricity to this country . . ." he began, and the lights went off at the television station. Bockarie and Mr. Saquee laughed. Their television was still on because it was powered by a generator. After several minutes, the television station regained power and the president picked up right where he had left off, speaking about the wonderful electricity they had brought to the country and other development projects in the pipeline.

"Now, that is pure comedy," Bockarie said.

"I had a feeling you would like it, man. That is why I watch this so-called news show. You really see what is going on in this country in the background of the news itself."

Bockarie wanted to mention that that was just half of what was going on, there were worse things that most people in the city would probably never know about—they had their own worries and desperation. But the match between Manchester United and Arsenal came on after the president's speech, and gradually the house was filled with men and boys who had come to watch.

15

THE NEXT MORNING, Bockarie left before Kula; his meeting was earlier. They decided to meet at Lumley Beach near Aberdeen after Kula's appointment with Pascal.

"Say good morning to the children for me, and I will see you later, my dear." He kissed her hand as he walked out of the room.

"That is all? Come back." She threw her arms around him and whispered that it was better now. "Now my luck and yours have mixed," she said when she released him. He turned to wave before disappearing behind the house to join the street that led to the main road.

Bockarie stood in the long queue to take a transport vehicle to Aberdeen. He was standing next to a young fellow who wore an ID card for Fourah Bay College, the best school in the country, around his neck even though it was a holiday. The teacher in Bockarie came out.

"Is college still on?" he asked the young man, who at first pretended not to hear him.

"No, sir. We are on holiday."

"So why are you wearing your badge?"

"This is authentic—you see the insignia on the lanyard. That is how you know it is not fake." He showed the writing to Bockarie.

"I have no doubt that you are a student, but why wear the badge on a holiday? Why wear the badge at all when you're off campus?"

"It is a sign of prestige. With this badge on, I can enter many places without anyone second-guessing me." And he moved closer to whisper to Bockarie, "I also attract a lot of girls." He laughed.

Bockarie liked the intelligence of this young man and his humor. "Do the young women also wear it the same way?" he asked.

"Yes and no. They have to be careful because an educated woman can be a threat to a lot of men, you know." His face got serious.

Bockarie and the fellow, who later introduced himself as Albert, had a spirited conversation about college life in Lion Mountain. Albert spoke about his frustrations with the way the university was structured. He referred to something called "legacy." It meant that the professors—most of them, not all—taught the same lectures over and over for years. If you were to take someone else's book who had attended college before you and read the notes, you would pass the exam. What really agitated Albert was that if a student asked questions beyond the scope of the professor's knowledge, it was looked upon as a challenge, as an act of disobedience and disrespect. You would be vilified and failed in that class even if you did well. "Educational blackmail," Albert called it. "As a result," he said, "you have to keep your questions and curiosities to yourself so you can graduate. And of course you would like to graduate after all the money you've paid. That's why this country doesn't move forward." He motioned for Bockarie to follow. They pushed their way into a packed vehicle, managing to get seats near each other.

"I am sure there are other reasons why this country is the way it is," Bockarie said, stretching his elbows to have the space he needed before someone else squeezed in.

"I agree, but the one I am speaking of is the one I am faced with." Albert lowered his head a bit to avoid another passenger's bag as it came swinging near him.

The vehicle started moving with no space left for even an ant, and half an hour into the journey, which was mostly spent in traffic, it was pulled over at a temporary checkpoint flooded with policemen. They asked everyone to step out of the vehicle.

"Oh, great, the tax collectors," Albert grumbled and searched through his pockets for something.

"What are you looking for?" Bockarie asked.

"My tax receipt. I don't have it." He cursed under his breath.

The police lined everyone up, including the driver, and demanded general state taxes to be paid on the spot. "Five thousand leones each."

People complained. Some said they didn't have jobs; some said they were students with no income; others said they had paid but no one told them to carry their receipts at all times. It didn't matter. Everyone was made to pay. Receipts were provided, but you couldn't tell which of them were real.

"Why are there so many different kinds of receipt?" a passenger asked.

"We have the old and the newly printed ones mixed. I ask the questions here, so keep quiet," the police commander responded.

An old man handed one of the policemen a receipt. The young officer started laughing and called his superior over.

"Sir, is this your tax receipt?" the superior asked.

"Yes, sir," the old man said.

"So your name is Kadiatu Kamara?" the policeman went on, chuckling.

"Yes, sir." The whole place burst into laughter. The old man couldn't read or write and didn't know that he had taken his daughter's receipt, not his son's, to show as his. So he decided to answer to whatever name was on the one he carried. Many people did such things, so the government began asking people to take passport photos and staple them to their tax receipts, an additional cost to the already struggling majority of the populace. Before the vehicle departed, the passengers watched the policemen share most of the tax money they had just collected among themselves. Bockarie and Albert shook their heads and laughed—the policemen stood under a sign that read SAY NO TO CORRUPTION! CORRUPTION IS A PUNISH-ABLE CRIME!

Bockarie exchanged mobile numbers with Albert before he got off the vehicle by the beach to wait at a Lebanese café for his appointment. He walked around the café a few times, hoping that whoever he was meeting this time would arrive before he entered this place. He didn't want to buy anything and was embarrassed to sit down and wait without even a bottle of water. But he could go around the place only so many times.

When he walked in, the waiters looked suspiciously at him, assuming that he couldn't afford anything. But whenever anyone white or with the aura of someplace abroad entered, the waiters rushed to serve that person. Bockarie sat himself down with a view of the ocean, and out of nowhere came the man who had called himself the representative of Mr. Kaifala. He still didn't introduce himself, but he greeted Bockarie with a firm handshake as though they were old friends, saying nothing. His mood was different from the first meeting, and Bockarie took this as a good sign. They sat quietly watching the cars drive along the beach road. There were young women and girls clearly hanging about the road to sell their bodies in broad daylight. Some looked younger than Miata. They wore next to nothing and some of their skirts were so short that if you walked by you saw everything. They had see-through shirts and red lips. On the other side of the road were some young men and boys who had come by the beach to relax, play some football, and dream about being able to sit on the restaurants' decks and eat whatever they wanted.

Sirens got everyone's attention. Two police motorcycles were coming down the road, clearing traffic. A 4×4 was behind them in the distance, speeding so much that everyone knew it was a government vehicle. The young women began to stand in ways that allowed them to open their legs even more, laying their hands on their breasts. The black car rolled into view and its license plate was a ministerial one. It pulled up next to some of the girls. A minister rolled down the window and called on two of them; they climbed into the air-conditioned vehicle. The tinted windows rolled up, consuming them. The motorcycles had stopped ahead and they resumed their horns. As the vehicle passed by, the young men who had seen what just happened high-fived one another, wishing they could be ministers or have some power.

"Wonderful example for the youth, eh?" The mysterious man looked at Bockarie.

"All the boys think that that's how you're supposed to use your power. They admire that sort of behavior. If the minister does it, especially in broad daylight, then it must be good." A well-dressed young man who had been sitting nearby pulled up a chair next to Bockarie and the mysterious man. He wore a brown linen suit that fit him very well and a white shirt with cuff links but no tie. "Don't tell me this is the first time you have seen such a thing, gentlemen," he said.

"It is for me. I am not from here and don't come by this way often," Bockarie said, staring at the confident and well-spoken fellow and wondering what he did for a living.

"You are very spiffy, our new friend," the mysterious man said. They went on about politics and world affairs and you name it. The young man was better informed than the two of them.

"What is your name, young man?" the mysterious man asked.

"Sylvester." He extended his hand to both of them. But as the vibrancy of the conversation waned, he asked, "Could you kind gentlemen help me with some money for food?"

The mysterious man and Bockarie looked at each other, perplexed.

"You look like you have money, not like someone who needs to beg for food," Bockarie said.

"I am actually on the zero-zero-one plan these days. If I am lucky, that will continue today."

"What is this plan you are speaking of?" Bockarie tuned his full attention to Sylvester, whose strength and dignity didn't reveal a slight bit of suffering. Sylvester smiled, revealing his dry lips and mouth—a sign of someone who hadn't had any food or water for a while.

"It is how my friends and I refer to those who are fortunate and can have one, two, or three meals a day." Sylvester paused and looked at the faces of the two men.

"There are those on zero-zero-zero, which means they have nothing to eat all day and go hungry. For example, you see that fellow over there. See how he walks. He is so hungry that you have to get out of his way. It is only the wind that walks him, as he has no more strength." Sylvester was distracted by the plates of food that a waiter was carrying to another table.

"Let's order you some food, Sylvester. Waiter, come here," the mysterious man called. Sylvester's voice became tainted with some excitement as he continued.

"So, there are those on one-zero-one, and we consider them lucky. Two meals a day! And for a good number of us, we work hard to either be on one-zero-zero or zero-zero-one meal plans. I prefer the latter, so I will take my food with me. For now, I will drink lots of water so that I will feel full."

Sylvester seemed happy to have educated these men. He told them that he and many others had to do all sorts of odd jobs to buy a few nice clothes and shoes, soap to wash, and sometimes a small bottle of perfume. People would think that they were not prioritizing their needs, but they were. A well-dressed and presentable young person wouldn't be mistaken for a thief or looked down upon. Most important, it provided him the opportunity to have an audience with someone in order to be able to ask for food or money to buy food.

"I wouldn't have been able to sit here if I had tattered clothes. You wouldn't have made my zero-zero-one possible today!" he said. His food came and he asked for a carry-away container.

The mysterious man ordered water for himself and Sylvester and mango juice for Bockarie. They sat together looking at the ocean, the persistence of the long body of water curling and breaking on the shore.

"I will leave you, gentlemen, and may our paths cross again. I won't have to explain myself another time around. It isn't always easy to ask for help like this, you know." Sylvester lowered his voice and left the men to their quiet moment. He adjusted his cuff links, picked up his food and water, and walked down the road toward the city center. The mysterious man got up and said he would be back in a few minutes. Bockarie watched him get into a vehicle that was parked in the sand, almost on the beach.

Bockarie began thinking this might not have been the best place to bring his family—or perhaps he was too hasty. He would wait to meet this Mr. Kaifala; maybe something good would come of it. Where could he and his family live, if not here? This was the capital city, after all, the pinnacle of opportunity, or so he had believed. He sighed.

The mysterious man returned and they waited.

Kula was wearing a beautiful white lace dress with an elegant matching head tie. Even her children were impressed—they told her she looked beautiful and wished her luck. She walked slowly to the junction to get a transport vehicle, rehearsing possible interview questions in her head. What makes you think you can do this job?

Are you qualified? How? On her way, the van she was in was pulled over and she, too, was asked to pay a tax to the policemen. She demanded the precinct, badge number, and name of the captain, so that if her receipt were fraudulent, she would know where to find him. They saw from her stare that she was a woman they didn't want to offend; rather than answer her questions, they just asked her to pay next time.

The van departed shortly afterward and she got off at a roundabout in Aberdeen, as Mr. Saquee had suggested. She walked the small hill to the Inamutnib Hotel, but she thought for a moment that she must be in the wrong place—the hotel sign was almost entirely in Chinese.

"Excuse me, sir. Is this the right hotel?" She showed the guard the piece of paper that she had written the hotel's name on.

"Yes, this is it indeed, but the Chinese are in charge now, which is why all their writings are everywhere." The guard motioned for her to enter and pointed her in the right direction up the hill.

At the reception desk, she asked for Pascal and they told her to wait. Thirst was spreading itself through her throat. She looked at the price for water and immediately put the menu back down. She didn't know water could cost that much. People came and went. The young lady at reception received several scolding remarks from a Chinese man who said a bunch of things in some sort of English that Kula had never heard.

"I am sorry to make you wait for so long. I am Pascal," a tall man introduced himself. He sat in the chair opposite her and asked for water to be brought to the table.

"Have you ever done anything in the hotel business?" he asked.

"No, but I was a nurse and there are similarities. They both deal with helping and pleasing people, making them feel comfortable," she said firmly but without raising her voice.

"Mr. Saquee did tell me that you are a very intelligent and

strong-willed person." He laughed encouragingly and continued with many other questions for about thirty minutes.

"So I will employ you on a trial basis for a month. During that time you will work alongside one of the staff so you can see how things are done. I am sure you will catch up quickly." He extended his hand to end the meeting.

"Thank you very much. I will do my best and I certainly appreciate this opportunity." Her handshake was firmer than he expected. He seemed surprised.

"You can start in two days. We will have your badge and uniform ready for you then. Please bring a passport photo the next time. I should tell you, though, that you will only get paid at the end of the month. Since you are in training, you won't be receiving pay every two weeks as the other staff. I know it is expensive to pay your way here and back for a month, but this is all I can offer now." He nodded to say his final goodbye and walked in the direction of his office.

Kula finished drinking the cold water and called her husband's mobile phone.

"Hello, dear. I am done." She smiled. "Okay, I will meet you there in a few minutes."

She put the phone back in her purse and left to meet her husband by the beach. The cool breeze entered her pores as she neared the ocean, walking with an elegance that distinguished her from many of the other women she passed.

When she saw him, she ran and threw herself in his arms. He held her for a while and kissed her before they started walking arm in arm along the beach barefoot, holding their shoes. They told each other their news. Bockarie, too, had gotten some work to correct papers for university students, or so he had been told, and would start the following day. He didn't want to anger Mr. Kaifala, who seemed reluctant to explain the details of the job and was in a hurry. The money would be good, though.

"So this Mr. Kaifala really exists and showed up after all." She took off her head tie to feel the ocean breeze some more.

"Yes, but there is something abnormal that I felt with him. Anyway, it doesn't matter." He rolled up his sleeves.

"Your work sounds way more exciting than mine. I am happy for you, dear, for us. It has been too long that you just stayed at home raising our children and me, if I may say so. We have to discuss, though, how to take care of the children." He kissed her again and used his body weight to push her into the coming waves. She jumped excitedly, laughing.

"Let's not think about it now, my dear. Let's just enjoy ourselves, perhaps even buy ourselves a drink at one of these beach bars." She pointed to a number of them along the sand. He agreed and they chose one and started heading toward it. En route, they saw a man dressed in a long white robe, a big cross dangling on his chest. He was saying some words that didn't make any sense and in front of him sat a number of women in white robes as well. He would take one of them after making lots of noises and dip her head into the ocean.

"They believe that he can pray for them to have good husbands!" a jogger said as he passed Kula and Bockarie.

"This city has so much to teach one every day. It is as though you are living several lifetimes every time you look around." Kula looked away at the ocean before turning to her husband again.

"What do you think? Should I go pay him to almost drown me in salt water for a good husband?" She laughed and started running in the sand away from Bockarie.

"Maybe he should dip me in the water so that I can become a good husband. Wait a minute, aren't I already a good husband?" He chased after her.

"Says who?" She convulsed with laughter as he neared her and threw her in the sand.

They arrived home late that night when everyone was asleep.

The night's air was pleasant on their faces since it seemed the city was opening up to them, showing them what it could provide them.

But the hand of the city is unpredictable, the hand of the country is even more capricious. Often shadows gather around the giving hand and break its fingers, spoiling the gifts.

Tonight, Kula and Bockarie giggled as they entered into their small room and slept in the clothes they had been wearing all day.

16

BOCKARIE WAS DISHEARTENED on his first day of work after he fully understood what his job entailed. Mr. Kaifala's operation, as he called it, was really a place that, in collaboration with some college professors, wrote thesis papers for students who could afford to pay for them. Of course, not everyone used this route to get an education, but the whole thing didn't sit well with Bockarie. He remembered the conversation he had had with Albert, the Fourah Bay College student who wore his ID card around his neck during holidays.

How can the country go forward with such practices? he asked himself. They were writing theses for people who couldn't even speak English well but would now have degrees ranging from bachelor to master's to PhD. The operation even had staff who would go to defend the thesis of their clients under false names and of course with support from the professors they had in their pockets. No one was getting any salaries at the college, so they were open to other options.

"Welcome, my good man. You are on trial for one month to see if you will keep our secret and also if you are able to write excellent papers for us! For now we will only give you money for transportation and for three meals a day. I am sure you learned the saying in school that 'an empty bag cannot stand upright.'" Mr. Kaifala showed Bockarie to his desk, where work was already waiting in a pile with research notes ready and bound for him to read. He wanted to ask if anyone in his office was really who they said they were. Mr. Kaifala didn't look like a Kaifala. In fact that morning while he waited in the reception area, two people had referred to Mr. Kaifala as Mr. Cole and Mr. Conteh. He had answered to both names with ease. Bockarie shook these thoughts out of his mind. He had to take care of his family and even the money that he would now get for transportation and meals could help him a lot by getting on the zero-zero-one meal plan and walking home after work. Food would be at home at the end of the day, so he would be able to save all that money for his family. He pulled out a thesis topic for a master's degree in international relations.

This person will probably never leave this country to do anything international, he told himself to justify his action. He started reading the research notes and even wrote an opening paragraph. It was not all that bad because he liked using his brain even though this was for the wrong reasons.

At lunchtime, when he stepped outside to get some air, he saw cars with government license plates and young Lebanese getting out of fancy vehicles to pick up parcels from the operation office. There were also regular-looking people like himself who came in for their parcels with sweaty clothes and dusty shoes, a clear sign that they had walked a long way and spent their last cents to get the semblance of an education. Maybe they were intelligent enough for what they were receiving. Who knows what the story was that had brought them to make such a decision. He couldn't enjoy the breeze with these sights and thoughts, so he returned inside.

At home that evening, he didn't say anything even to his wife about the reality of his job. He pretended to be happy and gave the money to her for safekeeping and to take care of the family. His children would start classes soon. Bockarie had decided to work for his current employer for only a month, and during that time he would look for something else. What he didn't know was that the work was so demanding that he wouldn't have any time to thoroughly search for something else. And in a city where the hand of opportunity did not come by easily, he would need to carefully and cautiously jump from one canoe to another before sounding the doorbell of his values.

The sky was at its bluest, and if you looked closely for a while you could see whatever your imagination thought dwelled beyond the body of the sky. Since the daily activities necessary to survive in the city were stressful enough, people looked at the sky only briefly and mostly set their eyes about themselves and on the earth to gain a strong footing so that the wind of despair didn't claim them quickly. Kula had looked up every so often to guess the time from the movement of the sun. It was her first day of work, from 3:00 p.m. until 11:00 p.m. She prepared food for the family and allocated chores to her children before getting ready. She would not see her husband until late and that made her slightly sad, but she distracted herself by spending some time with the twins, who were busy crayoning in their coloring books. She and her husband had bought an extra mobile phone that was to be at home for emergencies. She handed it to Miata.

"Is it all right, Mother, for Isatu to come and study with me?" Miata asked.

"Yes, as long as you do not invite boys." She had a way of sounding funny while being serious. Miata didn't respond, but Kula knew her words had found a resting place in her daughter's mind. She hoped.

As soon as Kula left home and got into the transportation vehicle, it started raining heavily. No one was prepared because the words of the sky had said otherwise. Water gushed into the van, thoroughly soaking everyone. The driver handed out small plastic bags so that passengers could at least wrap their mobile phones, money, and other things of value that were enemies of water.

"Water nor to fire me people dem so wunna nor vex," the driver joked, telling his passengers that water is not fire, my people, so do not get angry. As suddenly as the rain had come, it stopped and the sun brightly lit the soaked earth and beings. There was flooding on the streets on a bright sunny day. After disembarking, Kula called the emergency mobile phone and asked Miata to bring her some dry clothes and shoes that she would need after work because she wasn't allowed to take her work uniform home. She needed the shoes immediately because the ones she wore were now filled with water and making squishy sounds as she walked up the hill to the hotel.

"Get your brothers to look after the house and come before nighttime. I don't want you on the street when it is dark," she instructed her daughter.

"Yes, Mother." She hung up the phone. *She wouldn't need me to bring her shoes if we were back in Imperi. She would have just walked home barefoot*, Maita thought and shouted the names of her brothers, who were playing football nearby. They were unhappy about stopping their games and grumbled, but their sister paid them no mind. Isatu decided to accompany Miata.

"But I didn't tell Mother that you will be coming along," Miata reasoned with her friend.

"Don't worry. She will think it is a good idea that I came with you, especially if it gets dark before you return home." She waved her hand for Miata to hurry up.

Meanwhile, in the staff room, Kula squeezed the excess water out of her wet clothes to be able to use them to somewhat dry her hair. Quickly changing into her uniform, she put on her wet shoes that had refused to release their water. Standing up straight with determination, she went to the front desk to start work. Pascal gave her a quick tour and some instructions. Then he handed her over to another woman whose job was to teach her throughout the eight-hour shift. Her expression wasn't cordial and she ignored Kula the entire time. Pascal had gone home for the day, so she had no one to turn to. However, she decided to just observe and learn on her own.

A few quiet hours into the shift, a guest came from his room. He was clearly from the country but had been away for a while—or was, as the local parlance referred to him, a "JC" (Jus cam), just returned. Kula's colleague was on the phone, so he came to her and started shouting.

"I don't understand how anything works in my room. Everything is in Chinese. This is an English-speaking country, you know. Look at this." He showed Kula the air-conditioning remote that was all in Chinese. He went on, "I also ordered some cassava leaves and they told me they don't have any local dishes. But they have some general's chicken and other Chinese dishes. I would like to speak with the manager."

Kula looked toward her colleague, who was now off the phone, but she ignored her, leafing through some useless magazine. The Chinese fellow who seemed to run the place from the back came out to the reception area.

"I am the manager and how can I help you, sir?" He edged Kula aside, and it was at that instant that the other receptionist intervened to handle the situation. But the man refused to speak to her, insisting that he must speak to this manager standing in front of him.

"I want some cassava leaves, you know, food from this country."

"We don't have a chef for that. So no cassava leaves, okay," the manager said.

"You mean to tell me in this entire country you cannot find someone who can cook cassava leaves? It is bullshit and you know it."

"Mister, no bad words here. Please."

"And get some remote controls that are in English." He threw the remote on the desk and stalked away. The rest of the evening was quiet. People mostly came to ask for their room keys and dropped them off on their way out. Miata arrived just when her mother was beginning to worry about her.

"I didn't know you were coming with Isatu," she said, taking the bag from her, then greeting Miata's friend.

"I knew it would take a while because of the rain and wanted someone with me in case it got darker, as it is now." Miata avoided her mother's eyes.

"It turns out that I am getting off earlier, so please have a seat there in the lounge and we will return home together." Miata agreed, hiding the disappointment in her face from her mother. She and Isatu had planned on having a little excursion by the beach before returning to the eastern part of the city. Kula observed her daughter and Isatu from behind the reception desk while they drank the Coca-Cola she had bought them. They went on about something that made them laugh, almost choking on their drinks. She turned her eyes to her feet, which were now relieved from the cold shoes, though the stained wetness made her toes itch.

Within twenty minutes, the lounge was filled with many young girls whom Kula recognized as prostitutes. Older white men took some of the girls with them, but more kept coming. At one point, an old English fellow started chatting up Miata and Isatu. He invited them to his room. Kula wanted to jump from behind the desk and deal with the man, but she calmed herself and walked around the barrier to where her daughter and friend sat.

"Sir, you should be ashamed of yourself. These are young girls and this one is my daughter. I am sure you have a daughter their age where you are from. How would you feel if someone as old as you solicited her for sex?" she said, fiercely but quietly, so that her boss wouldn't hear her supposedly tormenting the customer. The man hurriedly left, heading back to where the rooms were. Behind him trailed some girls offering themselves for his pleasure. He put his arms around them and walked on. Kula made the girls move where she could see them directly from the reception counter.

Kula's shift went on for another long hour, and she hated every-thing she saw with the young women and girls and the older white men. She eyed Miata and Isatu hard each time she caught them look-ing at these interactions. As soon as her shift was over, she quickly went in the back to change. When she returned, there were some girls physically attacking Miata and Isatu, shouting at them to find their own location and that this was their territory. Kula grabbed one girl by the hair and the other by her arm and took them outside. She slapped them harder than they expected.

"These are my children and you think any other woman sitting in the lounge of a hotel is like you." She moved in for a second set of slapping. The girls took their high heels off and ran away, cursing at her as they went down the hill.

"This country is really not what it used to be. Not a word about this to your father." She pointed her finger at Miata.

While Kula was looking inside her handbag to make sure that her work ID hadn't fallen out as she was dragging those girls outside, a brand-new BMW sports vehicle pulled up next to them. The driver ran to the back door and opened it. A young man, no more than twenty-five years old, was sitting in the middle of the backseat like a king. He stepped out, a mobile phone at his ear, speaking and laugh-ing to someone, a white towel around his neck and carrying a tall bottle of water. He saw that Kula, Miata, and Isatu were looking at him. He handed the bottle of water to the driver, reached in his pocket, pulled out some notes, and handed them to Isatu and Miata. He walked into the hotel holding his jeans, which kept falling off his buttocks. The girls giggled and jumped until Kula turned to them.

"Do you need a ride to town? I just returned to pick up some papers from the office," Pascal called out from the nearby parking lot. Kula nodded and introduced her daughter and friend. The girls sat in the back of Pascal's Toyota and Kula in the front seat.

"I see in your face that you have questions about the young fel-low who just gave them money." Pascal smiled.

"Has everything gone wrong in this country?" Kula asked.

"Well, that is a big question. In short, a lot of things have been rotting away for a while, but let me explain to you what you just saw." His face got serious as he tried to start his car, whose engine took a while to respond.

"Here we are. The engine of a hardworking man always refuses to start at first!" He put the car in motion. The girls looked at their brand-new notes and whispered to each other, ignoring the adults. Pascal explained to Kula that she had just met a JC who had perfected "false life."

"I used to be impressed by these young men and wanted to be like them, wanted to go where they lived and actually stopped looking for any possibility of succeeding here in my own country. Until one of my cousins who lives abroad came home and told me the truth. He knew some of these guys. Mind you, not every one of our people are like these, but there are many with these false lives who send the wrong messages to our young people." He honked for the gate to be lifted. He went on after driving through the iron post:

"There are lots of people, mostly young men, who live in the United States or Europe. They had immigrated to various countries hoping to make good of their lives. However, when they got there, they saw that the realities weren't as golden as they had envisioned. So instead of coming back home, because of shame and worry about being called failures by their peers whom they had bragged to before leaving, they stayed wherever they were, struggling.

"But they came home to visit, after saving up for a year doing odd jobs, just to show that they were doing really well wherever they were. Some of them even shipped vehicles like the one you saw at the hotel for the two- or three-week visit. They would end up selling those vehicles to pay their way back. Most of them would have no more than three to five thousand dollars, a lot of money to blow off here. So you would see them all over town, at the beaches and hotels, and they managed to impress girls, boys, men, and women, who then started dreaming that they, too, would do well only if they went abroad, not knowing the reality behind it all.

"Now, there are those among this population who are serious and go to school, get an education, and work hard for their money. When they come home they do so quietly, without any of this false life. But they are few in number." The car slowed to allow the herd of motorcycles to go by.

Kula had been listening intently. "So they paint a deceiving picture of what their lives really are," she said.

"Exactly, my sister, but it is an enticing picture. And they do it year after year. They even ruin young girls to whom they promise things when visiting."

"So it is like a ritual of broken dreams that gets performed over and over." Kula's response deeply affected Pascal, and he could not speak for minutes, repeating her sentence in his mind again and again.

"I had never found the right words for it. It is exactly what you said. I am amazed." He drove quietly into the city cloaked with such darkness that its beauty had disappeared from the eyes. The moon and the stars had gone elsewhere tonight.

Bockarie and Kula had done all they could to take care of their family, but things were getting harder. The prices of goods kept going up, and two weeks into work they were running out of money to feed their children. They wanted Manawah and Miata to continue their summer classes, but they couldn't afford it anymore. They barely saw each other with energy in their bones for something other than sleep. Kula had also started working on weekends. They hadn't even had time to write home and, as the elders had warned, sleep started visiting them less and less because they were afflicted with worries of what tomorrow would bring. They did manage to keep their children in line, but they knew if their life didn't improve, they would lose them, especially Miata, to the enticements of the city.

Things became especially difficult during the last two weeks of the month before Bockarie and Kula expected to be paid. The family could afford only a few meals each week. A new kind of shame, pain, and discomfort found a home on their faces—the faces of parents who watched their children go to bed hungry night after night or dissatisfied with the little food they had eaten. Sleep also didn't like visiting children or human beings with empty bellies. Many nights, Kula and Bockarie would sit on the veranda whispering to each other about whether they had made the wrong decision to come to the city. In the countryside you could at least count on someone sharing food with you, or you could grow something in the earth in anticipation of when you had no money. They hadn't seen Mr. Saquee for a while because he was hiding from them, as he knew they were struggling and didn't want them to feel that he needed the rent that they were supposed to start paying after a month. Laughter, too, was limited, something that had never before happened in their family.

Finally the day came for Bockarie to be paid and he allowed himself a smile at the prospect of beginning to weed out the thorns of suffering that had blanketed his countenance. He arrived at the operation center early and went to work. At midday, he heard a loud pounding at the entrance to the office. It was unusual; people were usually somewhat discreet when they came to collect their papers. When Mr. Kaifala opened the door, he was thrown to the ground by a number of police officers and handcuffed. The police asked everyone to stand against the wall and put their hands up. They searched the area and took bags of cash with them, along with Mr. Kaifala. Even after the police had gone, Bockarie remained with his hands up against the wall, frozen with the pain that ran through his heart. He knew he wasn't going to get paid that day and didn't know when. The police hadn't come to raid the operation but to arrest Mr. Kaifala, who was suspected of being involved in smuggling cocaine into the country. Bockarie learned from his coworkers that a plane filled with cocaine had landed at the airport and was captured by the authorities. The investigation was unfolding, and many big men in politics and business had been arrested, while others had fled the country. The enigmatic fellow who had first met Bockarie on behalf of Mr. Kaifala told everyone that they must go home and they would be called when operations resumed.

Bockarie pulled the man aside. "What about my pay? I need that money."

"Didn't you see that they took all the money that was here? If we do resume, we will owe you a month's pay."

Bockarie raised his voice. "What if you don't resume operations?"

"Then you have had some experience here that you can put on your résumé!" The man laughed and walked off. Some of Bockarie's colleagues were gathered around a radio listening to a program about the cocaine plane. The argument took hold of the listeners and they, too, started debating. The issue was whether people should care about whether their country was used to bring drugs to Europe and the West. People disagreed on the matter.

"Why should we care about them, their children and families? They didn't when we had a war and all the arms and ammunition was brought from their borders to us," one of the debaters on the radio asked. Bockarie didn't pay much attention to it. He had his own problems, which no one else cared about.

He was supposed to meet Kula at her hotel so they could celebrate by sharing a large bottle of beer. How was he going to explain this to her? He stepped outside and was greeted with a gust of hot wind that he despised. He loved hot weather, but everything had become sour. His children would not eat today again. He walked to meet his wife.

She was waiting for him at the entrance to the hotel, and she was crying. She had been fired because Pascal and the Chinese manager had fallen out and hence anyone he had employed was let go as well without any pay. They held each other, Bockarie remaining stronger for both of them. She was not crying out of weakness but for her children. Their words to explain to each other what had happened were broken, and when they got home, their children heard only a broken story as hunger cut through them and their capacity to listen. All their faces were ravaged with the gathering shadows of hopelessness. Kula's face was stained with tears that contained the burden of yesterday and they rolled down her face, which had become older and rough with the worries of a broken tomorrow. Night was coming and tomorrow would arrive in one form or another. If anyone had told them that they would look back at this day while having conversations that mended the repetitive brokenness in so many lives, they wouldn't have believed it.

They had all been sitting quietly for nearly two hours. No one moved much except for Oumu, who was restless because she wanted to ask her father to tell a story but didn't know if it was appropriate. She thought about moments when she had heard stories from the elders. Something brought the voice of Mama Kadie to Oumu's mind. "Always press your bare feet to the ground and listen to what the earth says and what it has to give you for the day. She always has something, but you have to listen to receive it," Mama Kadie had said to Oumu during one of those times when the little girl had sat with her, peppering her with questions, which Mama Kadie had enjoyed because she knew the little girl was ready to receive the stories of the past, the ones that strengthen your backbone when the world whips you and weakens your spirit.

Oumu remembered these words now as her family sat together hungry and silent, the parents avoiding the eyes of their children. She looked at her family. Each person's head was bowed in defeat, or perhaps that was all they could do. She stood up from the little chair she had been sitting in near the wall by the door. She removed her flip-flops, bent down, picked them up, and placed them on her head. She walked outside and slowly pressed her feet to the ground, walking around the yard a few times before something propelled her feet toward the main road. It was where she had last seen Colonel. He had waved to her and placed his hands on his lips as he had done on the first day she'd arrived in the city. As he had instructed, she hadn't told the rest of the family that he was nearby.

Perhaps he might have some encouraging words for her, she thought, although she didn't really know what good that might do. As she walked, she hummed a tune that was sung at the end of a story she'd heard. It was a story about how, if you went to sleep without the story of the night having been told, you would wake up somewhere strange and it would be long before you came back to yourself. She hummed it quietly to herself, keeping it within, rather than letting it into the outside world where it would be drowned out by the noises of those struggling to end another difficult day. She stopped at the edge of the boisterous street where she had arrived and raised her head to look for Colonel.

He had been watching her the entire time, his frame in the darkness.

"Oumu, wait over there," he called from across the street. "I will come to you." He looked to see if there were any cars, and then quickly crossed to her, holding a basket of food. He handed it to her without saying anything more, but his eyes said she must take the food home to her family. She smiled, her lips so dry from hunger that they held on to each other, so that her smile was not as wide as the dance of her heart. They stood side by side for a bit, and Oumu gathered some strength and lifted the basket with her small hands to see if she could carry it. She set it back on the earth briefly.

"I will go back now before Mother and Father start to worry about where I am." She held Colonel's hand in the way that people much older did when they had more to say than situations permitted, in a

way that promised that the conversation would be sweeter and completed the next time around. Colonel crouched down to be at eye
level with Oumu. He whispered something in her ear.

"Tell them this when you think it is appropriate to do so," he
said. She nodded, turned around, and walked back to her family,
hastening her steps, balancing the flip-flops on her head without
even knowing they were there anymore. She entered the silent room
where everyone sat still, willing something—anything—to happen.
She set the basket down and pulled out some plates, and started
dishing rice and potato-leaves sauce with fish. The smell of the meal
brought back everyone from wherever they had been. They raised
their heads in shock, but with the hunger still in their throats, they
were unable to ask where Oumu had gotten the food. She took the
hands of her parents and brought them to the meal, then waved for
her siblings to come closer and gather around. She passed water in a
small bowl so that all could wash their hands before they started
eating together.

Kula made sure that the food was not too hot before everyone
dug in. They ate ravenously at first, at least the first five handfuls of
rice. Another silence ensued, but this time it was followed by sighs
of relief as the delicious taste of the rice and the sauce spread in their
mouths. They were all sweating because it had been a while since
they had had food in abundance.

They ate the rest of the meal more slowly, enjoying every bite as
though it was the only time they had ever tasted this simple meal.
Oumu stopped eating before anyone else and sat back in her chair
licking her hand. Then her parents stopped, followed by Manawah,
Miata, and then Abu, leaving more food for Thomas. He ate all that
was left and licked the plate clean. Each of them reclined against
the wall of the room, forming a circle, their palm-oil-laden hands
resting on their knees.

Oumu sensed that her parents would soon ask who had given
her the food. "The one who gave me the food told me to tell you

that the world is not ending today and that you must cheer up if you want to continue living in it," she said.

"Who is that?" asked Kula.

"Colonel," Oumu said.

Bockarie and Kula looked at each other and smiles passed across their faces. Before either of them said anything else, Oumu asked, "Mother, can you tell us a story?"

"I don't see why not." Kula sat upright, cleared her throat, and waited for the silence that invited all spirits to such gatherings.

"There were two brothers who decided to leave home and journey to another land. In those days, before one went on a journey, you performed a ceremony of cleansing yourself thoroughly by washing every part of your body and your heart. Therefore, on the day of the journey, the brothers went to the river and began washing themselves. They took out their hearts, cleaned them, and laid them on a rock to dry a bit as they scrubbed the rest of their bodies. It was believed that by washing one's heart, particularly before a journey, you allowed yourself to experience that journey purely.

"The brothers were playful and always joked around with each other, so they started playing diving games. Laughter took hold of them, and when they were done washing, they left, forgetting their hearts on the rock by the river. They realized this only after they arrived at the new land and couldn't find pleasure, understanding, or feeling in the new things that their eyes saw. The older brother touched his chest and realized that his heart wasn't there. His little brother did the same.

"They picked up their sack and started walking back home as fast as they could. When they reached the river days later, their hearts were still there, but the arrival of day and night had altered them and ants had eaten certain parts. The brothers washed the hearts and put them back in their places, but they could no longer experience things the way they had."

Kula finished and the silence deepened.

"So they must find a way to repair their broken hearts by relighting the fire that is now dull within them. They should live for that." Oumu's voice broke the silence and cleared it away. That is what happens when old wisdom and new wisdom merge, and find room in the young.

It is the end, or maybe the beginning, of another story.
Every story begins and ends with a woman, a mother,
*   a grandmother, a girl, a child,*
Every story is a birth . . .

ACKNOWLEDGMENTS

The writing of this novel was possible because of the support of family and so many people and places that gave me inspiration, strength, supportive feedback, and just their presence in my life during this journey.

With tremendous gratitude to my wife, Priscillia, who is my muse, and for her insightful feedback, which was valuable in sharpening my imagination to develop and reintroduce some of the characters in this book. Thank you, my love; you are my radiance of today and tomorrow. I am indebted to my grandmother, Mamie Kpana, for her wisdom, which she inserted into my memory and spirit as a child and until now. She is my philosopher of life and the inspiration behind one of the major characters of this novel. *Bi se kaka mama!* My mother, Laura Simms, whose unwavering encouragement, experience, and love for storytelling and writing continues to reignite my passion to write. For my other mother, Sarah Hoveyda (or as some would understand it, my mother-in-law), whose joy and enjoyment of every moment always grounds me and reminds me of simplicity and the beauty of it: متشكرم. Thank you to my cousin Aminata; her husband, Khamis (Mohamed); and my niece, Mariam, and nephews Reyhan Kamil and Ayaan Kamal for your mannerisms and languages that return me to the past, when I was a boy in my village, in my home. To my family in New Caledonia, my sister, Nadia; my brother, François; and my nephew Madiba, *merci beaucoup* for the happiness you brought me because of your presence during the long quiet hours of editing this novel in Brooklyn, New York. Madiba, happy man, you were four months old but your laughter was medicine. Thank you for sometimes kicking my computer closed to remind me that I needed a break and to look out the window with you and discover the world outside through your eyes and laugh with you.

To Sumaili, JV, Prince, and Valentin, for your questions, curiosity, conversations, your strength, love, and happiness you brought to me during the times we sat outside on the veranda in Bangui, Central African Republic, as I edited and you had your English lessons. These moments certainly played a part in how I wrote.

I have written this novel in my country, Sierra Leone, in Central African Republic, in Italy, France, and the United States. My gratitude, as always, to my homeland, to my people for shaping my purpose for writing and for the remarkable dose of inspiration. I am grateful to the Civitella Ranieri Foundation for granting me a fellowship in 2011 that gave me the space, time, and isolation I needed to begin putting together this novel. It was a blessing to be in Umbria, Italy, at such a magnificent location that gave my imagination fresher wings. In addition thank you to all the staff in New York and in Italy, and to my fellow artists I was in residence with.

My thank-you to the people of Central African Republic, to the city of Bangui, where I finished the novel and was inspired daily by the strength and resilience of those I encountered, and especially to the children who left an indelible impression on me of what it means to be human anywhere and at any time.

Ira Silverberg, I am forever grateful to you for introducing me to the world of publishing. Thank you, thank you.

I am extremely lucky to have an editor like Sarah Crichton, who is rare. As always, it is extraordinary and a pleasure working with you, and I am looking forward to more. Thank you all at Farrar, Straus and Giroux. I truly feel part of the family.

And last, thank you so very much to my agent, Philippa Brophy at Sterling Lord Literistic, for your trust in my vision and always looking out for my well-being, and also to Julia Kardon for always answering my many questions and for your patience and professionalism.

A NOTE ABOUT THE AUTHOR

Ishmael Beah was born in Sierra Leone in 1980. He came to the United States when he was seventeen and studied political science at Oberlin College, graduating in 2004. His first book, *A Long Way Gone: Memoirs of a Boy Soldier*, was a number-one *New York Times* bestseller and has been published in more than forty languages. *Time* magazine named it one of their Top 10 Nonfiction Books of 2007. Beah is a UNICEF Ambassador and Advocate for Children Affected by War; a member of the Human Rights Watch Children's Rights Advisory Committee; an advisory board member of the Center for the Study of Youth & Political Violence at the University of Tennessee, Knoxville; a former visiting scholar at the Center for International Conflict Resolution at Columbia University; a senior research fellow at the Center for the Study of Genocide and Human Rights at Rutgers University; cofounder of the Network of Young People Affected by War (NYPAW); and president of the Ishmael Beah Foundation. He has spoken before the United Nations, the Council on Foreign Relations, and many panels on the effects of war on children. He lives with his wife in New York City. You can follow him on Twitter at @IshmaelBeah.